Happy B[irthday]
Ella
    from
       Beverly
       Patty

WHITE COLLAR GIRL

WHITE COLLAR GIRL

by

FAITH BALDWIN

TRIANGLE BOOKS
NEW YORK

COPYRIGHT, 1933, BY FAITH BALDWIN CUTHRELL

ALL RIGHTS RESERVED

TRIANGLE BOOKS EDITION PUBLISHED JULY 1939
REPRINTED SEPTEMBER 1939
REPRINTED FEBRUARY 1940
REPRINTED APRIL 1940
REPRINTED SEPTEMBER 1940
REPRINTED OCTOBER 1940
REPRINTED JANUARY 1941
REPRINTED APRIL 1941
REPRINTED JUNE 1941

TRIANGLE BOOKS, 14 West Forty-ninth Street,
New York, N. Y.

PRINTED AND BOUND IN THE UNITED STATES OF AMERICA
BY THE AMERICAN BOOK—STRATFORD PRESS, INC., N. Y. C.

To Lena

WHO SAID SHE LIKED IT

WHITE COLLAR GIRL

CHAPTER ONE

THE shabby roadster rattling over the River Road wore, like service medals, casual signs painted nonchalantly here and there. Approaching it from the rear one read the warning "It Won't Be Long Now." But tonight it was too dark to decipher any such insouciant slogan, although the sliver of a new moon cast its faint exquisite light upon the lazy flowing of the river.

Summer nights are very lovely in the North. On the Canadian side of the river the lights in farmhouses shone, the whistle of a train sounded uncannily near. From the near shore there came the voices and laughter of campers, and the frantic barking of a dog.

The girl in the front seat of the car lifted her small face to the river wind. She said to her companion: "Look, Happy, someone's got a beach bonfire!"

Happy—otherwise known as Radford—Anderson, slowed down a trifle. He replied, in his slow, deep voice:

"We're near the Nortons' camp. Want to stop and go down?"

She said, "No," but added: "Let's turn off at

their road and park at the top of the hill. It's a glorious night. I hate to go back to the club, it's too hot for dancing."

"O. K., Linda, you're the doctor," he told her.

They turned into the road which had been made by the wheels of many cars and bumped their way in ruts and through stubble and stopped at the top of the hill. The trees had been cleared a little here, which was fine for scenic effect if dangerous to traffic. But Happy knew the way. The car ceased its spasmodic gasping and the two who sat in it were silent, looking over the river. Linda said:

"I must bring Susanna out here, first thing. I never tire of it, do you?"

"Nope," said Happy briefly. He lighted a cigarette and the tiny flare of the match in his big cupped hands showed her, fleetingly, the familiar mirthful face, the shock of light, unruly hair.

He tossed the match away. Difficult to see Linda, in the close starry darkness, but her face he had by heart. He had known her always, they had grown up together. So he knew, without seeing, that her eyes were gray and her hair a lovely curly tangle of clear bronze, and that against the clear pallor of her fine-textured skin her generous mouth was red and smooth, with deeply indented corners.

"When's the girl friend coming?" Happy wanted to know.

"Next week. She didn't," answered Linda, laughing, "give me much notice. Just a crazy telegram. 'Motoring up to spend the summer, family's gone abroad, I'm an orphan.'"

WHITE COLLAR GIRL

"That's a swell idea," Happy remarked, untangling his long legs; "suppose you hadn't wanted her? She sounds like a first class brat!"

"Well, she isn't," Linda said indignantly, "she's a knockout! You'll be crazy about her!"

"Who . . . *me*?" Happy snorted. "Fat chance. She'll probably high-hat the lot of us, anyway." He struck a dramatic attitude and falsettoed idiotically; "Who's your friend, Linda? What, a garage mechanic! Heavens, hand me my smelling salts!"

"I could whack you," Linda told him seriously. "Susanna Hudson's the last person on earth to be a snob. You'd never know she had money."

"Ah, *has* she money? I thought she was poor but proud. Now, you really interest me," Happy said solemnly.

"Happy, you're the biggest imbecile."

"Thanks, darling."

"Susanna's just **your** type," she told him wickedly.

"What do you mean, my type? You know my type. It's been the same since I carried your school books for you and had to fight half the male percentage of the class first to prove I wasn't a sissie and then because they all wanted the privilege."

"Don't be silly, Happy," she told him blithely.

"I'm not silly. I'm serious. I've always thought the world of you, Linda. I always shall. I wish to heavens I had something to offer you——"

She interrupted hastily:

"Happy, please don't propose to me again!"

"Well, it wasn't much of a proposal," he argued,

mildly astonished, "it was like saying I'd give you ham and eggs—if I had any ham—provided I had any eggs. I was just mentioning my preference."

She said seriously:

"It isn't your preference, really. You just know me too well. People always took it for granted that we'd dance a lot together and sit beside each other at dinners and all the rest of it. Then I went away and that gave me a new hold on your affections, you sort of had to get used to me all over again. Even if—if we could get married, I don't want to, Happy."

"Sure, you don't want to. Who the heck would want to marry me?" he asked her—or himself—sincerely. "But you *like* me, don't you?"

"Of course, I like you. But I'm not in love with you, Happy, nor with anyone else. And I don't expect to be, either. And you're not really in love with me, you know, it's just propinquity or whatever you call it. We'd better," she added, "start back now, Bert and Bess will think we've eloped."

"No chance," he grunted, putting the car into motion, backing carefully into the makeshift road and making a brilliant turn, "wish there were!"

He said, when they turned into the River Road again:

"Linda, it's pretty darned tough for you to—to have to give up all your plans. But I can't help but be glad, I always was a selfish lout."

"You're the most unselfish person I know, Happy," she told him sincerely, "and it—it isn't hard really. It was, at first. But I've gotten used to it. And I'm going to be crazy about my new job."

"When do you start?" he wanted to know.

"Monday. I've got my first sales talk all worked up. Want to hear it?" She went on without waiting for an answer, declaiming gravely: "There are eight million five hundred thousand women gainfully employed in these United States. Women inherit seventy percent of all wealth and property left by men, and are the largest recipients of dividend checks from the major corporations in America. . . ."

"Why wasn't I born my mother's only little girl?" mourned Happy.

"Don't interrupt," Linda bade him severely, and continued: "Women gamble, many of them accepting casual tips, through a desire to get rich quick. They lose, very often. What a woman, left with a small estate, or large, or a woman earning and saving, needs is to be told how to invest her money wisely, obtaining a maximum return with maximum safety. Seven percent with safety, that's what I represent!"

"Miss Anthony," said Happy, as her voice came to a full stop, "you are breaking my heart. At present I have forty-six cents, mostly Canadian."

A small and active brown bunny hopped into the road, blinded by the headlights. Happy swerved. Linda, bouncing, exclaimed heatedly:

"And the next time you take me riding, you needn't throw me into the river, either, Happy Anderson!"

"Sorry," apologized Happy as he regained the

road, "don't like running over bunnies. Look here, Linda, how'd you get this job anyway?"

"Through Mr. Pearson. You know, he's the district manager for the investment house of Marsden, Taylor, in Buffalo. He was in at the bank the other day and heard I was working in the Five-and-Ten. He came right down and dragged me out from behind the counter and took me to the Lawrence House for lunch. Jim Merton used to have this district, you know, but he's gone to New York," explained Linda, a little more wistfully than she knew, "so Mr. Pearson offered me the place. He says that the field hasn't been touched yet, especially in the farming districts. Lots of women won't even open their doors to men salesmen, you know. And because I'd been brought up in the banking business, so to speak, he thought I might be the logical person to take the job."

The lights of the Country Club shone ahead. Happy said, driving rather slowly:

"Well, good luck. Maybe I'll strike pay dirt some day and give you a big order. Anyway I'm darned glad you're out of the store, your mother was fit to be tied."

"I know, but what could I do?" She leaned closer to him and spoke with emphasis. "I wasn't through college when—when father died. And when I came home, I half expected to go back again. Then, when Bert found out things were in such a tangle and there was only the insurance left and the house— Happy, I just *had* to go to work. I wanted to take a business course, and there just wasn't any money to do it with. I thought I could earn and save enough. There aren't, you know, very many opportunities in this town, Happy.''

"*Don't* I know it?" he said glumly.

"Happy, I realize it's hard for you—if only you could get out——?"

"I can't," he said shortly. She was silent. She knew he couldn't. He had an extraordinarily selfish mother. Happy would, she supposed, spend the rest of his days in Lawrenceton, the most popular man in it and the most wasted.

They reached the club, a long low structure of gray fieldstone, and parked. As they approached the wide verandas two figures detached themselves from the gloom and called to them.

"Where the dickens have you two been?" Bert Warren demanded. "Bess and I were about to go home, the party's getting dull."

Linda and Happy went up the steps where Happy promptly found a large wicker chair and sank into it. He never stood up when he could sit down. The others grouped themselves about him, Linda perched on the porch railing, Bert Warren leaning against a pillar and Elizabeth Young on the arm of Happy's chair.

"I was trying to sell Happy a bond," Linda stated gravely.

Bert laughed. "Look here," he offered, "come around to my office, say, next year. I took a case on a contingency basis and maybe I'll win it, who knows?"

"How's your mother, Linda?" Elizabeth Young

asked, her charming serene face turned toward her friend. Linda smiled at her affectionately. "She's pretty well, Bess," she answered.

"Tell her I'll be over soon," Elizabeth said. She was the district nurse, a handsome clever girl, a little older than Linda, and engaged to be married to young Warren. Elizabeth had been the mainstay of the Anthony house ever since, at her father's death, Linda had returned from Bryn Mawr, to find her mother, never very strong, completely shattered by the shock, and the family finances in a particularly muddled state. Bert had been very kind too; he had taken their affairs on his broad shoulders. Everyone had been kind, she thought, during that dreadful and cruelly beautiful spring. . . .

"Pearson's a great guy," Bert said now, in reply to something Happy had said, "everyone likes him, he's worked up a good clientele for his house and Linda's just the girl to go after the savings in the sock. She'll get it if anyone can."

"My quota," said Linda, "for my first year is around sixty thousand dollars. That's because of the district," she continued placidly, as Happy whistled; "in a metropolitan district it would be, I don't know how many times that."

"Didn't know there was that much money in the world," gloomed Happy, "why don't you tackle Fred Jarvis? He could give you your entire quota and never miss it."

"His wife would miss it," Bert commented; "she doesn't think any more of a dollar than I do of my right eye."

"Speaking of the dowager and her right eye," Elizabeth said idly, "did you people hear that Dick Jarvis is coming home? He should be here this week, some time."

"No!" Linda toppled precariously on the railing. "Why, I haven't seen him since grammar school," she said excitedly. "I wonder what he's like now?"

"Oh, according to the way the unmarried females in this town are sprucing up," reported Bert, laughing, "he must be a combination of Abe Lincoln, John Gilbert, and J. P. Morgan——"

"With a dash of Rin Tin Tin——" supplied Happy.

"Funny," mused Elizabeth, "but I don't remember him. I must have known him though."

"Perhaps not," Linda told her. "You were away a lot, you know, and he went away to prep school at about the time the rest of us entered High. He used to spend his vacations in Canada with his mother's people. Then he went to Princeton and then to Oxford or somewhere. What's he going to do here?"

"He's going into the Fred Jarvis Pulp Mills to be groomed for general manager and then take over the works," Bert explained. "It seems that the old man is tired of going to an office or something. I heard tell that Mrs. Jarvis wanted to move to New York but Jarvis is dead set against it. This town's the apple of his eye, it's his private tennis court and playground and he intends to spend his declining years in it watching it fall into genteel decay."

"Bert," Elizabeth reminded him, "someone will hear you."

But he was off on a tangent and ignored her warning.

"It made me sick to see you go into that shop, Linda," he said violently.

"There wasn't anything else," she told him. "After all, I wasn't trained. And while I wasn't crazy about selling stationery and postcards, particularly during a Saturday afternoon rush, it had to do. It's been good enough for other girls in town."

Bert, given an opportunity to indulge in his pet topic, now launched forth, with gestures.

"I understand that," he agreed. "Unless you are trained—to teach, to nurse, all the rest of it—jobs are scarcer than hen's teeth here. Bad enough for the men, worse, I would say, as long as Fred Jarvis and Homer Manton and a few others with money manage to keep this place like their own private back yards. There hasn't been anything to it, for them. How many new businesses have come in here and succeeded in the last twenty years? Not one! An enterprising lad or two from down-state comes up here and starts something; but he finishes it on a train out! These people—they make me tired," declaimed Bert bitterly, "run around in Lincolns, manage the country club, manage politics, throw parties, take themselves off to New York for their wives' frocks, or to Paris for the daughters', send their kids away to schools and universities, spend their winters in Palm Beach or Miami and manage, at the same time to keep this town like something Rip Van

WHITE COLLAR GIRL 13

Winkle dreamed of. Why? Because they have to be the big frogs in the little puddle. They can't bear the thought of any progress which might unsettle them, change standards, shift values. They like Lawrenceton 'just as it is,' *ergo,* it remains so! Unless a man decides for a profession—to be a lawyer, doctor, minister—and even then he hasn't much opportunity—he hasn't a dog's chance. Look at Happy here. Smart lad, if ever there was one, the makings of a swell executive. What's he doing? Working in a garage, because his town offers him no better opportunity, and if *you* see any future in that you need to have your eyes examined!''

"Gosh, leave me out of it," implored Happy, in alarm.

"Bert's perfectly right." Elizabeth rose to her fiancé's defense. "Look at Mabel Morgan and Carrie Mathews——"

"You look at 'em, I'm not feeling so well," Happy interpolated.

"No, but seriously, Happy! Mabel's in the Goodie Shoppe—and Carrie's selling shoes at the Booterie—both of them wasted, both of them far too capable for their jobs."

"It's different here," Linda said slowly. "In a big city girls sort of fit into various jobs, work at 'em, or out of 'em, in more or less classified strata. Here, you do what you can, that's all, and one sort of a job is as good as another, so far as social position is concerned. Mabel may wrap up fudge in the Goodie Shoppe and concoct banana splits. Who cares? Mabel's the daughter of one of the best doctors in town. She didn't, as it happened, want to train or teach school or take a business course. But she wanted to be independent. So into the Goodie Shoppe she went; and I'll bet a cookie she still goes to the Country Club dances and has the men fighting over her from the stag line. Carrie's father's a minister and a scholar, but Carrie tries on shoes in the Booterie. No one thinks anything of it, do they? It's Carrie's hard luck that she isn't able to—'' Linda stopped suddenly, unwilling to conclude her argument—*"isn't able to leave her mother and go somewhere where she could find a position with a future!"*

The others understood. Linda went on, fluently, finishing her sentence aloud with scarcely a break—"it's her hard luck that she isn't able to get old Tad Perkins out of the shop, for she's twice the executive he is. Since her mother's breakdown she seems to run all the parish business, from what I heard last Christmas."

Elizabeth said:

"Well, we won't get anywhere with this discussion. When's your friend coming to town, Linda?"

"Next week I hope. It's a good thing for you that you have Bert where you want him, and that he's too good a lawyer to risk a breach of promise suit," Linda told her, laughing.

"I'll keep my eye on him if I have to take him around weighing babies with me," Elizabeth laughed.

"Gosh," said Happy, "two handsome strangers in the town at one time will be plenty too much! I knew there had been a different atmosphere on Main Street for a day or two. It feels like brass bands and banners, as if the Legion was about ready to put on the Labor Day show, a little prematurely.''

"Two?" asked Linda.

"Haven't forgotten Dick Jarvis, have you? You admitted a little while ago that you were burning to see him.''

"Just a trifle scorched," she amended, "but when I used to go to his parties—Happy, you went, too, you remember, don't you?—I thought he was *grand!* I'd stand in corners and stutter if he spoke to me. Sheer admiration. He never noticed me though, I was such a plain kid."

"You were not!" contradicted Happy loudly.

The others laughed. Linda's gray eyes danced.

"That's nice and loyal of you, Happy," she said, "but even if I have become a raving beauty since, I certainly wasn't one then, back in the prehistoric ages."

"I'm anxious to see him too," admitted Elizabeth.

"You and every other girl in town," her fiancé said sadly. "But if he thinks he's coming back here to pep us up, he's given himself a task. Regard what is known as Lawrenceton's younger set. Seventy miles an hour, once they're across the river, and bottles, bottles all the way. This may be the backwoods or the provinces but it can give the towns a swell run for their money."

"Dick's always been a sort of legend to this place," Linda said.

"Like our Only Movie Actress," Happy added.

"Yes, only now and then we do hear something definite concerning her, an interview regarding the Old Family Mansion, for instance."

They all laughed, recalling Dorine Dunne, who had gone to school with them too, and who had been born Dora and whose grandparents still lived on a small, bloodless farm, a few miles out, and whose family mansion consisted of a ramshackle if picturesque old house plus a couple of cow barns not quite up to present standards of sanitation.

"Local Girl Makes Good," murmured Linda, laughing.

"Bert, I've got to work tomorrow," Elizabeth said, "what time is it?"

He told her and Linda exclaimed in horror:

"And I have to be back of a counter," she mourned.

"When are you quitting?" Elizabeth wanted to know.

"Saturday night. But today's only Wednesday; no, it's Thursday. Come on, gang, let's get going," said Linda, rising.

They piled into the car which Happy had borrowed from his garage. Linda had resigned from the club, following her return home. But Bert belonged, and Happy, although not a member, had been pleased to supply "elegant locomotion" for the evening's dinner-dance party.

Riding townward, Bert and Elizabeth in the back seat, Happy and Linda in front, Elizabeth murmured, secure that the sound and fury of the engine would cover her voice:

WHITE COLLAR GIRL 17

"Linda's awfully game, isn't she?"

Bert squeezed her hand. "Next to you, the best sport I ever knew. She was all set for a real career, and her dad sure wanted it for her." He wrinkled his brows in the darkness. He said, for the hundredth time: "I'll never understand how it happened. Everyone thought Allan Anthony was, if not rich, then very comfortably well off. He'd been president of the bank for years, knew all there was to know about wise investments. And then, at the end of his life, to go off the deep end with a bunch of wild-cat speculations! Lord, it about floored me. The nastiest job I ever tackled was being executor to that—that mess. And having to tell Linda and her mother."

"If only Mrs. Anthony would move—they could get a cute little apartment somewhere and save. That house must be an awful expense," Elizabeth said.

"Sure it is. It eats up money in taxes and repairs. And they haven't much, you know."

He added: "Those women were great though. Not a word of complaint. Mrs. Anthony—gosh, she was crazy about him, wasn't she?—just held her head high and said nothing except—'he never speculated.' After that, she kept quiet. His death certainly just about killed her. And I sometimes wonder if it wasn't the facing of the financial facts that killed him," he said, low.

"Has Linda never said anything about the way you found things?" Elizabeth asked him.

"Why, no. She went through his private papers,

letters and things. I asked her if she found anything which had any bearing on the matter; she told me she hadn't. Here we are," he said, as the car turned a corner.

Elizabeth was dropped first. Then Bert. Linda said, leaning out of the car, "We had a grand time, Bert, thanks a lot."

He yawned openly. "So did I. We'll have to do it often. Only, I've called an early meeting at the office tomorrow——"

"What meeting? The Dead-Eye Dicks?" she inquired, remembering the masculine secret societies of her early days.

"Not exactly." He stood by the car and laughed up at her. "But since you were home last vacation a couple of bright lads and myself got tired of decorating the drug store corner and decided to form a Civic Club to keep us out of mischief. We like sticking our noses into local politics. I've urged Happy to join us but he's too gosh-darned lazy. Good night," he said, and turned toward the house where he roomed.

"Good guy," commented Happy, driving away, "he's smart enough to make an impression, even on Lawrenceton consciousness, if he gets a chance."

CHAPTER TWO

LINDA's house, set back from the street in its own spacious grounds, was not far away. The house itself was of slate-gray stone, neither old nor new. It had the high peaked roof, the occasional stained glass windows, the pompous ornateness, the solid appearance of the houses of its period. Vines softened the severity of its cold gray flanks. Tonight, as always, the door stood open.

Linda, on the porch, called back to her cavalier:

"Don't forget to come around, and be prepared to lose your heart."

"You can't lose anything you don't own," he told her. "That's why the recent Wall Street disaster didn't bother me at all."

She heard him laughing over the sputter of the starter as she opened the door and went into the square hall and up the stairs, and stopped to see if her mother's door was open. It was.

Mary Anthony lay in the great old-fashioned bed, a bed so big that her fragile body seemed lost in it, reading. She looked up and smiled at her daughter.

"Have a good time, Linda?"

"Yes—" Linda came in and perched on the side of the bed. . . . "But I'll be dead tomorrow."

"I'm glad you're going out more. I've wanted you to. Your father would have wanted you to." The small face, white against the whiter pillows, quivered with a grief the passing of the days could not lessen. "And I'm so glad about—your new work. You'll be happier, Linda."

"I think so, too." She said, after a moment: "We must try and give Susanna a good time."

"Jessie Jarvis wants to entertain her," Mrs. Anthony said.

"What?" Linda rose and looked down at that older, faded, replica of herself. "Of course, she would!"

Her tone was exceptionally bitter. Mrs. Anthony said mildly:

"I don't know what has gotten into you about the Jarvises, Linda. Fred was one of your father's closest friends . . . and Dick will be home soon—"

"You, too?" asked Linda reproachfully, and laughed. She leaned over to kiss her mother. "Good night," she said, "Susanna will be all right. She'll fit in anywhere."

On the following Saturday, Linda was watching the clock which would release her from her duties. Saturday was the big day of the week. People came into Lawrenceton from the smaller towns, came for the most part in cars; cars of all makes and vintages; came, too, from the outlying farm districts. The movie houses were crowded to capacity, the stores and streets swarmed with people. Whole families wandered through the aisles of the shops; fathers, mothers, grandmothers, sisters, cousins and aunts, with a small string of various-sized children trailing, excited and weary, behind them, like the animated tails of comets. The Five-and-Ten did a rushing business on Saturdays. Linda, toward the close of the afternoon, was limp. She pushed back the heavy hair from her forehead. The day would never end, she thought. She heard two young men talking, near her counter. One said, laughing, "Is it always like this, Dick?" and the other replied, in a voice which was perfectly and equally strange to her: "Always, and especially on Saturdays. Thought it might amuse you."

"Broadway has nothing on this," said the first man cheerfully. "Hey, look at the postcards. I'll get some and send them to all and sundry. Cross marks the body, wish you were here, or words to that effect. Pretty girl, there, too, behind the counter," said the young man, even more cheerfully and quite audibly.

Linda stiffened a little. A girl, near her, the daughter of her mother's grocer, giggled and pushed her scarlet tipped fingers through her thick, washboard-waved coiffure. "That's Dick Jarvis, isn't it?" she whispered.

It was, of course. While his friend looked over the postcards, selecting them for their garishness rather than their beauty or fidelity to nature, Linda regarded Richard Jarvis, who was rigid in rapt contemplation of an entirely atrocious vase, made of something remotely resembling china and stuck all over, like a larded pig, with bits of impossible and varnished shells.

No, she would never have known him. And yet—there was still the wave in the brown hair which as a boy he had detested, there was still the stubborn cowlick. His eyes were dark, she remembered that. But she had last seen him as a small, sturdy boy, practically toothless. Now his dental equipment was complete and he affected, she noted with a smile, a small, brushed up mustache which was, she admitted, becoming enough. Also he had grown out of all recognition. He was as tall as Happy now, but less haphazardly put together, more compactly built. There was great strength and a touch of arrogance in the set of his shoulders. His clothes, if not New York, were London.

"May I have these, please?" asked his friend, smiling into Linda's abstracted eyes.

This young man was short, stocky, a bit on the plump side. He had a cheerful and insolent face, and the pink skin of a baby. Richard was bronzed . . .

Linda made change, put the postcards into an envelope. The young man said, caressingly, leaning closer: "You look like a *very* nice girl——"

Richard moved nearer, said shortly: "Here, none of that, Mike." Linda, flushing, looked up at him and smiled. The words on her lips were never spoken. Jarvis took the shorter man by the shoulder, said briefly, "Let's get out," and moved away, making no sign of recognition. "Isn't he a knockout?" breathed the girl at the next counter, sighing. "Looks for all the world like Jack Gilbert, don't he?"

"No, he doesn't," Linda replied shortly. She was smarting all over. She heard Dick's hurried, annoyed explanation as he and the temperamental Mike made their way through the crowd to the door, "You can't do that sort of thing here, old man, it just isn't done." She could see Mike's quirked head and amused, unbelieving expression.

He had not known her.

Why should he know her? It had been years since they had seen each other.

But she had known him.

Perhaps he had known her; or realized she was someone with whom he had once had some sort of contact. Wasn't it "being done," in his crowd, speaking to girls with whom one had gone to school and then found, after a lapse of years, behind counters in the Five-and-Ten?

He was a snob, just like his mother!

Arrogant, like his father!

She hated him. She wouldn't speak to him again —if—if . . .

He'd probably thought she was flirting with him as well as with his friend . . .

"You look like a very nice girl."

The creature hadn't, of course, meant "nice." The opposite, exactly the opposite!

Her cheeks, pale with fatigue, burned as if they had been soundly slapped. She straightened out the stock on her counter. Her hands shook. "Didn't you use to know Dick Jarvis?" asked the girl next to her curiously.

"I went to school with him, ages ago," Linda responded briefly.

"Why didn't you speak to him?"

"What for?" she asked uncompromisingly, and then because it hurt to say it, hurt to make the admission, forced herself to go on. "He probably wouldn't have known me anyway."

Why was she so angry? It was no crime for him not to know her. She admitted to herself that there was no reason on earth why he *should* know her. She hadn't really expected him to. She had meant to say: "You're Dick Jarvis, aren't you? I'm Linda Anthony."

He'd remember then; remember the name; he had no reason to forget the name. The Anthonys, she thought, lifting her chin, were as good as the Jarvis' any day in the week; better; as respected in the town, in that part of the state; quite as well known.

That's what she'd planned to say, in the fleet moment; and what she had expected in return was a lighting of his eyes, a smile. "Linda—not really Linda, the kid I used to go to school with?" Laughter and contemplation across a counter. "What in the world are you doing here, Linda—didn't mother write me you were at Bryn Mawr?" And then he'd remember father and speak of him . . .

That was the way it should have happened. But it hadn't happened that way. Oh, she didn't mind his not remembering—what she minded was the cool sliding of his glance over her, the utter unfriendliness, indifference, call it what you like. "You can't do that sort of thing here, Mike, it isn't done."

WHITE COLLAR GIRL

Flirting with a shop-girl wasn't done.

Prig! she thought furiously.

He'd come back to the town, to work in it, to take over, some day, his father's place. He didn't regard it as refuge, as "his own back yard." He regarded it as a stupid little place, narrow, unexciting. He was too big for his town.

She was filled with an immediate loyalty toward her birthplace; its slow, curious charm, the windings of its great river, its trees and little hills, its wide green pastures, its kindly, normal people. She thought, distressed: I was feeling a little too big for my town, too. Well, I'm not any more!

She went home, desperately tired. She thought, it's my last day anyway. Monday—Monday she'd start out, fresh and new, driving over to Boone to talk to Mr. Pearson, to get her final instructions. After supper, cooked and served by Myra, the maid of all work, she telephoned Happy.

"Busy?"

"Don't be sil'."

"Come over and look at my Ford, will you?"

"If you're trying to sell it, I'll offer you seventy-five cents."

"Thanks, I'm not selling. I have to use it in my business," she told him.

Happy arrived and she spent an hour with him in front of the barn, which had been converted into a garage, while he tinkered with the car, which was of a very ancient vintage. "She'll run," he announced, rising.

"That's great. We got a good price for father's

car but I'm glad we didn't get anything for Leaping Lulu,'' she admitted, as Happy dusted himself off. "Come back into the house. I want to show you Susanna's picture."

She led him into the living room and displayed a photograph. "Isn't she pretty cute? voted the prettiest girl in our class."

"What! With you there?" He tossed the photograph on the table. "I don't care much for the blond babies," he said. "Better team her up with Dick Jarvis. He's home, you know."

"At last!" she mocked.

"You're dissembling," he accused her.

Suddenly she was furious.

"I am not! Sometimes I think people in this town are crazy," she said violently; "just because Dick Jarvis has money and more education than he can handle."

She stopped. Happy's astonished eyes were upon her. "Here," she commanded, "let's try out Lulu, we can stop at the Goodie Shoppe for a soda."

Happy, jingling the coins in his pocket, said, "Well, I've thirty cents." As the car started, he added, "But I was saving fifteen of it to treat your friend!"

CHAPTER THREE

Susanna arrived in the golden dusk of a gorgeous June evening. She arrived in a long, underslung roadster of impressive foreign make, painted an eye-aching scarlet. The rumble was full of luggage. The front seat was practically empty as Susanna occupied very little room. Susanna wore a white frock, a scarlet béret, and a little scarlet coat. On the seat beside her was a wrap of summer ermine for, as she afterwards explained, "How did I know it wasn't snowing in the North?"

She was not tired although she had driven three hundred miles or so that day. She had put herself on the Albany night boat the evening before and had collected enough material for laughter during the trip to last her the three hundred miles. She had phoned and wired en route; was certain of her welcome.

Susanna's small decorative head was not as fly-away as her yellow, carefully careless curls. She had speedwell blue eyes, deceptively childlike in their saucer roundness and naïve expression. Her nose wasn't much. Her mouth, which she treated with unnecessary crimson, was shaped rather like a Valentine kiss. She said, clambering out of the roadster and seizing Linda in her astonishingly capable arms: "Golly, I'm glad to see you!"

She explained that her trunks would follow by express. "Trunks!" exclaimed Linda. "Why not?" asked Susanna. "Don't they use trunks up here? Oh, Linda, this is the swellest place!"

"Well, of course, they use trunks. But I was thinking of your plural," Linda explained, "and if you've brought a lot of clothes, duck, they won't do you very much good."

"Just a few little old rags," Susanna defended herself. "Linda, I suppose you think I'm crazy barging in like this. But honest to Peter, I couldn't go abroad with The Parents. I wouldn't mind if we went funny places and did interesting things and stayed in *pensions*. But, no, we have to go to hotels, and travel with couriers. That's the worst of having a hotel man for a father, all the other hotel men turn out the guards for him and have brass bands playing. If we went to Siam it would be the same. We'd stop at the Ritz."

Mrs. Anthony asked helplessly, stemming this flow of chatter, "The Ritz—in *Siam?*"

Susanna and Linda laughed wildly. Linda said kindly, "Don't mind Sue, mother, she's always like this. It doesn't mean a thing."

Presently Susanna and her hand luggage had been installed in the room next to Linda's. Linda said: "You'll have to share a bathroom with me; and with mother, as far as that goes. This isn't Siam!"

Susanna replied: "That's grand. I'll love it. Gosh, you're a good scout to take me in. How are

WHITE COLLAR GIRL

the men around these parts? I mean, *what* are they?"

"There's a lawyer, a very nice one, but keep your paws off him, he's bespoken," Linda replied gravely. "Then there are a couple of nice soda jerkers and a few lads home from college. Married men, all ages, plenty of them, but this isn't New York. Besides, they mow lawns in their shirtsleeves and that isn't romantic. There's Happy," she mused aloud.

"Happy? What is it, a dog or a canary?"

"A six-footer. He works in a garage," Linda said solemnly, but Susanna was not to be caught that way. She exclaimed joyously:

"Great. Perhaps he'll tell me what's wrong with my bus. She had coughing spells on the way up And the Smith Brothers couldn't help her."

"You've forgotten Richard Jarvis, Linda," Mrs. Anthony, curled up on a window-seat, reminded her daughter.

"So I have. Now how in the world did I come to do that?" mused Linda with exaggerated remorse. "To be sure, Dick Jarvis. Young, rich, handsome, the catch of the county."

"How dull," complained Susanna, who was darting around the room, her arms full of stockings, lingerie, perfume bottles and photographs of personable young men, "sounds like a matrimonial paper advertisement."

She stopped still, stockings trailing from her arms, a scent of Matchabelli and Caron surrounding her like an aura. "Jarvis? Dick Jarvis? Any relation of Fred Jarvis? Oh, golly, he must be, they come from here!"

"Not far," corrected Linda. "Yes, his father's name is Fred. I forgot you knew them."

"I don't—but Mother does. She met Mrs. Jarvis abroad. They used to write to one another and Mrs. Jarvis was at luncheon at the house once, while she was passing through our little town," giggled Susanna. "It was the year before I went to Bryn Mawr. I went out to lunch. I decided she must be somebody because Mother got out everything but the gold plate for her," reported Mrs. Hudson's only child gravely.

"Too bad," Linda commented, "she'd adore the gold plate."

"Linda," said her mother mildly, "I'd rather you didn't talk that way about our friends."

There was a small pause. Susanna hurled herself into it gallantly with the effect of a large brick falling into a silent pool.

"Look here, Linda, is it true that you're selling bonds or something? I mean, when I phoned your mother said you were out on the road. For a wild moment I thought you were traveling in BVD's!"

"It's perfectly true. I've just started. Can I sell you one, darling?"

"Have you a nice one, with curly hair, for about ninety-eight cents? I'm ahead on my allowance, eighteen months."

Linda laughed. Susanna hadn't changed. She said:

"No, but, honest, it's a great job. I was terrified

WHITE COLLAR GIRL

the first day I went out muttering sales talks under my breath. But I like it a lot, so far. You'll have to come along with me, some time. By the way, what in the world will you do with yourself here, Sue? This is the original Deserted Village.''

"Sleep," Susanna answered briefly, "and flirt and drink sodas and take your mother buggy riding. I'll get along, don't worry."

Mrs. Anthony left the room to see about supper. "I'm starved," Susanna had said. Susanna sitting on the floor trying vainly to match stockings, looked up. Her eyes were understanding, blue pools of something very like compassion under the halo of blond hair.

"Lindy, you've been having a rotten time!"

Linda tried to smile. Her under lip shook. She set her teeth in it.

"That store business—it wasn't so hot?" asked Susanna.

"No, I hated it. But it's all over now. I had to do anything at first. I wrote you——"

"Yes, I understand." Susanna was silent, her hands idle in the tangle of sheer silk. "It's pretty darned hard on you. Sure I haven't messed things up, coming up like this?" She waited, but barely, for Linda's emphatic negative, and then went on, flushing: "I mean, expense and all that? When I said that about my allowance I didn't mean—I mean —Father would be awfully glad to—Oh, Lord, I'm being crude and brutal," she said, desperately, "but, Linda, I don't want to be a burden on you, lamb."

"You won't be," Linda accused her, comprehending perfectly and suffering no wound to her sensitive pride, "the little you eat!" She laughed outright and looked down at the other girl affectionately. "The only thing that worries me is how in the world I'm to entertain you. There's the Country Club, of course. I don't belong any more but most everyone else does and we can manage that all right. Then, lots of our friends have camps. Ours," she stated, "is for sale."

"Don't fret about me," advised Susanna. She rose up on her round knees to embrace the knees of her friend. "Is there a miniature golf course here? I'm swell at vest pocket golf, you know that!"

She dug in a purse and flourished bills and a check book.

"I'm not as poor as I said I was. This isn't even allowance. I said to Dad: 'See here, if I were going abroad, I'd be pretty blamed expensive. Clothes and all.' And he agreed—with deposits. So I've enough to play several games and buy gas for the car and take you out to lunch, now and then."

"That's good." Linda looked at her for a minute. Then she said honestly: "I'm glad you've come. Awfully glad. I was getting peevish and crabby. I don't know why."

Susanna knew why, but said nothing. She had been the repository for Linda's confidences for a considerable length of time. She knew Linda's ambitions by heart; and that heart ached for her friend, was wounded for her. She muttered something—

a bit of feminine profanity—something about "a darned old shame." Linda smiled. She said gently: "I'm all right, Sue, I'll get adjusted."

Susanna thought, privately, that everyone got adjusted sooner or later but that the process wasn't interesting; and in Linda's case, it seemed unfair.

Happy, having been duly informed of the impending event, arrived in the evening, to regard for himself the materialization of the ostentatiously spurned photograph. Susanna greeted him with a shriek. "Linda," she remarked reproachfully, "why didn't you tell me about this Big Number?"

Linda said she had told her. Happy looked from one to the other of the girls. Susanna, swinging in the shabby canvas swing on the side porch, touched the creaking floor boards of the veranda with a negligent toe. She said briefly: "I hope you're not much of a business man. Linda tells me she is. I've got to relax after a hard year's work."

Linda snorted.

"Very hard," Susanna went on severely, "and I never could relax alone. I hope you're a gentleman of leisure?"

"Sure I am," responded Happy in hollow tones, "I work in a garage."

"Oh! Are *you* the garage man?" Susanna asked in tones of profound delight and interest. "How's business?"

"I am. Rotten."

"Good. I've always wanted to know something about the inside of my bus. If I break down on the road I'm as flat as a bum tire unless some great big he-man comes along and lends me his assistance. I'd like to learn why the wheels go round," said Susanna. "Maybe some time, if you're not busy, your boss will let me play around the junk pile and learn who's who in the best engine circles?"

"He'd love it," Happy told her, grinning, thinking of his employer, who was his mother's cousin, a large fat amiable gentleman with a fixed dislike of hard work and a marked susceptibility where youth and beauty were concerned.

"Then, that's settled," said Susanna, swinging contentedly. "I see where I'm going to have a large summer."

That night she wandered into Linda's room clad in a wisp of batiste and lace fancifully and idiotically called a foundation garment.

"Linda," asked Susanna, her fair hair burnished with a vigorous brushing and standing out around her small, pert face like an aureole, "why the dickens didn't you tell me you had anything in tow as swell as Happy?"

Linda, mending a run, looked up from her sewing. She was tired, her eyes were heavy. She sighed a little wearily and replied in some astonishment: "I don't know. I've known Happy all my life . . ." her voice trailed off.

Susanna, perched on a hassock, clasped her hands about her knees and regarded her friend with limpid, azure eyes.

"That explains it. He's a knockout and you don't know it. A natural! A born comic," said Susanna with conviction, "and don't you love the way he stands on one leg like a stork?" She giggled. She asked presently: "Not crazy about him or anything, are you, Linda?"

Her tone was a trifle too careless. Linda looked up, the gray eyes wary. She replied, however, with absolute honesty: "Why, no, Susanna, I'm not. I've sort of gone around with him ever since I can remember, and I've always been awfully fond of him, but——"

"Sure?" asked Susanna urgently.

"Sure. But why," asked Linda, amused, "all this cross-examination?"

"I think he's swell," said Susanna elegantly. "I could have me a time with that lad. Only, I don't happen to like poaching on anyone else's preserves —anyone I like, I mean," she added honestly and hastily, "and I thought if this were one of those hay-ride, choir-stall, barn-dance matches back in the old home town, I wouldn't throw any monkey wrenches. But if you don't want him——?"

She broke off and regarded Linda quizzically. Linda said immediately:

"I don't. He's yours."

She wouldn't have been human had she not added mentally—*if you can get him!* After all, Happy had been a fixture for a long time, part of her background. Always there, somewhere, with his long legs and placid pleasantries, his unfailing good humor, his effortless life-of-the-party attitude, his inarticulate understanding and affection. She didn't, of course, "want" Happy. Yet did she want anyone else to want him? She was transfixed by this unusual idea and wondered silently if she had become, without knowing it, a dog-in-the-manger sort of person.

Susanna said carelessly:

"Of course, he's cuckoo about you. I saw that right away. But I think it's one of those propinquity things. What he needs is a good shaking up," decided Susanna with a complacency which would have been maddening, Linda thought, in anyone else, "and I'm the baby to administer it. Just as long as you don't mind."

Do I? Would I? thought Linda puzzled. Aloud, she said:

"I don't know whether I mind or not; but go ahead!"

"You're a grand person," Susanna said delightedly. "No, I don't think you'd mind. You didn't, you know, talk about him, ever, when we were together. Or sleep with his picture under your pillow!"

"Happy's?" Linda laughed outright.

"There, you see!" Susanna regarded her in triumph.

"Oh, go to bed, do," implored Linda affectionately. "You must be half dead after your trip."

"Not me," denied Susanna confidently. "I could drive to Toronto this minute and never know it."

Linda thought, And so she could. She said again: "Well, I'm tired. Hop along with you. Remember, I'm a working woman."

Susanna departed. After a moment she stuck her curly head in at the connecting door. She asked:

"What about this Jarvis creature?"

"Oh, you'll like him," Linda replied with conviction.

"That means—you don't?" asked Susanna shrewdly. "And if so, what's the big idea? Why should I go around liking your pet hates?"

"I don't hate him," Linda told her slowly; "he just doesn't matter, that's all."

"Oh, I see," said Susanna and chuckled.

Linda went to bed fatigued and exasperated. Staring into the soft darkness of the summer night, framed by the open window, she thought, But he *doesn't* matter! Why should he?

Happy? Susanna hadn't meant that, of course. Naturally Susanna couldn't imagine herself anywhere for any length of time, without a flaming "heart." She'd picked on Happy, heaven alone knew why. It didn't, of course, mean anything. But if it did, it couldn't mean anything to herself, Linda, could it? She honestly thought that out, lying there. She admitted, eventually, half asleep, that it couldn't. But it gave her an odd empty sort of feeling, as if Susanna had threatened to remove, say, from her life a piece of worn but comfortable and fondly regarded furniture.

On the following morning Susanna decided that her car needed immediate attention. Laughing, Linda directed her to the garage where Happy was to be found and set out herself, in her Ford, to call on some prospects sent her by the home office. She returned in the afternoon, having made no sales, and rather discouraged. On her way into town she picked up Dr. Meadows, her family physician, who had been out taking a constitutional. She drove in, talking about her new job. He was interested; so much so that she stopped at his familiar office and came away with an order for a thousand dollars. On the street, before she turned her corner, she saw Happy, lounging his way toward home. She stopped the Ford and hailed him. "Why so glum?" she inquired.

"It's that Susanna," he complained bitterly.

"What about her?" asked Linda, with foreboding.

"She turned up at the garage this morning, got around Bill like nothing on earth, asked for Tony's overalls, and started taking that costly toy of hers to pieces. She got it back together again, with eight things missing. Then she made me take her to lunch, fifty-fifty. What a girl! Can't you send her back to New York?" he pleaded.

"Certainly not. What's more, you'd be desolate if I could!"

"Who, me? Gwan, you're crazy!" But he said it without conviction. After a moment his long face brightened. "She's kinder cute, isn't she?" he asked and fled.

On her arrival home Linda found Susanna soaking in the bathtub, reading a motion picture magazine with one eye and gnawing a large pilot biscuit. Mrs. Anthony called her daughter across the hall into her room.

"Jessie Jarvis phoned," she said dramatically. "She wants you and Susanna to come to dinner Saturday night. Dick's guest is leaving Sunday."

"For heaven's sake!" exclaimed Linda. "She certainly has her ear to the ground!"

"Susanna's arrival was in last night's *Planet*," Mrs. Anthony told her. "I met Minna at the A and P a day or so ago and told her we expected a guest——"

Minna was the star reporter, rewrite man, social editor and poetess of the Lawrenceton *Evening Planet*. Linda groaned.

"I don't want to go to the Jarvises," she said stubbornly.

Her mother asked slowly:

"Linda, why? You know perfectly well that after all you have to make some effort to amuse Susanna, now she's here. The Jarvises can do so much for her," she added, irritated. "What on earth is the matter with you? You've always liked Fred Jarvis, you used to make a point of seeing him, vacations, if you could."

Linda paled a little. She said: "I know." She looked at her mother. The kind and gentle eyes were full of nervous tears. She surrendered. "All right, we'll go," she said, and went back to Susanna, hating herself—wishy-washy idiot!—and desiring a number of things: that the Jarvis family would go to Canada; that they'd jump in the river; that Susanna wouldn't stay; that she had never come.

But she didn't mean that.

That evening, listening to Susanna discourse wisely on carburetors and feed pipes and magnetos and free wheeling, Linda knew she hadn't meant it;

and later when she and Susanna, out on the veranda, were talking over "old times"—not so old really, but to Linda so far away—she knew that having Susanna with her was one of the best things that had ever happened to her. Susanna was a specific against melancholy.

Susanna, as it happened, encountered Dick Jarvis on the following day. He came into the garage where Happy intermittently occupied himself and was presented to Susanna. That young person, lying underneath her car, in a pair of overalls much too large, rolled from her back to her stomach, wiggled out as far as her shoulders and grinned at young Mr. Jarvis from the stone floor. "Excuse my glove," apologized Susanna.

She was perfectly filthy. She had a gay bandanna around her curly hair and her wide small face was smudged with grease and recalcitrant lipstick.

"Isn't she the limit?" asked Happy in the negligent tone of a fond parent. "Get up, Susanna, and give the nice gentleman your hand."

"Don't disturb her," said Dick hastily, and Susanna, regarding her very soiled hands, chuckled. She also eyed Dick recumbently, with a wicked expression, yearning and impish. He wore such very nice white flannels, his shirt was so obviously heavy and spotless silk.

She scrambled to her feet. "Control yourself," warned Happy, unfavorably impressed with her expression.

She did so, with an effort. At lunch time, home, cleaned up, she held forth to Linda.

WHITE COLLAR GIRL

"I've met this King Richard."

"Dick Jarvis? Where? When?"

"Under my car. At least I was. He wouldn't, the big stiff, although I urged him, 'Come on in,' I said, 'The gasoline's fine!' Hear we're going up to dinner at his house? Won't that be an occasion? Happy's going, too," said Susanna, as an afterthought.

Later, when she had a moment alone with her friend, she said:

"Give me Happy any day in the week. This boy Jarvis is a severe pain in the neck."

Perversely, Linda questioned her.

"Why? Don't you think he's awfully good-looking? Most people do."

"Do you?"

"I'm asking you," said Linda.

"Oh, so-so. Never cared for male beauties, myself," yawned Susanna. She then proceeded to lead her friend on, maintaining the while an expression of utmost angelic simplicity. Almost idiocy.

"Snob, isn't he?"

"No, he isn't," denied Linda flatly, "everyone likes him a lot."

"You don't."

"I didn't say I liked or disliked him. He just doesn't matter to me, that's all."

Bess and Bert came around to call that evening. Happy was there. Happy was always there. Happy and Susanna sat in the swing and giggled while Bert discoursed on small town politics and particularly upon Fred Jarvis.

"What's the dirt?" demanded Susanna of Happy.

"Most of it was on you this morning." He laughed aloud. "Dick's face was a picture. When he came in I said, 'Susanna Hudson's here . . . best-looking girl who ever hit this town.' He said, 'So I've heard.' News travels fast, you know, Sue. He asked me to dine off the Jarvis platinum with you all, Saturday night. He's a good guy. I accepted, blushing. Then he asked: 'Where's Miss Hudson? I'd like to meet her,' and I said, 'There, under the red car!' and he said, 'My God!'"

Susanna chuckled. She asked, lowering her voice: "What's wrong between him and Linda?"

"Nothing that I know of," Happy replied, astonished. "I don't believe they've even seen each other since he came back. Come to think of it, she's acted sort of upstage whenever he was mentioned, lately, but I don't know why. She said, when we first heard he was honoring the Home Town, that she was keen to see him again."

"Dirty work at the crossroads somewhere," Susanna muttered.

CHAPTER FOUR

LINDA, Susanna and Happy went to the Jarvis' on Saturday night in the red roadster. Susanna exclaimed as they turned in at the massive gate posts and approached the house which stood, overlooking the river, at the end of a long drive. There were acres of tended gardens known throughout the state and the house itself was of frame, long and low, with a great deal of veranda space. Mr. Jarvis was fond of explaining to his guests that the original small farmhouse which his grandfather had built had been preserved in the present larger structure.

Susanna washed and, in as much of her right mind as she found expedient, looked delicious enough to eat in a silly little frock which matched her hair, and blue absurd ribbons which matched her eyes. Linda, who because of her father's expressed hatred of mourning had not, to the town's amazement, put on black at his death, wore the frock she had bought in New York before the last Easter holidays. It was coppery in tone and brought out all the lights of her bronze hair. Entering the living room, listening to Mrs. Jarvis' elaborate greetings and to their host's genial greeting, she was conscious of an accelerated heartbeat, a feeling of vast distaste for the evening ahead and a wild desire to escape entirely.

Susanna was hailing Dick Jarvis with a shriek. "How do you like me with my face washed?" she was demanding.

There was in Linda's brain a confusion, words and pictures, she said to herself idiotically. She saw another girl, an obvious "import" as Happy remarked to her later, who turned out to be one of the Canadian Jarvis'. She saw the fatal Mike, rubicund, cherubic as ever; she saw Dick Jarvis, a blur of flannels and blue coat, coming forward, smiling; she heard Mrs. Jarvis', "You remember Linda, don't you?"

He was saying, holding her hand in his own, thinking that this girl in the copper-colored gown had the most disturbing pair of eyes he had ever seen:

"I hope she remembers *me*. Do you?" he asked Linda.

She said, "Yes," with a remarkable finality and flatness of intonation that caused Susanna to glance at her sharply.

Now she was meeting Mike. "May I present Dick's friend, Mr. Towers?" Mrs. Jarvis was fluting.

A maid appeared with cocktails. There was that last minute hunt for chairs and end tables which happens in the pause between introductions and drinks. . . . Susanna and Happy established themselves on a sofa. The Canadian cousin was somewhere else, while Mike inserted himself into the chair beside Linda and Dick Jarvis, very much puzzled and taken aback, hovered over them conspicuously.

"Run along, Dickie, and sell your papers," ordered Mr. Towers amiably, "I'm in conference." He looked at the glass he held; he looked at Linda. Linda favored him with a smile. "Now where," he said, "have you been all my life?"

"Here," she told him, slim shoulder turned to exclude Jarvis from the conversation, "New York, Bryn Mawr . . ."

Dick said, with a desperate attempt to include himself:

"Mother told me that——"

She was deaf; she was unutterably rude. She smiled at Mike Towers again. And Mike, noted for a columnistic memory, permitted himself a whispered scream.

"For heaven's sake," he remarked—and he was equally noted for his lack of tact. "It was *you*—in the comic Five-and-Ten!"

"It was I," responded Linda, with perfect gravity and grammar, "and a very nice girl, too, at least you were kind enough—" She broke off, laughing, and he laughed with her.

Richard said, flushing: "I never dreamed . . . I didn't recognize you, Linda!"

"I didn't recognize you either," she answered sweetly. He knew she lied. He regarded Mike's empty glass. "There's a dividend in the shaker," he suggested persuasively, and Mike rose with alacrity. "While you're over there," remarked Dick, "you might see how Rose is getting along. She simply adores New York men!"

Rose was the Canadian cousin. Mike ambled toward her after a vindictive look at his host.

Dick sat down in the place involuntarily vacated by the aggravated Mike. He inquired persuasively: "Are you angry with me?"

"No. Why on earth should I be?" she asked coolly.

"For not knowing you!"

She laughed outright.

"Why should that upset me?" she demanded.

"Well, of course . . ." He flushed, hesitant. He agreed: "Why should it?" Indeed, if he had insisted that it had, he would have written himself as vain and imbecile. He told her: "I'm awfully sorry —why didn't you speak? I heard about your dad, Linda. I was sorry."

She rewarded him for that, with a direct glance and a murmur of thanks. Yes, very disturbing eyes. Not stormy now; sad. No, not sad any more, cool, remote, a little faintly mischievous.

"Your mother wants us," she murmured, with obvious relief.

Dinner had been announced. They left the lovely spacious living room for the dining room.

The dinner party was not exactly a howling success. What howling there was was done by Mike, Happy and Susanna. Mr. Jarvis, pleasant, a little abstracted, carved the roast and made himself agreeable. Mrs. Jarvis talked, Nice, Cannes, Juan-les-

WHITE COLLAR GIRL

Pins, Lucerne, London and other fanciful places, to Susanna.

The Canadian cousin, who was vivacious and pretty, was engaging as much of Mike's attention as possible. Dick, separated by the width of the table from Linda, looked at her across the elaborate array of linen and lace, roses and silver candelabra, and thought he had never seen dark hair as warm in tone or gray eyes as cold. Yet they weren't cold when she looked at Susanna—or Happy.

Later they had coffee in the living room, the French windows open to the scent of roses and to the cool, small wind from the river. The room was an extraordinarily pleasant mélange of old and new. Much inherited furniture had been preserved, polished to mellowness, yet the room was entirely modern in accent, in grouping, in the glazed chintz of draperies and upholstery. Susanna looked about her appreciatively. "It's beautiful," she told her hostess, "and so restful."

"Do you like it? I'm so glad," said Mrs. Jarvis and launched into a rather entertaining description of the three New York interior decorators she had coaxed up to "do the house over," a year or so before.

Mr. Jarvis settled to a long talk with Linda. He talked of her father, ". . . finest man I ever knew," he said sorrowfully, tapping the spoon against the tiny cup he held. Linda inclined her head, her eyes hostile. She listened courteously enough, very still. But she was still only on the surface. If he doesn't stop, she thought desperately, as the pleasant voice went on, slow, emphatic, I'll scream.

Happy and Dick were talking short wave radio receivers. Mike and Rose were arguing about ice hockey and during a pause in which Mrs. Jarvis drew her husband into her conversation with Susanna, Linda managed, quite literally, to escape, crossing the room to look at the built-in radio which was part of a modern bookcase. "Neat, isn't it?" asked Dick, following her.

Dick turned a knob. "This is WJZ in New York," said the announcer. They were broadcasting dance music; very lively strains poured into the room. "How about it?" asked Happy, grinning at Susanna.

Dick said, as Susanna left the older people and went out on the tiled porch with Happy, revolving in his arms, laughing, her face upturned, "Linda?"

She shook her head. He said urgently: "Just to show I'm forgiven?"

Mr. Jarvis called genially: "It doesn't seem very long ago, Linda, that you were coming up here to parties and Jessie was doing her darnedest to make Dick dance with the pretty girls. He doesn't need asking twice now."

"Linda?"

She stepped out on the veranda. There were lights shining faintly, across the wide sweep of the river. Dick said, smiling down at her: "That's a waltz—do you remember dancing school and old Miss Burnes, with the long, red nose—*one*—*two*—*three*—*one*—*two*—*three* . . . ?"

She laughed and permitted him to take her into

his clasp. Waltzing, the music came to her dimly. She looked away from her partner, through the many glass windows, out to the river. He said, "I'd forgotten how little you are."

Later, they returned to the others, for contract. Mr. Jarvis played with a frowning intentness, Mrs. Jarvis talked an erratic and excellent game. The six young people cut in, in couples.

"Golly, I love this place," said Susanna to Happy.

"I wish you did, really," he told her, grinning.

"Oh, but I do."

"It's all right for a visit," he said, "or, did you mean, this particular house? It's the only one of its kind," he warned her solemnly.

She put her curly head on one side and looked up at him.

"It's all right to grow old in," she informed him, "but for my part, while you're young, love in a cottage seems indicated. Less—interruption," said Susanna.

"You're a little devil," Happy told her with emphasis.

He said to himself, astonished, casting an almost frightened look at Linda, as, playing with Mrs. Jarvis against Dick and his father she sat, her bronze head bent over the cards in her hand, "Is it possible I'm falling for this bit of blond fluff?"

No, it wasn't possible. Why, only a little while ago . . . what had he said to Linda, out on the River Road? He flushed, remembering, and Susanna exclaimed with delight: "Penny for your thoughts.

Ten cents. A quarter! Bet you couldn't tell 'em out loud, in public!''

Dick and Linda were out of the next game, Rose and Mike playing and Happy and Susanna going back to the porch to dance. They didn't dance, as it happened. "Must have dropped dead," said Dick, "suppose we look-see?" Protesting, Linda followed him, but beyond the French windows he stopped, his back to the room. "It was an excuse really—" he said and nodded to where Happy and Susanna were standing in a dark corner, regarding the river and each other. "Look here, Linda, how about being friends?"

In the dim light she observed him coolly, her head a little tilted; red lips, disturbing eyes. Dick caught his breath. She asked:

"Why?"

"Why not? Look here, what have you against me? Surely not that idiotic affair of Mike——"

"Mike's very nice——"

He muttered: "Blast!" He said: "Oh, he's all right. Linda, why are you so evasive? Surely I can be forgiven? How was I to know you? You'd grown from such a slip of a thing, all eyes and long legs, into the—the loveliest——"

Susanna came toward them, maize organdy skirts swinging. "Isn't that the swellest river?" She indicated it. "What are you doing, Mr. Jarvis, signing on the dotted line?"

"What do you mean?" he asked, astonished.

"Linda. Oh, she's no Five-foot Shelf. Just a little bond and security salesman, didn't you know

WHITE COLLAR GIRL

that?" She looked about her. "Can't we sit down?" she demanded plaintively.

The wicker chairs had been pushed aside. Now Dick dragged them forward and they made themselves comfortable. Susanna went on, after demanding a cigarette, "Sure, she's headed for Bigger and Better Business, didn't you know?"

"The child's cuckoo," murmured Dick.

Linda was indignant.

"It's perfectly true!" she said.

"Look at that moon," Susanna ordered Happy. They were engrossed immediately, looking at each other. Dick laughed.

"A security salesman—you—in a town like this where *men* have tried and failed! You can't separate the average man in this town from his money," said Dick didactically, "and the others, well, they've already made their investments."

"Is that so?" Linda sat up straighter. She said, after a moment. "All right, I'll make a bet with you. I bet that during the first month I'm with the firm I'll sell five thousand dollars' worth of securities. It doesn't sound like much, but you yourself said——"

He turned and looked at her. There was a moon; he saw her as a pale, fragrant shape beside him, her eyes looked enormous and very dark.

"Five thousand . . .? There aren't five thousand cents *not* working in this place," he said confidently. "All right, I'm on, what's the wager?"

"If I win," said Linda, her heart thumping, "you'll give me an order for—double!"

"Ten thousand?" He whistled. He had it. Not, of course, from his rather new salary, but safely in the banks, a legacy from his mother's people. Besides, he possessed a very liberal allowance.

"Very well," he agreed after a moment, "and if you lose——?"

Her heart raced. "If I lose?" she prompted him.

"I'll let you know the stakes then. Are you game to take it up—blind?"

There was a pause. She lifted her chin and answered him with a vivid and reckless defiance. "I'm game!" said Linda.

"If you knew what you're letting yourself in for," he warned her.

"I'm not afraid," she said.

But she was—a little.

The next morning she started out, with her list of prospects and her little sales talk, feeling she had set herself a double goal. She continued to feel it as the days went on and she worked hard, permitting Susanna to go her own sweet way. But Susanna was never at a loss for entertainment. She met the Nortons, a very charming young married couple and picnicked frequently at their camp. She was with Happy as much as was humanly possible. Sometimes she saw Linda only in the evenings.

Linda got orders. Her friends were entertained, many of them giving small orders. "Help, here comes the Security Salesman!" they would announce when they saw her coming. "Linda, I have a broken ankle, so I can't write my name."

Pearson encouraged her, by phone call, by letter. She was starting out very well. But she was dissatisfied. At night, after Susanna was asleep, she read financial papers, she read books on finance, sitting up sleepy-eyed, in bed. She *had* sold securities, right off the bat. But to her friends, people with money, people willing and able to help her out. Her list of friends would be exhausted, sooner or later. She had not yet tackled strangers. Hard to tackle strangers. Hard to arrive at a strange house with a brief-case and have the door closed in one's face . . . thanks, no book agents. But it would be through strangers and not through friends that she would make the majority of her sales. Or so she hoped. And through her awakening interest and ambition there ran an undercurrent of desire— to win her bet. She saw Dick Jarvis rather often. And now and then he asked her: "How are things coming, Linda? Going to be ready to pay up, at the end of your first month?"

She'd be ready—but it would be Dick who paid.

On the last two days of the month Linda made one sale and lost one. She arrived at the house of a stranger, a farmhouse between Boone and Lawrenceton, too late. Another firm had sent a representative to that same house only a week before. Going away, she climbed into the Ford and started it and sat there being shaken half to death, thinking. She'd had this name on her list for ten days. She'd been afraid to come, afraid to try out her newly acquired powers of persuasion among strangers.

Because she had been afraid someone had gotten in ahead of her—and she had lost. All in the game, she supposed, but it was hard to be philosophic about it and to grin and bear it. Because it had all been her fault, through timidity and lack of confidence and stupid repressions.

She set her little jaw and drove home. She was tired. The sale she had made had taken three hours of hard talking. The sale she had lost had taken about three minutes. One was as tiring as the other.

It was the end of the month, and she had sold three thousand dollars' worth of the issues offered by her house; had done, Pearson assured her, very well indeed; but—she had fallen short of her own goal, the goal she had set herself.

Susanna was down at the Norton camp that last night and expected Linda to join her. No, she wouldn't go. She'd stay home, and rest, and read, and line up her prospects. She had a farmhouse she was planning to visit; and a rather rich man, a retired merchant in Boone, was also down on the list. It was said of him that he had twenty or thirty thousand idle, uninvested. If she could only get a tenth of that she'd try to be satisfied. Dick would have forgotten it was over, the first month's trial. She'd have to tell him, she couldn't back out, but tonight perhaps, she needn't . . .

He came at dusk, shortly after she arrived home. Her mother murmured at him for a few moments and then left them alone.

"Aren't you going down to Nortons' for the night?" he wanted to know.

"No."

"I am. Susanna's there," he said.

She looked at him quickly and looked away. His face was quite grave but there had been a smile in his voice.

"Change your mind, do. You don't have to keep office hours. What are your plans for tomorrow?"

"I'll be out, working."

"I see."

"It's awfully warm," she said desperately, "suppose we go out on the veranda?"

He followed her in silence. She sat down in a big wicker chair and invited him to take the swing. The veranda gave on gardens. People passed, talking, on the street in front of the house. The trolley ambled by, on its own sweet way, taking its time. Someone's radio was on, full blast. The dusk was full of the summer sounds and scents. It was July . . .

Vines screened them, surrounded them with a green, pale gloom. He asked carelessly:

"How's the work going?"

"Very well. I like it a lot." Her heart was beating so fast that her own words came muffled to her ears.

He asked, tossing his cigarette to the floor, setting his foot on it, while she thought, ridiculously, he's awfully untidy, I'll have to pick that up before Mother sees it. "The month's up, isn't it, Linda? Tell me, how well did you do?"

She told him defiantly:

"Three thousand, in round figures."

He whistled.

"You never did! I never expected—" He broke off. "I ought to let you go scot free. But I won't. Linda, you've lost your wager. You've lost. I've won. Linda, are you ready to pay me?"

She said, Yes, in a small but firm voice. Why was she so frightened; why did her heart race so; why were her lips dry and shaking?

He had risen from the swing. He was standing close to her. He was saying softly:

"You don't like me, do you? Or if you do, you fight against it. Why? What have I done? You've been as rude as possible to me since—since we met again. Oh, courteously, softly rude. I know. Now, I've won my wager . . . your wager, really. I'm going to do something I've wanted to do ever since I saw those gray eyes of yours looking at me as if I were something even the cat wouldn't bother to bring in; something I've wanted to do since I saw your mouth, set in a straight line. *This* . . ."

He lifted her bodily from the chair. Held her upright, in his embrace, bent his dark head to her own and kissed her mouth—a long, hard kiss, with tenderness . . . a kiss all ardor, all seeking, all a sort of wild male anger . . .

Then he let her go; and waited.

CHAPTER FIVE

He did not have to wait very long.

Linda spoke, trying to control her voice:

"You'd better go now. I'd just as soon you never came back!"

She was tremendously disturbed. She knew, as well as she knew anything, that she had—liked being kissed by Richard Jarvis; and she had hated it. She had liked it because, during that long moment when his mouth had conquered her own, in a hard, remorseless pressure, she had felt an immediate, unthinking response which had held her as in a slow, strange enchantment, turning her knees to water, sending the blood rushing through her body, warm, enervating. And she had hated it because she *had* responded, responded to a caress without tenderness, without . . . love.

Dick said: "You *could* be a better sport! After all, you lost!"

She had lost: more than she knew; more than, at that moment, she dared to realize. She leaned against the veranda rail, the vines on the latticework, cool and green, touched her, whispered to her, with the passing of a vagrant breeze.

"It was *cheap*," she said to him frantically. "I—I might have known. Ten thousand dollars, against a kiss!" She tried to laugh, shakily, scornfully. "You haven't progressed much from the kissing games of your childhood, have you?" she demanded.

He did not answer. She could not see him clearly for the growing darkness and the mist of angry tears in her eyes. She could, however, see that he put his hand to the small Gilbertian mustache which he wore so becomingly and, as Linda thought, so affectedly, with a rather uncertain gesture. He urged engagingly:

"Don't be sore at me, Linda. Lord, I never seem to be able to get off on the right foot where you're concerned! It was a joke, wasn't it?"

"It wouldn't have been a joke if *I'd* won," she said stubbornly.

"You won't change your mind about going to camp with me?"

She answered: "Hardly." She added: "You'd better go now, you'll be late."

He thought: I'm mad about her . . . I have been all along, I didn't know it. He thought: I wish I'd never made that confounded bet. He thought further: No, I'm glad I did . . . *glad* . . .

Aloud, he said: "All right, I'll bring Susanna with me when I come up in the morning."

On the steps he paused.

"Sure you won't reconsider?"

"Reconsider what?" she asked him, from the doorway.

"Forgiving me."

"There's nothing to forgive," she said, and then, as he took a step up and toward her, she added: "I was foolish to—take it that way. As you said, a poor sport. You see, it wasn't important enough to matter. Just rather silly."

Now, at that, he was back beside her, he had her wrist between his strong fingers.

"Linda, are you trying to goad me into—?" His face was very near her own, his dark eyes absorbed, demanding.

She did not attempt to free herself. She looked at him merely, her head thrown back, gray eyes mocking. He freed her and said, stupidly, boyishly:

"I don't suppose it *was* important. After all, it can't be the first time you've been kissed!"

She smiled. He could see the glimmer of it flash across her small white face, secret, infuriating.

She said: "It wouldn't be very flattering of you to assume that I had *not*, would it?"

He swore, deliberately, under his breath. Now she opened the door and, definitely, stepped inside. From the windows she watched him dash down the steps, climb into his car, slam the door and jam his foot on the starter with an unnecessary violence. She heard the protesting sound of gears handled with savage annoyance. The car shot down the driveway, turned into the street on two wheels, and disappeared.

Her mother said, mildly, "You decided not to go to camp?"

"Yes. Tomorrow," explained Linda, "I've got

to go over to Wilson, I'll leave, I suppose before Susanna gets home."

Elizabeth Young and Bert came in during the evening. They played bridge, robbed the ice-box, left early. "Gosh, you're getting absent-minded," Elizabeth reproved Linda, during the game, and afterwards out in the kitchen when the older girl's hand shot out just in time to prevent Linda from emptying a full bottle of milk into the sink. "What's on your mind?" she asked her, laughing.

"Nothing except securities," laughed Linda, flushing a little.

During the evening, Linda, without much interest, listened to Bert's recital of the various things that were rotten in Denmark. He had been consulted, as legal adviser, by two young men from Syracuse, who had capital enough to start a promising business and wished to build a small factory in Lawrenceton, with the hope of enlarging it later. Bert had advised against it. "No use," he had told them, "trying to buck the powers that be." He now expatiated upon the subject, the "closed corporation," of Jarvis, Homer Manton and one or two of the other wealthy residents.

Elizabeth said, doubtfully: "Yes, but if we get the bridge to Canada they simply can't help progress—progressing, can they?"

"If!" snorted Bert.

The bridge project had been in the air for several months. A number of towns had put forth their claims and the site had not been decided upon. It seemed to Bert Warren and to a number of other people that Lawrenceton was the logical place for the bridge. Where the bridge was built would come, inevitably, traffic, tourists, business, progress, money.

Linda heard, and, much later, remembered the conversation, but ten minutes after Elizabeth and Bert had departed, she could not have repeated a word of it. When she was in bed she lay wide awake, trying to think.

But she couldn't think.

She never wanted to see Dick Jarvis again.

But she had thought that before; and she had seen him again.

He could go away, to schools, to universities, to Europe; he could come back to his home town and treat her as if—as if—she could put no words to it mentally. She didn't, she told herself, mean anything to him. Just . . . a small town girl with whom he had played in school, whom he had returned to find behind a counter in a five-and-ten-cent store; whom he thought he could treat lightly, cheaply . . .

She felt her entire body burn with outraged blood.

Mrs. Jarvis had always talked of Dick's "conquests." Linda had heard her, from the time Dick first went away to school. "The girls are just crazy about Dick," Mrs. Jarvis would say complacently. "It's awful, the way they run after him, long distance calls, wires, special delivery letters!"

Well—she wouldn't run after him. She'd run away from him.

No, she wouldn't run away. She wasn't afraid of Dick Jarvis.

But she was afraid; not of him, of herself.

She'd given him the impression that—that a good many men had kissed her. That hadn't been true. Of course, there had been Happy, on rare occasions—not recently. And one or two others. But ...

She loathed girls who kissed and told; girls who kissed and didn't tell; girls who went lightly from one pair of masculine arms to another.

Dick must think her one of them.

Not that she cared what he thought.

She turned over and laid her face against the soft curve of her arm. She was tired, she should sleep. She couldn't sleep. She didn't want to think ... of that strange long moment, mindless and enchanted. She tried to close her mind to it, to think only of how angry she was, how wounded ...

Susanna turned up directly after breakfast, before Linda was ready to start out for Wilson, twenty miles away.

"Why didn't you come last night?" she demanded. "We had a grand time, including a hot dog roast on the beach. And we all went swimming."

"Wasn't it awfully cold?"

"Sure, it was cold. I nearly died. Why didn't you show up?"

"I reached home late, I was tired and didn't feel like it," Linda explained.

"Oh. . . . What did you do to Dick?"

Susanna was busy drinking more coffee. The ride up from the Nortons' had made her hungry again. Myra was muttering in the kitchen and Mrs. Anthony was with her making out the day's orders. Linda was sitting at the table with Susanna.

"I didn't do anything to him, except tell him that I couldn't go," she answered.

"Is that so? Well, he acted like a man who has found a new bootlegger and gone in heavily for samples! He came down there like a thundercloud, wouldn't explain why you weren't with him, just said you'd changed your mind . . ."

"I told Dolly Norton I mightn't make it," Linda began.

"Oh, it was all right with her; she was sorry, of course, but not peeved; that place is Liberty Hall," Susanna said, chewing reflectively on a piece of cold toast. "But Dick! Sudden storm and then all sunshine. Singing around the place, getting up crazy games. He's a nut, I tell you! He made us do charades, the swimming party just before supper was his bright idea, then he wanted to know if we didn't want to play Post Office. Everyone yelled at the idea. He said he thought it was a popular game up here in the wilds! Then he started beauing all of us around, Dolly, Nellie, everyone—even me. . . ."

"What did Happy say to that?" asked Linda. She was smiling a little. *Post Office!*

"Happy? Happy wasn't there, he didn't come either," mourned Susanna. "He told me he couldn't continue to accept people's hospitality the way he had been doing lately and not do anything in return."

Linda looked at her, wide-eyed.

"Happy? Why, he's always gone everywhere,

done everything, everyone adores having him, he's the life of the party!"

"Well, he isn't any more. Sits around and glowers, bad as Dick was, the first part of the evening, yesterday. I know what's wrong with him," declared Susanna, "he's trying to keep away from me. All right, let him try!" she added with menace.

"Who—Dick?"

"No, idiot, Happy. . . . But I'll fix him," she said viciously. "He can't get away with that, even if I *am* crazy about him!" She looked guilelessly into Linda's startled eyes and went on: "And I know he's crazy about me. Linda, say you don't mind!"

"Mind? But, of course, I mind. I don't believe it for a moment. What on earth will your father and your mother say?" demanded Linda wildly.

"You *do* mind! Oh, Linda!" and Susanna set down her cup and went, actually, a little white.

"Idiot. Not for myself. But your mother—and your father!" She had a mental vision of them both: Mr. Hudson, short, white-haired, with the skin of a baby, and very shrewd eyes; Mrs. Hudson, short, thin, devastatingly smart, and, in common with most mothers, anxious for Susanna to make a "good" match. She saw them, and beside them she saw Happy, lounging against the ramshackle door of the garage, his hands in his pockets and, if not a literal straw in his mouth, then giving that effect.

It would never do. She said so—aloud. Susanna made a profane sound. Susanna argued:

WHITE COLLAR GIRL 65

"What's eating you? What do Mother and Dad matter? They think I'm the cat's, don't they——?"

"They do. That's just it."

"Well, then," inquired Susanna in triumph, "wouldn't they want me to *be* happy—not to mention *have* Happy?"

"Oh," said Linda, distressed, "it isn't that serious, is it? How could it be—in this length of time? Susanna, I don't know what to think of you. If I believed this, for a minute, I'd send you home packing!"

"No, you wouldn't, darling. Besides, I wouldn't go. I'd get someone to take me in. The Jarvises perhaps. Mrs. Jarvis is quite sold on me," confided Susanna wickedly. "Besides, what has time to do with it? Happy suits me. He talks my language. I adore the way his hair grows, and his long legs and his voice. He's the only man I ever met I'd be happy with anywhere. The others—well, I could have been happy with 'em just as long as they stayed put—see what I mean? . . . But yank 'em out of the surroundings I knew them in, I'd be bored stiff. It isn't so much being happy with a man anyway, it's being unhappy *without* him!" stated Susanna profoundly.

Linda stared at her a moment.

"Assuming that you are serious," she began, and then broke off to exclaim helplessly, "but I can't believe it—do you realize that Happy Anderson is in no position——?"

But Susanna interrupted.

"To marry me? Sure, I know. He's said so, half

a dozen times, not, I assure you, in so many words. As far as words go, his intentions aren't honorable, in fact he hasn't any intentions!"

Linda urged her stubbornly.

"Do try and be serious."

"You said I couldn't be!"

"I mean, about the situation. If he hasn't said anything then how do you—I mean—" She stammered and floundered hopelessly.

"Go on, say it! Say, 'How do you know he cares tuppence for you, you brazen minx?' How does anyone know?" asked Susanna, in her turn; and at the change in her tone Linda looked at her, observing the alteration in her expression with mingled feelings of envy, pity and terror; for Susanna in that one brief moment, grew up, became entirely a woman, grave, a little remote. But only for the moment. The moment passed, she was her elfin self again. "Of course, I know. For one thing, Linda— swear you won't be sore?" She paused, head perked on one side and regarded her friend with anxiety, "Swear?"

"Of course I won't be. What, then?"

"Well, he told me about—*you!*"

"About me?" Linda flushed, her exquisite skin was rosy red. For the life of her she could not control the angry sparkle in her eyes, the sensation of hurt, of annoyance, of anger even. . . .

"I knew you'd be!"

At Susanna's expression, partly triumph, partly contrition, Linda laughed until her sides ached. She couldn't help it. Hurt and anger evaporated. On with the new love, off with the old, make a full confession! Up to that moment she had not really believed that Happy had permanently deserted his old colors. Now she admitted it, to herself, a little ruefully but without malice.

"Sue, what did he say?"

"Nothing. Oh," she admitted, "that's not true, of course. He wouldn't like me to tell—it was just how fond he'd been of you, all along; how fond he was still, how you never had cared for him—really—*that* way; and how he hadn't realized that anyone else could attract him until——"

"Until you came along, in a red roadster?"

"Well, something like that. He—he didn't come right out with it, you know. And—and this was several days ago. He's been thinking things over since."

"What, for instance?"

"He hasn't told me. But I *think* he's thinking that I've a good deal of money, or will have some day," announced Susanna straightforwardly.

"Sue Hudson!" Linda sat up very straight. "Happy's job may not rate very much down in New York and your friends down there may think he's a hick and all that, but let me tell you one thing, if you believe he's interested in you because of your father's money, you're pretty much mistaken!"

She spoke with spirit. Her cheeks were redder than ever and her gray eyes held an angry light. Susanna smote her pink palms together.

"Attaboy, Linda. You got me wrong. That's what I meant, what you said."

"What? You even *talk* like Happy!" groaned Linda.

"I meant—he's realizing I've got a lot of money—and so he's laying low. If I want him to propose to me I'll have to do it myself," declared Susanna, gone suddenly Irish.

"Oh . . . I see," said Linda slowly. She added, "I believe you're right."

"A little thing like that would never bother me," Susanna said outrageously, "only, it would be more fun to make him. I think I can if I try hard enough." Her eyes danced.

"Linda," said Mrs. Anthony, appearing dramatically, "have you any idea how late it's getting?"

"Golly," said Linda, jumping up, "I must get after the elusive prospect. Want to come to Wilson with me?" she asked Susanna.

"When will you be back?"

"I've no idea. I'll probably eat lunch out. There are several people I want to call upon."

"Then I can't go," Susanna decided. "I told Dick I'd lunch with him at the tea room and then, at four, when he's through work, we were going to shoot a round of golf."

"I see," murmured Linda.

She drove the Ford to Wilson, where she spent several hours persuading a large, stubborn, suspicious widow that the securities she held were on the verge of crashing, and came away exhausted, but having gained her point inasmuch as Mrs. Meaney had consented to have her securities analyzed, and if it were proved to her satisfaction that her income was in danger, she would then consider selling, to reinvest with Linda's house. After that period of *sturm und drang* Linda went to call upon the mother of a college friend in order to hear how Daisy was getting on in Montana on her dude ranch vacation. She departed, after a good luncheon, with an order for a thousand dollars' worth of a conservative issue, rather dazed, for she had never thought of Daisy's mother as a possible prospect. From Mrs. Revere's she went to the office of a business man who was on her list and walked out of it twenty minutes later, breathing hard and with a spot of angry color high on either cheek. For the business man, who was old enough to know better, had refused to think that "a pretty girl like you" was seriously interested in securities. So Linda had spent a frantic five minutes dodging around desks and things. It had been lucky, as the gentleman observed, that his staff was out for a late lunch. Not as lucky for him as he fancied. Linda left him nursing a smarting cheek and a wounded pride which hurt him more than the excellent aim of a small firm hand. But Linda took with her the knowledge that she could draw a line through *that* "prospect's" name forever.

Back in the car, she chuckled, remembering his outraged expression, his small, mean mouth pursed to—"My dear young lady—!" and, then, "You little wildcat!'' closely following upon a line beginning "Look here, baby!"

She laughed again, recalling his protruding eyes and his large stolid figure, particularly entertaining when in full gallop around the desk. Such things, she reflected, were bound to happen. . . .

Men . . .

On the way home she stopped at a farmhouse between Wilson and Lawrenceton; a small, shabby house set back from the road. Mr. Pearson had spoken to her about the woman who owned the farm. She was a widow and ran the farm as best she could with five children to bring up and only a small sum of insurance in the bank. "If you could persuade her," suggested Mr. Pearson, "that she will derive a better income from investments . . ."

The house was spotlessly clean, as was the tired woman who admitted her. Linda looked about the best parlor, a conglomeration of the worst of golden oak and mission furniture and really fine old pieces. Everything was dusted within an inch of its life. She saw two of the younger children playing on the porch, an older girl washing. The boys, Mrs. Hopkins told her, were in the fields.

She shook her head when Linda stated her business. She was poor, she said. Making ends meet was difficult. The children helped, but in the fall they went to school. There was a grade school nearby but for two years the older children had walked four miles in to high school. Sometimes they got lifts. Winters, when the snow was deep, they went on snowshoes. Sometimes they didn't go at all. Bob, the oldest boy, was through now, as she couldn't afford to let him finish but she'd like Ella to finish and maybe teach or something.

Linda explained to her the reason for her coming. Investments weren't, she explained, for the rich only. They were for the poor as well. Mrs. Hopkins would, by investing carefully, get a greater return on her little bit of money than by leaving it where it was. If the farm went well, she could afford to reinvest the dividends.

She left, late that afternoon, having set a day to return and drive Mrs. Hopkins into town where she would withdraw the majority of the insurance money and give it to Linda for investment. "You look honest," said Mrs. Hopkins, "and smart. I never had anyone explain things to me the way you have. It's hard, being a woman alone; with children. There was a young man here once or twice, but I shut the door in his face. I'd heard too much about these gold bricks and fake oil wells and men robbing widows and orphans. But a girl like you wouldn't harm anyone. I remember your father. When we had to put a mortgage on the place, I drove in with Howard—my husband—to the bank to sign the papers. Your father was a good man."

Linda left, driving home deep in thought. She felt—responsible. Something of the real responsibility of her job came to her then, for the first time. She thought, I must talk to Mr. Pearson about her; and see what I can do, other ways.

She planned to raid her friends' attics and clothes closets. If the children could be outfitted with proper clothing during the year it would go a long way toward lightening Mrs. Hopkins' burden. Also, she could take books and magazines out to the farm. Mrs. Hopkins liked reading, she said. But the library was pretty far away. "I don't get much time, but now and then, of an evening, it's nice to have magazines to look at . . . for the stories and the recipes and all."

Mrs. Hopkins should have the magazines; and the children the clothes.

CHAPTER SIX

DURING the crowded days Linda was very busy. She saw little of Susanna and was grateful that it had been agreed between them, at the beginning, that her guest would entertain herself. Susanna managed that nicely. One week-end, however, Linda took time off and, with Susanna and the Nortons, motored to Canada. It was not until she had accepted the Nortons' invitation that she learned Dick Jarvis would be going, too, in his own car. Her impulse was to draw back. But she conquered it. As if I'm going to let him think I'm so afraid of his fascination that I'd avoid him!

She had no cause for worry. At the last moment Susanna elected to drive with Dick, so Linda went with the Nortons and their guest, a pleasant young actor, originally from Iowa but now of Broadway and Hollywood. His name, whether given by his sponsors in baptism or not Linda could not determine, was Maxwell Gordon. He regaled her during the trip with tales of Dorine Dunn, for whom he had once been leading man. The picture had been *Her Secret Sin* and when it had been shown in Lawrenceton a couple of years before, there had been standing room only.

"She comes from here," Linda told Gordon.

"She does?" He looked at her, smiling. "Oh, that's so, family mansion and all that."

"Ruined farmhouse," commented Bill Norton briefly.

"Not really? I've seen her do some pictures in which she wears sunbonnets and ginghams, yet she seemed hardly to the manner born. Was her father a Canadian Mounted, by any chance?"

"Well, no!"

"That's funny. I thought she inherited it."

"Inherited what, for heaven's sake?"

"The knack, gift, talent, or what have you. You see, Dorine always gets her man."

"She may get 'em," remarked Dolly Norton, who was dark and pretty, "but she doesn't marry 'em."

"Dear me, no," said Gordon, "she has to remember her public!"

He was brilliantly malicious at Dorine's expense. Bet a cookie, thought Linda shrewdly, that she got him, too. And didn't want him!

She thought, I'd be enjoying this, the ride, the hotel at Montreal after, and all that if it weren't for —Dick.

Yet she need not have troubled. He hardly spoke to her, rarely detached himself from Susanna's side. Mrs. Norton murmured: "Looks like a bad case . . . what about Happy?"

"Oh, Susanna's pretty fickle," said Linda, laughing. But she laughed with her lips and her slim white throat and not with her stormy gray eyes.

She shared a room with Susanna. Susanna said:

"I don't see how you could keep from falling for Dick! I've changed my mind about him. He's swell and he knows how to give a girl a whirl, doesn't he?"

Linda said nothing; and if Susanna chuckled wickedly into her woolly blankets, Linda didn't hear her.

What she hadn't heard also was Susanna's conversation with Dick, as they drove at an entirely infernal speed along the Canadian roads.

"Look here, Dick, my lad, I want you to do me a favor!"

"Listen is obey. Shoot."

"I want you to pay me serious attention."

Dick grasped the wheel firmly and looked at her, grinning.

"Do I not, Oh queen?"

"Hey, be serious. I want you to indulge in a very heavy flirtation."

"With whom?"

"Me," said Susanna, her fair hair concealed under a bright green bandanna and her hands in the pockets of her white linen suit.

"Well, I might consider it," he drawled, doubtfully. "What have you to offer?"

"Nothing, darling, but a good bluff. I haven't fallen for you, if that's what you mean, and you needn't try out any line on me when we're alone, 'cause you don't mean it, and I don't mean it, and hurrah, ain't we got fun! But something's got to be done about Happy."

"Oh, Happy! Am I to be John Alden or something, or is it Cyrano?"

"I don't know, and anyway I think they're saps," quoth Susanna, "but Happy has to be brought to his senses."

"You mean brought out of them?"

Susanna giggled.

"Have it your own way. It won't be hard to bluff it," she mused, "because you do dance well and I think you're very good-looking—if you like the type—and I'm not so bad myself—if you like the type!"

They looked at each other and laughed. She asked abruptly:

"You—you're sort of keen on Linda, aren't you?"

He flushed and the smiling mouth straightened. He kept his eyes on the road ahead. After a moment he replied lightly:

"How in the world did you ever discover that, Philo? I thought I concealed it so well."

"I'm serious," said Susanna stoutly, "so don't try and get away with the wisecracks. I know you're keen about her. What's the matter with you two, anyway?"

He muttered with authentic gloom: "She can't see me for dust!"

"I'm the little vacuum cleaner," said Susanna, delighted. "Look here, practice up on this heavy affair while we're away on this jolly old trip, will you? Even if Happy isn't here, Linda is."

"Linda wouldn't care if—if——"

"Perhaps not," said Susanna; "honestly I don't

know. I can't make her out and that's the sober truth. But there's no harm trying. How about it?"

He flashed another grin at her.

"Oke. And it won't be so hard either," he said gaily.

"No, but you can save the ardent expression for an audience," she informed him, "and now, dear Mr. Jarvis, do tell me a little about the history, geography and geology of the country over which we are now—For heaven's sake, look out for that hen!"

That was the conversation, with the result that Dick and Susanna were practically in each other's pockets, mooning through meals and dancing together as if each were dying, afoot, and only held upright by the firm clasp of the other. "Hot stuff," murmured Bill Norton.

Linda was a little sick. She might have known. . . . Anyway, Susanna was a blond demon. Linda felt very sorry for Happy. She remembered Susanna at the breakfast table saying gravely: "It will last, it's got to last." Was this the way it lasted?

Susanna was a darling but when it came to men . . . She simply couldn't resist adding a scalp or two to the many dangling, invisibly, from her slim round waist. Only it seemed a pity that Happy's thick fair thatch should repose among the others. Happy would take it hard. It didn't matter about Dick. He'd live through anything, including Susanna!

Returning home, Linda worked harder than ever. The securities of the suspicious widow had been analyzed and had now been sold out, through the house, and just in time to save her from a severe loss. In gratitude she gave Linda the order for reinvestment, adding a considerable sum to that realized on the sales.

Linda went for Mrs. Hopkins and took her to the bank and saw her draw out most of the insurance money under the horrified eyes of the teller. The sum was safely and conservatively invested and there were plenty of magazines at the Hopkins' farm now, and shoes, mufflers, underwear and outer things for the children as well. Mrs. Hopkins said, brokenly, "I don't know how to thank you—I don't know how we got along without you."

Linda told Pearson: "If anything happens to that woman's investments I'll—I'll go out and *drown* myself. I can't tell you how I feel!"

"Nothing will happen," said Pearson soothingly. "It's the best bit of business she ever did in all her life. I'll tell Mrs. Pearson about those kids."

Toward the end of August several things happened. Susanna, since the Canadian trip, had had the run of the Jarvis place. Mrs. Jarvis regarded her fondly. "It would be *so* satisfactory," said she at tea with Mrs. Anthony, "if anything came of it— I would be pleased. Dick should settle down and Susanna is charming."

Mrs. Anthony repeated this, dutifully, to her daughter. Linda said nothing. Her mother asked, after a moment, "Do you think it's serious?"

"How do I know?" asked Linda crossly. "I begin to think that nothing Susanna ever does is serious!"

Happy came to the house, ostensibly to see Linda, now and again. He looked older, paler, a little thin. His smile was not as ready, his wisecracking had suffered. He would look hungrily about the room. "Where's—Susanna?" And Linda would be forced to answer, over the ache in her heart, an ache which she assured herself was all for Happy, "Golfing with Dick," or "Motor boating with Dick," or "Up at the Jarvises' . . ."

"Gee," said Happy, one evening, "I'm going to get out of here!"

"Out of where?" Linda regarded him with astonishment.

"Out of town. . . . I—I can't stand it much longer, Linda!"

He made no further explanation. She knew. She put her hand on his and he took it and held it, hard. "I wish," he said, "I wish——"

Again, he got no further, but again she knew. "I wish I could forget Susanna and go back to loving you, Linda."

But he couldn't; they both knew it.

"I can get a job somewhere——"

"Your mother——?"

His mother had always held him, tenacious, unwilling that he should leave her. He had had opportunities, before. Now he shrugged.

"She'll have to get used to it," he said.

"But, Happy—" Linda hesitated, then she went

on determinedly, "Sue won't stay much longer, you know."

"What difference does that make, she's poisoned the whole place for me," he murmured. "I used to drift along happy-go-lucky, not caring much. Now, everything's different, I can't be content."

Linda tried to talk to Susanna. "You're hurting Happy," she said. But Susanna tossed her little head in a spirited fashion. "What of it?" she demanded, with what seemed to Linda unnecessary harshness.

One night, they went again to the Jarvis' to dinner. Linda had fought against it. Happy had fought against it. Somehow they had been beaten down. They went and suffered each in his own fashion, grimly. Susanna was in high spirits and had never looked prettier.

After dinner she disappeared into the gardens, with Dick. Mrs. Jarvis smiled complacently and folded her hands upon her silken stomach. Jarvis inveigled Happy into a game of Canfield and Linda listened, unheeding, to the radio.

A male tenor, who sounded like a female contralto, announced, from Chicago, in honeyed accents that his old pal had stolen his best gal. Mr. Jarvis won his game and regarded his opponent triumphantly. But Happy rose, with a strange and stricken face, and departed abruptly for the long front terrace, through the French windows. "Well, I'll be darned," said Fred Jarvis mildly.

A moment later Dick came back, alone. He was smiling. He dialed for dance music, and succeeding, drew Linda out to the screened porch. She found herself in his arms, the last place she wanted to be. Or rather, the one place she was determined not to be.

"Come on," he urged her, "dance . . . don't let the innocent bystanders know how you feel about me."

"Where's Susanna?" she demanded.

"Where she ought to be. With Happy."

"With Happy?"

"Certainly, why not? He came at just the right time. She was about to dissolve into tears on my shoulder. Instead, he offered his. She was beginning to be afraid that her little game wouldn't work."

"What game? What are you talking about?"

"The oldest game in the world, darling," he said mockingly, "the poor kid's been out of her head because Happy had given her the air. Pride, and all that sort of thing. Now, it's all right. He can have a job in the mills, if he wants it, I told him so, though I can't see Susanna—however, that's her own affair."

"But——"

"Don't talk. Dance. Must you be so stiff, little ironing board? Even if you hate me, you can dance with me, can't you? Shut your eyes and pretend it's someone else."

She said, after a moment, shortly:

"That's enough. I'm going back to your mother and father."

She was disturbed, feared that he knew it; disturbed by his nearness; by the dimly lighted veranda, by their isolation and the haunting music. . . . He said: "Very well, I can't hold you here by force."

She asked a little wildly:

"Why—why——?"

"Why, what?"

"Nothing. I'm going indoors."

She did so, and he followed. Presently, they were playing contract. Mrs. Jarvis asked: "But where's Susanna—and Happy?"

"They'll be along presently," her son told her, dealing the cards.

Susanna came in. Eyes like blue stars, hair like ruffled spun gold, cheeks like early roses; and with her, Happy, a little sheepish but carrying himself as if his body were a banner; hand and hand, the two of them. Linda's eyes filled with foolish tears regarding their perfectly obvious condition.

"Congratulate us!" cried Susanna, radiant.

And that was that. Finding her there, sitting close to Dick in the gloom of the garden, Happy had started to speak, and then, stumbling away, had heard her voice: "Come back here, Happy. Dick, run off and find another playmate, will you?" Her shaken small voice had tears in it, and Happy had capitulated.

"Happy, why are you so mean to me?"

Childish, absurd. But it settled things. He loved her; he told her so, stammering. But he wasn't good enough. He didn't even have a decent job. Her father and mother would never consent.

WHITE COLLAR GIRL 83

"Let's talk about that some other time," sighed Susanna, in his arms. "Golly, but you were difficult!"

"I thought that Dick——"

"Oh, bother Dick. Forget Dick, forget everything but—me."

The old romantic stage setting, gardens and a slim silver sliver of a moon, the murmur of a river flowing by, pulled inexorably to its goal, a wind in the trees, fragrance from flowers, and the girl you love in your arms . . .

To put it mildly Mrs. Jarvis was distressed. She was disapproving and disappointed. She wrote that night to an address which Susanna had inadvertently given her, a letter full of apologies and "I thought you ought to know," and "of course, there is nothing against the boy, he's a very nice young man but——" "but——" and talk of "families" and "prospects" and the like.

But Susanna didn't know that Mrs. Jarvis *could* write, as far as that went she knew nothing at all; she was not of this world.

She refused to listen to Happy's protestations. She simply said soothingly: "We can talk that all over later, angel. Meantime——"

"Dick will get me a job in the mills; he said so, last night."

"All right. Then we'll go house hunting."

"But, Susanna, my dearest, you absurd little— what on earth will your family say?"

"You aren't marrying the family."

"I won't," he said stubbornly, "marry you without their consent. I have no right to, Susanna. I can't ask you to sacrifice——"

"*Will* you be still and kiss me?"

He was; he did; but the letter caught a fast boat from New York. And the fast boat was the *Bremen*. And the letter reached Mrs. Hudson and she read it. And a cable arrived for Susanna.

Coming home via Montreal. Sailing tomorrow. Will pick you up in Lawrenceton.

Susanna read the cable. She handed it to Linda. Her small face was rather pale. She said, "The old cat!"

"Who?" asked Linda, bewildered.

"Dick's mother. She wrote . . . I wondered why she wanted to know where they were stopping. Oh, darn it!"

"Sue, they had to know some time!"

"Yes, but I wanted them to know from me. I wanted to tell them myself. I wanted them to meet Happy without any—any biased opinions reaching them first.

"Well, it's done now, it can't be helped," she concluded, hopelessly.

For the time remaining to her she flaunted Happy as if he were a trophy. She went to see his mother, his cousins and his aunts and remained merry and gay and casual in the face of the most marked hostility and the hollow question: "Have you considered how Radford will support you?"

Radford! The name always made her laugh. He

WHITE COLLAR GIRL

was Happy . . . to her . . . with her. But not as happy as she wanted him to be. She had told him about the cable; and he'd said: "It means trouble?"

"Perhaps. Are you frightened?"

"No." She saw the hard outline of his jaw. Happy had—grown up, lately. He had never been quite mature before. "No," he said.

"Promise not to let them bluff you, Happy. Promise that, whatever happens, you'll hold me, fast and for always."

"Always."

"Like this?"

"Like this."

And Dick Jarvis said to Linda, during a little truce when they talked of their friends and not of themselves: "It's the best thing that ever happened to him, he's never had the incentive, before. She's supplied it. The incentive to get ahead, to do something in the face of no matter how many obstacles. She's made him discontented, the right sort of discontentment. That's been the trouble with him all along; he was—contented."

Linda agreed with him. She thought, puzzled, faintly wounded: He's right. I was never that to Happy—a star, a goal, an incentive, a cause for discontent. I was just part of the picture. No, he never loved me, really.

She wondered how many never loved their wives perhaps, really, but thrown together, drifted into marriage, propinquity, youth, affection, contentment, the contributing factors.

This conversation took place at the Country Club

the night before the Hudsons were due to arrive in Lawrenceton. "No, you needn't put them up," said Susanna, packing furiously, "let them go to the hotel. If they go to the Jarvises', I'll kill them. I've taken rooms at the hotel for them anyway. And if they expected me to meet them in Montreal, they were very much mistaken."

Susanna gave the dinner. It was a "sort of announcement dinner," she said, and indeed no one present at the club that evening could mistake her proprietary airs toward Happy. There was a good deal of laughter and conversation and toasts were drunk in a forbidden beverage, obligingly supplied by Dick.

He and Linda had been dancing and had left the room and gone out on the links. It was a very warm night. He had spoken of Happy then, cupped palms about the flare of a match. He threw the match away and they walked, talking, over toward the first tee. He said, abruptly, daring to say it because tonight Linda had been friendly, kind even:

"Linda, have you forgiven me?"

She answered, on her guard: "I thought we weren't going to talk about that any more."

He started to say, If—if of your own free will, you would—I'd know you'd forgive me; but he never said it, for she went on composedly:

"Susanna will be leaving tomorrow. I intend to work pretty hard, the rest of the summer . . . and afterwards. You see, your mother's been very kind to Sue, Dick. I mean, I couldn't refuse her invitations."

WHITE COLLAR GIRL

"You mean, you don't care about seeing me any more?" he demanded.

"Oh, if you put it that way——" she said, and laughed.

A thrill of pure, dark anger took him. He said suddenly: "Let's go back to the club."

CHAPTER SEVEN

THE Hudsons arrived in a new motor car and went to the hotel, as they had been coolly directed to do by Susanna in a wire which reached them at the dock. They spent the night in Lawrenceton and held a conference in the hotel bedrooms, mildly astonished that they had not been able to engage a suite.

Mrs. Hudson, for once mislaying her poise, was, for the most part, in tears. Her husband, who was a beardless Santa Claus in appearance, temporarily lost his suavity and general air of benevolence, and stormed fruitlessly at the smiling and unruffled Susanna. Her first encounter with her parents was without other audience. Later, Linda was pressed into unwilling service. Mrs. Hudson said hollowly: "And we are so fond of you, Linda!" which caused Linda to sink into an abashed silence which secretly infuriated her. Why on earth should she be made to feel that she had played the rôle of an illegal Eros? It was not her fault, that Susanna had flamed into town in a red roadster and attached herself with the placid serenity of a barnacle to Happy!

At first, the Hudsons flatly refused so much as to see Happy. "Pooh!" they said, and "Bah!" or words to that effect. "Nothing but infatuation," they said. "Pack your things and come home with us to New York where men are financiers and have their names in the Social Register."

But Susanna was sweet and Susanna was stubborn. "I love him," said Susanna, "he loves me. No one has ever loved anyone as much as we love one another. *Ergo,* we shall be married, with your parental blessing."

"She's a mule," stated Mr. Hudson, with unfatherly grimaces.

"She's a donkey," deplored her mother, not at all maternally.

Eventually, after something resembling supper, which was hastily consumed under the curious eyes of transients and permanents, Mr. Hudson, accompanied by his wife and daughter, marched himself up to the Anthonys. He hoped, he said, that Mrs. Anthony was a sensible woman. He doubted it. He doubted if any member of the uncertain sex was sensible. He glared at his wife. "If you had insisted that Susanna go with us to Europe, none of this would have happened."

Mary Anthony proved disarming. She said gently that, yes, she realized Susanna was very young and that, yes, she realized also that Susanna and Happy hadn't known each other very long. But they were dear young people. Happy was a dear boy, she had known him all his life. Generous, frank, kindly, he had what she insisted upon calling a "beautiful nature," although at this Susanna groaned and said audibly: "If I believed that, it would all be off. I could never live up to it!"

Mrs. Anthony intimated that she was sorry that Susanna's visit to Linda had ended in what appeared to be a family feud. But it was not her fault, or Linda's. *Love,* explained Mrs. Anthony firmly, and that was that. Susanna embraced her. "You're a darling," said Susanna.

Mrs. Anthony went on to say that she personally would welcome Happy as a son-in-law were she in Mrs. Hudson's shoes. Praise could go no further. Mrs. Hudson, painfully smart, magnificently massaged, her graying hair coiffed close to her little head, stared at her hostess. Mr. Hudson cleared his throat and looked apoplectic and Susanna went out to telephone Happy.

He arrived. Susanna ushered him in. Her sweeping gesture swept Linda and Linda's mother out of the room. Susanna planted herself firmly upon her two small feet beside the long and lanky lover she had selected. She said defiantly: "This is Happy. And I'm not going to give him up no matter *what* you say!"

Happy was quick to sense hostility. But anyone would have sensed it in this case, be he thick-skinned as an elephant. He flushed, a very little, and then smiled that crooked and engaging grin which caused Susanna's heart to do an Immelman turn every time he produced it.

"So you're the young man!" boomed Mr. Hudson, unnecessarily.

"I have that honor," replied Happy. He squeezed Susanna's cold little hand; he said, with disarming sincerity, "I understand perfectly that you're not overwhelmed with rapture over this."

"Sit down," barked his possible future father-in-law. Happy sat. Susanna, casting defiant glances, perched herself on a hassock, her bright head near Happy's angular knees. The usual cross-examination ensued: *Who* are you? How old are you? Who are your people? What is your family record? What business are you in? How much do you make? Can you support my daughter? and so forth and so on.

Susanna interpolated, airily: "As if that mattered; *you've* plenty of money!"

She addressed herself to her father. Happy went brick-red. He said shortly: "That doesn't concern us, Susanna." And Mr. Hudson looked at him with something approaching interest and respect.

Happy, as well as he could, explained the situation. The town: the general stagnation of it, which had been so ordered by the Few and so deplored by the Many. The lack of opportunity. The unwillingness of his family to allow him to seek elsewhere for a job. He said quietly: "I work in a garage."

This was no body blow to the Hudsons. Mrs. Jarvis had already apprised them, apologetically, in curly writing, of this dread secret.

"Happy," stated Susanna, "would make good in any job."

Mr. Hudson looked dubious.

Happy said gravely, leaning forward:

"I love Susanna, Mr. Hudson. But I have told

her that we cannot be married without your consent——"

"Brute!" interrupted Susanna, while Mr. Hudson brightened and Happy went on.

"If—if circumstances were different, I wouldn't bother about anyone's consent, but Susanna's," Happy said quietly. "But in this case I—" his eyes were very blue and direct, he looked much less boyish than usual—"I'm not a fortune hunter. I'm not interested in any money Susanna may have or will have. If she marries me, even with your consent, she'll have to live on what I make. I can't ask her to do that now, naturally, as I can hardly live on it myself." The irrepressible grin flickered out again. "But I don't intend to separate her from her family. I've no right to."

Out of this muddle Mr. Hudson appeared to grasp something which made sense, at least to him. He nodded and thrust a gold cigarette case at the younger man. Happy accepted a cigarette and rolled it thoughtfully between his fingers as Mrs. Hudson interrupted sharply.

"We had other plans for Susanna—"

"If you're thinking of those saps back home—" Susanna flared.

"You didn't always think them—saps," her mother reminded her delicately.

"I do now. After Happy, they're all saps!" said Susanna.

Happy, with an unpremeditated gesture of tenderness, dropped a large, brown, calloused hand upon her shining head. He said:

"If Susanna really loves me, she'll stick to me. . . . Look here, Mr. Hudson, couldn't you put me— on probation?" He smiled again. "I mean, give me a chance to prove myself, to clear out of here, get a job and work? And when I've made good—and I don't mean by that that I'll be a young man in a novel, coming back with a couple of millions in a few months—but when I've shown I can really amount to something, perhaps you'll reconsider?"

Susanna said, "I want to marry Happy *now*!" Her chin quivered, her eyes filled with tears. Happy said uncomfortably: "It's better not, Susanna." She touched the brown paw with her lips, rose, ran across the room and cast herself, weeping, into her father's arms. Holding that soft bundle of electric stubbornness and sweetness, Mr. Hudson looked over the head of his spoiled child and cleared his throat.

"That's fair of you, Mr. Anderson. Suppose we make a bargain. Suppose I give you a job?"

Happy said, scarlet: "I didn't ask for that, sir. That's not what I meant."

Susanna cried, muffled, "Take it . . . take anything . . . can't you let your old pride down even half an inch?"

She removed her face from her father's solid shoulder. She sniffed. Her little nose was pink. Her cheeks were wet, tears sparkled on her lashes. She shook her father fiercely with two small strong hands and cried at him accusingly: "If it's because he's small town—what are you," demanded Susanna, "but small town? Yes, and mother, too!

Don't you know that small town boys make good, and that most men who do make good were never born in your darned old New York!"

Amazingly, Mrs. Hudson began to laugh, unsteadily. Her eyes met her husband's. They were from the Middle West. A long way from it. They had grown up together in a hot and busy little town. They had, even, sung in choirs. Their first year of married life had been spent on a main street in a frame house, and Mr. Hudson had run the lawn mower in his shirtsleeves. . . .

"I give in," said Mr. Hudson, "Mr.—what on earth does she call you?"

"Happy."

"His name," confided Susanna, "is Radford. But don't let that upset you."

"Well, Happy," Mr. Hudson smiled reluctantly, "I think you have the makings of a good hotel man."

"Who? Me?" Happy looked bewildered. Presently he laughed. He asked: "A bell hop?"

"Well, not exactly. I meant what I said." He had meant it. This lanky boy had an engaging personality. Quick, too, Hudson judged, on the uptake. And a born untangler of difficulties, or he, Hudson, was no judge. He had a mental picture of Happy grinning engagingly at irate old ladies, prima donnas and Big Business Men. He said briskly:

"I'll give you a chance, both of you. You, to prove how good you can be; Susanna, to prove——"

"I don't need to!"

Her father shrugged. He went on:

"We've recently taken over a hotel on the West

Coast. I'll send you out there, you can learn the business. When you've learned enough to make it worth my while, you may come back East. I'll find a place for you. And you and Susanna can be married."

"Oh," said Mrs. Hudson; and, "Oh," said Susanna. Happy rose. Mr. Hudson rose, and Susanna left his lap unceremoniously. Happy held out the big brown paw. Mr. Hudson shook it. "It's a bargain," said Happy. "I'm pretty darned grateful." His eyes shone, he carried himself very straight. Susanna wept, uncomforted. "The West Coast! Oh, Happy, I know you'll never write . . . you don't *look* as if you ever wrote." She brightened. "I know girls," confided Susanna, planning visits, "in Los Angeles, San Francisco, Fresno—"

"No, you don't," said her father. "You'll stay home with your mother and me. That's part of the bargain."

Happy said, rather low: "Let me try, Susanna. Your dad's right, you know. I've got to make something of myself——"

She thought, the lovesick and fatuous child, it would be hard to improve upon what he had already made. But she put her hand into his and vowed, with steady lips, "All right, Happy, I'll wait."

He believed her. So, strangely enough, did her mother and father. They thought, astonished, She means it—she will wait.

Later, Linda and Mrs. Anthony returned to the room and Happy and Susanna vanished out on the porch. Mrs. Hudson made a baffled gesture. Yet she rather liked this young man, she admitted it to herself. Mrs. Anthony suggested softly: "Let them alone, they are saying good-bye." She smiled faintly. Hard to say good-bye when you are young and in love and every parting is the little death the poets call it. Hard. But not as hard as saying good-bye when you've grown old together and good-bye means a long eternity, waiting, housed so impatiently in the lonely, no longer valuable flesh. . . .

"Love me always?"

"Always, Susanna . . . darling, I'll make good."

He spoke no word to her of the scene which was to follow, the scene which would be staged for him by a selfish and reluctant mother, but Susanna guessed. She kissed him, murmuring: "She's going to take it awfully hard."

"I know."

But this was his chance; his chance not only for happiness with Susanna but his chance to put an end to drifting, to watching the world hurry past from the loungers' seat, in front of a corner drug store.

Happy left, promising to return bright and early in order to see the start, the procession, from the hotel. The Hudsons' new car had been purchased in England, had toured in accustomed haunts, and, brought back with them in the hold of the boat, it now slept, or stood wakeful, in the strange surroundings of an American garage, surrounded, until late at night, by the awe-struck visitors. It was a powerful car, sleek, a little arrogant. . . .

Susanna, who had recklessly planned that she and

Happy would drive to New York in her roadster, now refused to take it with her. Happy, she declared, could drive it down, next week, when he kept his appointment with her father. In this manner she insured herself against not seeing him again; otherwise, she told Linda, it would be just like the wily Hudson *père,* to ship his new responsibility off to Los Angeles *incomunicado,* rushing him from one train to the next in the dead of night. . . .

She spent what was left of that memorable night at the Anthonys', perched for the most part on Linda's bed, exclaiming, alternately, that she was so happy and so miserable.

Linda congratulated and condoled. "Don't worry, Happy'll make the grade."

"As if I didn't know that! Linda, I'll be so darned lonely. Give up your simple-minded job and come to New York with me for the autumn and winter."

But Linda refused to take the departing guest seriously. "I like my job, it's grand. And besides, I couldn't leave mother."

"Bring her along," urged Susanna hospitably, "there's plenty of room."

There was. The Hudsons occupied the very large penthouse atop the newest Manhattan Hudson Chain Hotel, on Fifth Avenue.

Early on a sunny morning Happy appeared to escort Susanna's luggage personally to the hotel, from which the spectacular start was to be made. The trunks would follow by express. Susanna weeping openly, careless of any stranger who might be up at such an ungodly hour, clung to him, and thrust out one hand for Linda's comforting grasp. She had already said farewell to everyone in town, yet Dick Jarvis ambled by, having forced himself out of bed with the unusual aid of an alarm clock. Susanna left Happy long enough to tell him the tragic yet hopeful news. "That's great," said Dick heartily. Mrs. Hudson was fussing over the disposal of bags and things. Mr. Hudson was haranguing his long-suffering chauffeur-courier who traveled, at a price, with the ménage. . . .

"Linda, darling—Good-bye, Dick, old thing, don't take any wooden money. Happy—Happy, I'll see you next week."

Handkerchiefs, damp, fluttering. Susanna's perky face, smiling, tearful; Happy watching her go, his eyes determined and hungry. Dick and Linda standing at last alone upon the curb, watching Happy climb into the little roadster and drive it, with uncommon care and tenderness, to his garage.

"Well!" said Linda, on a long breath.

Dick looked down at her.

"They're in love," he stated firmly.

"You astonish me," she said.

"No, but I mean it." He asked curiously, "Do you think she'll stick?"

"Of course, she'll stick!" said Linda aggressively. Yet she had not been quite sure of it until confronted by masculine doubt.

She had not seen Dick since the recent evening at the country club. Now, an awkward silence fell between them. She said, after a moment: "I must go home. I persuaded Mother not to get up to see Sue off, and although Sue and I had coffee together, I feel in immediate need of breakfast."

He suggested: "The hotel diningroom is open, or will be soon. I wouldn't object to ham and eggs myself."

He thought, How few women look pretty this early in the morning . . . the sunrise test, so to speak. Even Susanna had looked faded and worn under her careful cosmetic touches. But then, Susanna had been crying. Linda's small face was pale but her lips glowed red and her eyes were gray and unfathomable pools. He liked the way her bronze hair curled at the nape of her neck; he liked the trim suit she wore, brown skirt and coat, maize sweater. He watched her as she hesitated, trying to make an excuse. No excuse would do. He took her arm and escorted her up the broad shallow steps to the hotel porch with its deserted rocking chairs. Short of making a scene before the avid eyes of the desk clerk, she could not escape.

The diningroom, save for a few heavy-eyed salesmen, was deserted. Dick ordered with lavishness, over Linda's protests. Fruit, ham and eggs, buckwheat cakes and coffee, "lots of it!"

She said: "I ought to be home."

"Well, you're not. The Nortons are throwing another camp-party this coming week-end, I'll stop for you."

"No, I can't, I'll be busy."

He asked fretfully, "When will you take a day off?"

"When I've sold another ten thousand dollars' worth," she said, laughing and then stopped, remembering a wager.

His face did not change. He replied, lifting his coffee cup, "Well, here's how, I hope you do, it's time we got acquainted!"

"Acquainted!"

"Well, why not? When we do meet we spend most of our time fighting——"

She set down her cup. She replied carefully, although her heart beat with a sickening rapidity.

"That's because we're naturally antagonistic."

He looked amused.

"You think so, really?"

"Yes."

"You may be. I'm not." He leaned across the table, to the deep interest of the observant waitress who had known them both since they were knee-high to hop toads and who now drew nearer to murmur ingratiatingly, "More coffee, Linda? Dick, I'll bring you a plate of fresh cakes."

"Thanks, Gertrude——"

Gertrude departed to create excitement in the kitchen. Dick said:

"You're by far the most attractive girl in town, you know."

She flickered long eyelashes at him.

"I like," he announced, "my new job. It's rather fun. I had to battle with Dad at every turn, of course. He can't see changing anything; and some of his methods are as antiquated as—as blushing.

But I enjoy a good fight. Perhaps," he suggested, and smiled, "that's why I enjoy *you*!"

He was absurdly good-looking. He wore his clothes like nobody's business. His dark hair, with the suspicion of the wave—he had battered everything save the suspicion out of it, not long before, with military brushes and water—his engaging smile, his lean brown face and well-cut features . . . Linda, aware that her eyes had been dreaming far too long came back to herself with a jerk of annoyance.

Better have it out.

She looked at him now, no longer dreamily but directly, squarely. She said:

"It's all been very silly. Quarreling and then— being magnificently courteous—I—I live in a rather different world than yours, Dick."

"What, in Lawrenceton?"

"You know what I mean," she said, "I have to work." Remembering why she had to work her face hardened subtly. Not that she minded working, she liked it. But her father would have hated—she went on steadily: "You've all the time you want to play around. I haven't. I can't keep my end up with the Nortons and the others any more. I haven't time for golf, for many dances, for camping parties. You——" she flushed a little, the "antiquated" gesture of the abashed blood—"you like to—amuse yourself with me, because——"

"Well, go on, because?"

"Because I don't fall for it, like the others," she stated flatly.

His face was entertaining but not entertained.
She said strongly:

"You know they do. Dick Jarvis, son of Fred Jarvis. The catch of the town. Lawrenceton, Princeton, Oxford, Paris, Rome. . . . Coming home, condescending to the hoi-polloi, amusing himself with a job that's a sure thing, able to take any girl out and give her a whirl—" She remembered Susanna's words. "Of course they fall for it. I don't, that's all. Crown Prince stuff!"

He said soberly:

"What a pleasant person you think me. You don't like me, do you, Linda?"

"Not particularly," she said lightly. "I think you're attractive to look at and all that. But your attitude infuriates me."

He said softly:

"When you lost your wager . . . and paid up . . . I thought, for a moment, you liked me, rather."

He looked to see her redden; she paled, instead. She said, low:

"That wasn't very fair of you." She fixed the disturbing eyes on his own, and went on slowly: "If you mean I—I liked you to kiss me, you're right." She ignored his small exclamation of more than triumph. She went on: "I *did* like it. But I didn't like *you*. There's all the difference."

He was startled into abject silence. Linda explained:

"I'm young, healthy, a little lonely. Well, go on, look shocked. Men kiss girls they don't care for and like it. Why shouldn't girls?"

He said: "Why not, indeed?" but his dark eyes were outraged and astonished.

"Because," she said bravely, "because I responded to you, for a moment, that doesn't mean that I—like you. After all, you've kissed dozens of girls, without caring, without even thinking. I was perfectly aware I came into that category."

"You were never more wrong, in all your life!"

"I think not. You know," she said, "you kissed me . . . out of meanness, with malice aforethought!"

"Linda, for heaven's sake!"

She pushed her plate away. She said definitely:

"You were angry. Anger's an emotion. You can release it in a kiss, I suppose, after all."

He said dimly: "I'm pretty crazy about you and you're making me madder every minute!"

"There, you see!" She regarded him with animation, although her heart raced. "That's what I do to you. Make you mad! That's what you do to me. That's no basis for friendship," she told him.

"If you'd give me a chance . . ."

He was perfectly aware that he wanted to kiss her again, now, immediately, under the pale blue eyes of the hovering Gertrude. She was right, she infuriated him, but it was a heady sensation, it was a fever in his blood. What a girl!

Linda rose.

"I have to get back to Mother," she said, "and, don't you think we've done all the talking necessary? I haven't," she told him, "time for you.

There isn't any sense in it, is there? And you haven't time for me, really."

He followed her out of the diningroom; paid his check; exchanged pleasantries with the clerk; said, out on the steps, "I'll drive you home."

"Thanks, I'd rather walk."

"May I phone and come see you, some evening?"

"Why?"

She walked away, smiling very slightly. Yet she didn't feel like smiling. "I'm pretty crazy about you." Crazy. That's what it amounted to. She angered him, she piqued his pride. One girl who wouldn't fall. Well, she'd told him, straight from the shoulder.

He stood staring after her. Later, at the office, sitting at his desk, listening to the pedantic report of some clerk or other, he had an idea; and grasped it by reaching for the telephone.

When Linda returned home that afternoon, after a fruitless series of calls, the only bright spot in the day being a short visit with Mrs. Hopkins, she found a message waiting for her. "Mr. Pearson wants you to call him up at his home as soon as you come in."

She telephoned Pearson and his quick, brisk voice came over the wire. He had had an inquiry, he told her, from one Richard Jarvis . . . wasn't that Fred Jarvis' son? Young Jarvis was thinking of making some investments. Would Mr. Pearson please put him in touch with his district representative?

WHITE COLLAR GIRL 105

And if so, would the representative call upon him at his office in the morning? At ten?

Linda stammered. "Dick Jarvis? But—how perfectly ridiculous!"

Pearson said, mildly astonished: "Why ridiculous? Go after the business, Linda; it may mean his father, too. A stroke of luck, I should say."

Luck!

She hung up the receiver and bit her lip. How exactly like Dick! Making it impossible for her to refuse. She listened all evening to Happy discoursing on Susanna and presented him with Susanna's picture until he would have one of his own. In a few days Happy was leaving for New York and points West. "Linda, wish me luck."

She did, but in an abstracted manner.

When she walked into Dick's office at the mill the next day, the light of battle was in her eye. Two could play at that game.

She was met by a sour secretary, a woman she had known most of her life, and ushered into the office with no ceremony whatever. Dick sat behind the old-fashioned roll-top desk, blatantly golden oak, and motioned her to a chair beside him.

"I called up Mr. Pearson," he began.

She said: "It wasn't necessary, was it?"

"Quite. If I hadn't you wouldn't have come. You aren't, after all, such a good business go-getter. You would rather lose the business. I have," he said, leaning back in his chair, his face serious, "a sum available for investment. What has your house to offer?"

It was sublimely idiotic. From her brief-bag she hauled forth certain printed matter. She talked steadily; she explained; gave figures, percentages. He listened gravely.

"I am content to leave it in your hands," he said, when she paused for breath.

He took out a check book, a special account check book. He told her, pen poised: "I am ready to invest—ten thousand dollars."

In spite of herself, she gasped. He wrote the check. He said, "I'll hear from you again?"

Her hand was steady, taking the check. She thought frantically, I'll turn this over to Pearson, let him handle it.

Dick took her to the door. He bade her a courteous good morning. But his hand fell on her shoulder, lightly. He said, and laughed:

"Does it—wipe out the wager, Linda? And— does it leave you free to come to the Nortons'? I'll stop for you, Saturday noon."

She departed, furious tears in her eyes. She wouldn't go to the Nortons', she'd die first.

If she disliked him before, she loathed him now.

Ten thousand dollars!

A bribe, a greasing of palms. It meant less to him than a hundred dollars to her.

She found, on returning home, that Pearson had called her up. Dutifully she reported to him grimly. He said gaily:

"A couple more like that and you'll do more than go over the top. You're in line for a bonus, as it is. Going to invest it, Linda?"

She told him, rather shortly, that she was.

No, she would not go to the Nortons'. Dick could call her a poor sport and worse, if he wished. She wouldn't go and suffer under his dark, mocking eyes. He had less than no interest in her business ability, he was interested only in getting the better of her, in waging his private war with her under the imbecile cover of a "business" deal.

After all, she did not go to camp. Mrs. Norton's mother died suddenly and the party was canceled. Linda, sorry for Dolly and doing all she could to help, drew a small selfish sigh of relief.

Happy left for New York and Dick decided to go with him in Susanna's roadster. Linda, learning this from Happy's mother on the street, wondered why she did not feel more relieved.

He sent her a silly postcard of Ellis Island. He wrote: "Cross marks my room. Absence makes the heart grow fonder, Linda, if I thought it didn't I wouldn't have gone away."

At least, he had enclosed the card in an envelope. She had that much to be thankful for. She tore it across and across and dropped it in the wastebasket.

Dick had been gone for three days and Linda was on her way to a nearby, noisy, county fair with Elizabeth Young and Bert Warren when she heard the first rumor of coming elections. Bert told her, driving over to Boone:

"Have you heard that Fred Jarvis intends retiring from all active business and running for mayor, next fall?"

"No." She looked at him, astonished. "It isn't

true, is it? Fred Jarvis! Why on earth does he want to be mayor?"

"It's obvious. More fingers in the pie. Before he's through he'll have this place the world's most celebrated deserted village. He'll be able to turn it into private golf links and toboggan slides for himself."

Elizabeth said:

"The Civic Club wants to run Bert."

"Bert?" Linda regarded him, her eyes shining. "Bert! But that would be wonderful!"

He said gloomily:

"I can't afford it, really. But if I got it, Lord, I'd show 'em. We'd clean up this dump, put it on the map . . ."

She reminded him, slowly:

"You've a powerful opponent."

"Yes, and votes can still be bought. He controls almost everyone in town. Owns plenty mortgages, more than pulls his weight."

Linda said, thinking aloud:

"I've come to know a lot of people, out of the town but still in the city limits. I—I think I'd have some influence."

Elizabeth said stoutly: "Me, too."

Bert stopped the car on a side road. Goldenrod grew, waist-high, there were drowsy insects humming in the hot September sun. They could see the river, lazy, blue, and the great white clouds sailing in a clear sky. Cows stood knee-deep in pasture, and a barefoot kid went whistling by, a pup at his heels. . . .

"You'll work for me, Linda . . . go on my committee?"

"Of course, I will," she promised, radiant.

Elizabeth looked at her, a sidelong glance.

"Dick Jarvis will use all his influence against Bert and for his father," she began.

"Well, surely that's natural enough," her fiancé told her tolerantly and blindly.

But Elizabeth paid no attention to him. She was looking at Linda.

Linda lifted her chin. "He may control the mill vote and that of the younger female population," she challenged, "but . . . there are ways and means . . . all the voters aren't marriageable girls!"

"If Fred Jarvis gets in as mayor," Bert told the two seriously, "it will be the worst thing that ever happened to this town. It will mean digging its grave."

Linda said:

"He won't get in. *You'll* get in, Bert!"

Her eyes danced. If Dick had liked a good fight, he'd have one now.

She said slowly:

"Election isn't until a year from this fall. We've lots of time. Almost anything can happen between now and then," prophesied Linda.

CHAPTER EIGHT

Dick Jarvis, returning from New York, presented himself at the Anthony house with very little delay. He was provided, he announced, a little maliciously, with an adequate excuse, as Susanna had sent all sorts of messages to Linda and wished them delivered, so to speak, by word of mouth. "But you don't need any excuse to come see us, Richard," Mrs. Anthony exclaimed, in mild astonishment.

They were in the living room, that warm autumn evening. Dick flashed a bright, dark look at Linda. Linda said nothing, leaning back against the comfortable, shabby upholstery of her chair, tired from a day of trekking all over the countryside without much result. However, it wasn't often that she returned home without results: without a fairly substantial sum on the credit side. And she was discovering that she was doing more than trying to sell securities; she was rapidly becoming the repository for confidences . . . prospects telling her of what they had lost or gained financially, of their hope to save, to build up an adequate income, were growing confidential, and Linda was hearing of young people's ambitions for themselves, of old people's ambitions for their children; she was hearing complaints and expectations; she was getting an insight into the needs and lacks of the district which she had never dreamed she would possess. And because Bert Warren appeared interested in any phase of life that touched Lawrenceton, or the county, she sometimes told him these things and occasionally he made notes on a scrap of paper and listened to her thoughtfully, nodding occasionally or breaking into indignant exclamations. Elizabeth, always present at these informal conferences, often had her own data to add to Linda's. As school nurse she went into the families of the children and both heard and saw a good deal.

Linda, looking at Dick Jarvis, thought, Everything's been so easy for him always. Everything will continue to be easy. He lives in this town, he is part of it, but he is only a spectator, after all, he just scratches the surface, he doesn't want to plow down deep into the town life. He's afraid maybe of the things he'd turn up. . . .

Her hostility toward him was partially based, she admitted unhappily, upon the very attraction which drew her and which she fought against.

Mrs. Anthony said: "It's extraordinarily warm, isn't it? Suppose I make some lemonade—you'd like that, wouldn't you, children? Why don't you go out on the veranda?"

"I'm comfy here," said Linda and, rather rudely, yawned.

Dick grinned. "I'm not," he announced firmly, and rose and stood over her. "Here, stir yourself and let's go out and watch Lawrenceton on its way to the movies," he told her.

She went, of course, she could hardly do anything else, and established herself in the old swing while Richard, in a wicker lounge chair beside her, produced a pipe, asked for permission to light it and presently sat stretched out smoking in solid comfort.

"Why don't you go to the movies with me some time?" he wanted to know. "That's what all the boys and girls do here, isn't it?"

She said flatly: "I don't like the picture house. It isn't safe."

Richard raised an eyebrow. "What do you mean, not safe?" he inquired. "And what house?"

"There are only two and just one where the new pictures are shown," she informed him, "and that's a fire-trap."

"Girl, you're crazy!"

She saw his slow flush, and then remembered that his father owned the building, having built and leased it in order to keep certain chain concerns from getting a foothold in the town and bringing with them an amount of competition.

She said defiantly:

"I'm not sorry that I made that break. But I'd forgotten your father owns the place. You might," she suggested, "speak to him about conditions there."

"I'm sure you must be mistaken," he told her, a little stiffly. "I haven't been in the place, as it happens, since I came home, but there are fire laws and inspections, you know."

Linda said nothing, eloquently. Yet he was perfectly sensitive to her silence which mutely accused him of his father's quite well-known, if unofficial, dictatorship over fire and police and other civic departments in the town. He burst out, finally, with a recklessness he could not restrain.

"Look here, Linda, what in the world have you got against us—my family, I mean? I admit your attitude toward myself, although I don't understand it and can't believe it's justified—but just what's wrong with the rest of us? You used to be like—like one of us, when you were a kid. Dad's always been fond of you, he was such a close friend of your father's."

"I know that," she replied shortly; and was silent a moment longer. Upstairs, locked away, was a little strong box, which she had owned since her schooldays and her first treasurer's job. There were certain letters in it. She had found them, going through her father's papers. She had not spoken of them to Bert Warren. As an executor they did not concern him; as a friend, still less. She thought of them now.

"What's the Big Idea?" he was urging impatiently.

Of course, her mind echoed scornfully, you couldn't imagine anyone taking an opposite stand from that of Jarvis and Company! She found herself talking with great rapidity, and some heat.

"It isn't personal—" she began; but it was, in part. "It's this. Your father and his particular crowd of rich older men have run this town too long. They've made it, because it suited them, into a stagnant backwater, jerkwater sort of a place. It's time younger men came in, and, without selfish motives, cleaned it up—made it a place with a present and a future instead of a place with a past. Just because your people and a few of their friends have money, Dick Jarvis, and are content to live in lovely old houses and lord it over the rest of the townsfolk is that any reason why people, not as fortunate, and a lot more ambitious for themselves, and the town, should be held back, smothered, by the influence your father and Homer Manton and a handful of others exert?"

"Why, Linda," he replied, as she stopped to catch her breath, "I don't understand you, honestly, I don't. No one cares more for Lawrenceton than Dad . . . no one has its interests more at heart. Look at the things he's done for it, the new park, the ball field—the contributions he gives to charity, to the churches . . ."

He floundered into an amazed silence, less offended by her attack than sincerely astonished.

"Oh, parks!" she flung back at him, "and ball fields and charities! Money—that's all! He hasn't, has he, done one single thing that contributes to the town's business progress, its real rock-bottom welfare?"

Richard rose and knocked out his pipe against the railing. He leaned there for a moment, his hand clasped about the smooth warm bowl.

He said, after a moment:

"You've been talking to Bert. Bert's all right,

but he's gone goofy where this town is concerned. He imagines it could become the most important manufacturing center in this part of the state. He's cuckoo, of course. That's out of the question. Moreover, it would be ruined, if it did . . . all its charm would be gone, it would be a commercial proposition entirely filled with factories and slums and an emigrant population——"

"Charm preferred," she murmured, "to established progress?"

"Well, why not?" He looked toward the small white blur of her face. He said, with assumed carelessness:

"I suppose you know there's a chance of my father's running for mayor at the next election?"

"Yes, I know it." She was silent a moment. Then she said quite gently:

"You'll hate me for saying this but I honestly believe if he is elected it will be the worst thing that ever happened to Lawrenceton."

"Linda!" After a long moment, he went on: "I don't hate you. Sometimes I wish to God I did. I can't understand—anything . . . you—your attitude —your unfriendliness."

"I don't expect you can," she said soberly. "It isn't that I'm unfriendly, really, it's just that—we live in different worlds, we have different standards, different ideals. We don't——" she remembered Susanna's statement about Happy—"we don't speak the same language."

"That's absurd," he said violently, "and you know it. Look here, what on earth have you against poor old Dad? Why, this town's part of him. He's crazy about it, he wouldn't live anywhere else for anything in the world."

"Of course, he wouldn't," she agreed, "but that's why he wants to keep it the sort of place in which he happens to like living. He doesn't think that other people might want it changed, that's all."

"He's done a lot for it," Dick insisted stubbornly. "Look at the mills—he takes care of his people— doesn't he?— takes a real interest in them, offers hundreds good, steady employment. . . ."

"Oh, they'll vote for him," she remarked carelessly, "but just the same I give you fair warning. When election campaigns start, I'll be working against the Jarvis interests."

He was tremendously taken aback. Then he laughed. "You," he said mockingly but with an undercurrent of tolerant tenderness, "you—you're hardly old enough to vote!"

"Oh, yes, I am," she contradicted, "and perhaps by the time elections come around, I'll be influential enough to——"

"Linda, you don't mean it, you can't mean it. Your father's friend!"

She said strangely: "Yes, my father's friend. I—recognize that, Dick."

He said, coming nearer to her and leaning closer:

"I'll campaign for my father. You know that?"

"Of course—you should," she told him, and laughed a little.

"I take it—it's war?" he asked rather quietly.

"Yes."

Her tone was inflexible. They stared at each other a moment through the thick warm darkness. They did not hear people passing, talking, laughing on the street. His hands went out, touched her shoulder. *"Linda . . . ?"*

She said, "Yes?" again without stirring, but her tone was broken now, a mere breath of a whisper. He asked low:

"Why do you infuriate me so—why do you oppose me at every turn? This business about my father. That goes deep. Not that I care which way your political fancies turn, although it would be pleasanter to have you on our side. But—you're trying to hit at *me,* aren't you—through any issue, no matter how trivial or important?"

She replied, after a moment:

"I don't think so, Dick. . . . No, I don't think so. You see, I really believe what I said. It hasn't anything to do with you——"

"Are you sure?"—his hold on her shoulder tightened—"very sure? I'm not. It seems to me, God knows why, that we are out to hurt each other, that we can't get away from it——"

"You're hurting me now," she told him breathlessly.

His hands relaxed, fell to his sides. Mrs. Anthony came through the door with her quick light step.

"Dick? Linda? It's so dark I can't see you. Would one of you come and help me with the glasses?"

The curious spell which had held them both was shattered. Mrs. Anthony sat with them until the last cookie crumb was gone and the tinkling pitcher empty. Then Dick rose to go.

When he had gone Linda went up to bed. She tried to write Susanna but her pen slid from her hand and she thrust her fingers through her heavy hair, conscious of a headache, a feeling of tension at the nape of her neck.

That she disliked Fred Jarvis for reasons which were important to herself, she knew. Yet her motives in opposing him with what small strength she might muster against his tremendous influence were guiltless of that dislike. She had learned enough about him, his methods in the town, to cause her to throw her weight on the other side, quite apart from her personal feeling. But Dick—where did Dick come in?

She thought desperately, To be fair, I've got to separate him from all this.

CHAPTER NINE

HAPPY, arriving on the West Coast, began bombarding Linda with postcards, sent air mail. So like Happy, that last touch. He sent her pictures of zoos, trained seals, public libraries, and Hollywood main streets, always with a cross marking his exact alleged position and a "wish you were here," before his signature. Susanna wrote, lonesomely. Her parents had taken her to Bar Harbor for the short remainder of the season and she and her mother would go to Hot Springs or Pinehurst for the autumn. She said, "Can you *bear* it, my dear, *actually?*" Her father, she also wrote, had "loosened up" on the dress allowance proposition and for the first time in her brief, but colorful, career she was permitted to buy all the clothes she wished. But even a plethora of French hats could not make up for Happy's absence. "Golly, Linda, it's the real thing, honest it is! I go around in a daze. I meet lots of people, lots of men. No one matters, trees walking, that's all. I've even taken to reading poetry and I write Happy three times a day, like taking a tonic. He's not so hot on the return mail end but I know he misses me. He likes his job,

Dad's getting good reports, which seem to disconcert him somewhat."

Linda, reading the letters, envied Susanna. To Susanna, impatient and impulsive, waiting seemed unendurable. But waiting, thought Linda, must be a sort of yearning rapture when you were sure, were sure.

The season slid abruptly into the gorgeous autumn of the North Country. Skies were deepest azure, and the river a blue and silver torrent under gay winds, and an ugly gray-green, white-capped expanse under storm. All through September the goldenrod grew high, fields of gold starred with the amethyst of small wild asters, and woodbine turned wine-red, tangled ruby, on the rail fences. There were clear days and days without wind when all earth seemed suspended in blue warm space; and with the magnificent setting of the sun and the silver approach of stars there was a warning chill; and the Northern Lights sang through the heavens.

By the end of September the trees had started to turn, especially in the thickly wooded area of the foothills.

Linda was working hard, she was out practically every day, taking her panting but faithful little car over the rutted backroads, invading farmhouses and scattered cottages, driving through the main streets of the small towns, carrying her brief-bag, and her message, everywhere. She was going out a good deal too, on Pearson's advice: to church suppers, to card parties, to the Country Club. "You must show yourself everywhere," he told her seriously, "for everyone you meet is a potential buyer."

At first, this edict bored her. Later she became interested, increasing her circle of acquaintances rapidly and widely. Through Elizabeth Young she prospected among the teachers in town and out of it and with marked success. Her orders were small but in the long run mounted up. And hearing, through one of these women, that the most successful small town beauty parlor in the northern part of the state was in the nearby town of Benville, she made a trip over there and, later, an appointment and returned to have a facial, a manicure and a finger wave. Not that she needed these refurbishings but, by so doing, she grew to know the plump, smart, middle-aged woman who owned and ran the place and who, after her third visit, confided to her that she had dropped a large portion of her hard-earned savings in the recent market manipulations. "You'd better," said Linda, "get out of the market and into investments."

Before Christmas Madame Leona had "gotten out" of the stock market and had invested, through Linda, to the tune of fifteen thousand dollars. "I wish I'd known you sooner," she said regretfully. Linda, figuring up the cost of her various beautifying visits, found the transaction well worth her while. And Pearson was pleased with her; so pleased that gratifying letters came to her from the home office and early in the winter she made a trip to the city, staying with cousins of her mother's, in order to talk to the partners of her house and come away stimulated and pledged to do more, as time went on.

Another successful venture was that of an old patient of Elizabeth Young's and through her, her father. Linda was becoming known, in her district, as "the girl who sells bonds," and before spring was a familiar figure not only in her own town but in others. They teased her a little at the bank, but cordially, as her personal account grew. "Just like your father," they told her, and the president said, "We're proud of you, Linda." It was like an accolade.

It was inevitable that she would often encounter Dick Jarvis. He too was going out more, "mingling," explained Bert, "with the hoi-polloi, for the first time in his life!" He was interesting himself in the families of the mill people and exerting himself to supply doctors and hospitals, food and clothing when needed during the fall and winter of real distress among the people. Elizabeth Young, hearing of the insurance system he had put through, commented thoughtfully, "I didn't know he had it in him," but Bert responded, "He wants his old man to be mayor, that's all."

Linda listened, watching Bert's keen clever face across the table in the Country Club. She had rejoined. The dues could be managed, it was good business. She argued, shifting her glance to the polished floor and the people dancing: "I don't think it's entirely selfish, Bert. After all, it wasn't Dick's choice to stay up here for the rest of his natural life you know. I suppose he has to find something to do."

She wondered vaguely why she had defended him and with such a sincere belief in the veracity of her statement. Bert raised an eyebrow at her. He said, after a moment: "Maybe you're right. He's very popular, they tell me, getting more so all the time. Still there are disaffected people at the mills. The son of the former manager—who'd hoped to have his father's job some day—is a member of my bunch. He says that doctors and hospitals and insurance can't make up for low wages and family politics. He's right, of course. I have never approved of a paternalistic organization. Too much like the stern poppa who is liable to disinherit you if you don't walk the chalk line he's laid down. I'd rather Jarvis, too, gave less personal interest, gave fewer baskets at Christmas and paid higher wages . . . to our own people. He hires a lot of Canadian labor, you know. It's cheaper. They live just over across the river, no trouble to get here."

"There's Dick now," said Elizabeth warningly.

He was coming toward them, smiling, his eyes on Linda. She knew an illogical relief that she had worn the new frock which Betty Warren, who ran the New York dress shop, had bought especially for her, on her last buying trip to New York. Madame Leona, at Benville, had persuaded her to try a new make-up also. A pearly dusting of finely bolted powder over face and neck, shoulders and arms, a bright lipstick, a charming smudge of creamy eye-shadow on her broad lids. And her hair was entirely lovely, tucked up, now that it had grown longer, into a mass of small flattering curls at her nape, tendrils on her forehead and curling back of her little ears.

"Dancing?" asked Dick, after the greetings had been exchanged.

Linda rose. Dick said: "Bert, you look as if you needed exercise. Why not shoot some indoor golf with me?"

"Where, at the Goodie Shoppe?" asked Bert, laughing.

"No, I've been fixing up a sort of gym-recreation place for the men down at the mills, we've got a small course laid out in it, it isn't bad, suppose you take me on after hours?"

"Great stuff," said Bert. His eyebrows shot up again as he regarded Dick and Linda vanishing, reappearing in the maelstrom of the dance floor.

"He is going in for High Things," he told Elizabeth.

Elizabeth smiled. She said nothing, but she thought a good deal.

Dancing, Linda observed demurely:

"Welfare work suits you, Dick, I never saw you look better."

He asked, deftly swinging her out of the path of a cumbersome couple:

"Was that meant to be a dirty crack? Don't waste your breath. I'm having a swell time."

"What does your father think?"

"He *thinks* I'm crazy. He *knows* I'm spending too much money. What of it?"

"He'll change his mind. You're adding, of course, to his personal prestige and popularity."

"You think I'm doing it just for that?" he demanded.

She said nothing, regarding him with those disturbing eyes. His arm tightened a little. "I wish I could always dance with you—and not talk," he muttered. "You infuriate me when you talk. But dancing with you is pretty close to——"

"If you say heaven, I'll scream," Linda interrupted, "you sound like a very bad song writer."

"I won't say it, then. Lord forbid that you should scream. But I may think what I please. What do you hear from Susanna?"

"Plenty."

"Still faithful to Happy?"

"Why not?" she challenged.

"Quite . . . but again, why? I should have prophesied that she'd forget him——"

"Well, she hasn't. And Happy's making good," Linda told him in triumph. "All he needed was to get out of here, you know."

"I suppose so. You're making good, too," he told her. "I hear about you wherever I go. I understand you've been talking to some of the mill people."

"Some have managed to save," she said.

He disliked her tone a good deal, but said nothing. The music ceased, and the applause began. Standing there, a moment, very close, facing each other, he asked abruptly:

"How about the movies?"

"I've told you——"

"But Dorine Dunne is coming, next week. Surely you couldn't miss that?" He sighed sentimentally. "When she first started to make the grade I kept her picture on my bureau. Autographed, too. Come, Linda, don't be catty."

"I hadn't uttered a word!" she told him indignantly.

"You didn't have to. Your brows went up, the corners of your mouth went down and your little nose assumed an angle. Dorine's all right, think of the honor she confers upon this town!"

"Yes, and her grandparents still on that wretched old farm," Linda said, "and her own aunt dying for want of surgical care. It makes me sick."

Later, returning to the table, Dick remarked lightly:

"Linda's going to see the Dorine Dunne picture with me Wednesday night—let's make it a party? Dinner out here, early, and then to the cinema? How about it?"

"That will be jolly," said Elizabeth, smiling. "I've not seen her in a couple of years."

Bert grunted:

"She makes me tired."

"Come, you're dissembling, because Bess is watching you," Dick accused him; "she's the cutest little blond trick——"

"Her hair is red now," Linda reminded him.

But the party was arranged. Why on earth had she consented? She hadn't consented, she told herself afterwards, he had just taken it all for granted.

Wednesday arrived. All morning Linda had been out on the road, stopping at noon, by urgent request, to have a cup of tea with Mrs. Hopkins. There had been a heavy snowfall, and the roads were just passable. Mrs. Hopkins exclaimed on seeing her struggling out of the car, her arms full of books and magazines. "I never thought you'd make it. It's cleared off fine but the roads must be terrible."

"They are," said Linda, "but I'm used to that. I was dug out one day not long ago, on a back road to Willton. But if you keep to the highways the snow plows get busy and clear them in no time."

"I remember," Mrs. Hopkins said reminiscently as she took Linda's things and settled her in a worn rocking chair in the kitchen, "when there weren't any snow plows. And when I lived with my folks in town and we had wooden sidewalks. You're too young to remember that. They used to go off like guns in the middle of the night when there was a sharp frost. And the houses, too. It was pretty exciting to wake up on a clear night, with the thermometer way below zero, and hear the noise."

She bustled about, getting Linda tea and homemade jam and setting a frying pan for bacon and potatoes on the stove. Linda had grown very fond of this little, courageous woman with her problems and her unceasing efforts to make ends meet and to save against the rainy day which was bound to come. She had not seen her since before Christmas. Mrs. Hopkins was trying to thank her now for the things she had brought over, the toys and clothes, the small tree and trimmings.

"How are the children?" Linda wanted to know.

They were all right, her hostess told her, the younger boys were going in to the movies this evening. She didn't let them often, but children had to have some fun out of life. A neighbor was going, would take them and bring them back.

"I'll be there myself," said Linda, "I'll keep an eye on them."

"This Dorine Dunne, as she calls herself!" Mrs. Hopkins sniffed. "What they ever see in her! Brat, I call her. She sends her grandma silk dresses and fancy underwear but she'd let her starve before she'd send her money. Lottie's crazy about her, she's movie struck, like the rest of the girls around here."

"How is Lottie?"

Lottie was the sixteen-year-old on whom Mrs. Hopkins set "such store," for whom she was working, day in, day out, in order to keep her in school so that she might some day teach. . . .

Mrs. Hopkins shrugged.

"She's not content," she said unhappily, "she wants to stop school and go to work."

"But that's ridiculous!" Linda said.

"I know it. She's been going with some of the girls who clerk at the mills. She says, what's the use of keeping on with her schooling when she could be earning money now. She wants pretty clothes, like other girls, I suppose. I can't hardly blame her," said Mrs. Hopkins, sighing, "but she does worry me."

WHITE COLLAR GIRL 129

"I'll see her and talk to her," Linda promised, worried in her turn.

When she returned home she stopped at the high school and waited outside, reading, until the girls came out. She didn't see Lottie, she must have missed her in that helter-skelter, sweatered, mittened and overshoed crowd. She went into the big building, which was shabby and a little tired looking, as if the fleet careless passage of youth through its halls and doors for so many years had wearied it, and searched for Helen Carter, who, she knew, was in charge of Lottie's classroom. She found her, sorting papers, and moving with an air of fatigue about the room.

"For heaven's sake, Linda, did you come for some higher education?"

"Not exactly."

"You're not trying to sell me anything, are you?" asked Helen suspiciously, "because I'm broke. I cherish the thought that you did manage to sign me up a few months ago, that's something to fall back upon!"

"I can get you a nice little bond at ninety-eight now," Linda told her teasingly.

"No, you can't. Not unless you'll take a note for it." She laughed, in a tone of discouragement. The desks were battle-scarred. Linda leaned against one and said: "I was looking for Lottie Hopkins. Her mother's worried about her."

"What's wrong? Oh, but she hasn't been to school today. She's home sick. She's been out so often lately," Helen complained, "I thought I'd drive over and see Mrs. Hopkins myself but I haven't had time and I'm tired to death at night. It won't be long now to February graduations, to say nothing of mid-years. I almost give up when I think of it. Seen Bess lately? When are she and Bert taking the plunge?"

"I'm seeing them tonight. In the summer, I believe," Linda answered absently. She was thinking fast. No use telling Helen yet. No use talking to Mrs. Hopkins. Out sick? Well, she wasn't, Linda knew that. Playing hookey, of course. But why? To hang around the shops, to go to the movies! But someone would be sure to see her.

She left the school, more than vaguely disturbed. Somehow the Hopkins family had become her responsibility. She must find Lottie within the next day or two and have a serious talk with her.

She went to the club for an excellent dinner. The roads had been cleared and Dick's car made good time. It was again Wednesday dance night and they had time for a dance or two before returning to town. The conversation was general enough, and both men entertained themselves by talking raptly of Dorine Dunne's graces and allurements, Bert with his tongue distinctly in his cheek and Dick with an overdone solemnity.

They found seats, in the middle of the house, but were separated, in couples. The news reel, a short— Dick said, "I'm getting excited." A roar went up from the children in the house as Mickey Mouse fled across the screen. "Yes, I'm having palpitations. You'll have to hold my hand, Linda."

WHITE COLLAR GIRL 131

"I'll send out for spirits of ammonia," she told him.

"That's darling of you," he assured her, "but I'd rather you held my hand. Everyone's doing it, as you'll see if you look around you."

There were, she observed, plenty of young heads leaning against young shoulders, plenty of giggling and whispering and handholding in the dark. She thought: Something's wrong, I don't know what it is. In the city, perhaps there's an excuse, the poor kids haven't any place in which to make love. But here—well, I don't know.

"You disapprove?" he whispered as she shrugged herself more erect and took her eyes from an unabashed couple ahead of them.

"Not exactly. But somehow, it's too bad . . . I mean, *cheap*," she told him.

"Not for Dorine," he said, as the usual cast and headlines flashed on the screen and the synchronized music began. He laughed outright at the title . . . "Passion's Plenty . . ."

Two lanky boys struggled down the aisle looking for seats. The usher, coming to meet them, flashed her torch upward, on their faces. "Oh," said Linda, "there are the Hopkins kids."

She was on the aisle and so leaned out to speak to them, watching them settled across from her. The picture went on.

It was halfway through when they smelled smoke. . . .

"*Fire!*" screamed a woman, half hysterical, in the front row. The stampede began. Dick had

Linda's arm. "There's no danger," he was saying, but his voice shook. "Keep steady. There's Bert and Bess . . . ahead."

They were making their way toward the nearest exit. A narrow exit. It was blocked. Someone, the manager, jumped up on the stage, shouting above the tumult. People cursed, screamed, wept, prayed aloud. It was entirely horrible. Linda was almost at the exit when she turned and tried to fight her way back. "Have you gone out of your mind?" Dick shouted at her.

"The Hopkins boys!" she gasped, almost stifled with the smell of smoke. A bright tongue of flame shot up, above them, somewhere in the gallery, or where the projection machine was. "One's pretty little. . . . Dick, let me go—I promised . . ."

He followed, and found her, a little further on with an arm around each of the frightened lads who had traveled the same route she had, more slowly. "You're all right," she was saying.

They'd not been far from the exit. Now they found themselves out in the street. The fire department was clanging its way toward them; had stopped. The police were there. The crowds had gathered, women wringing their hands. . . . My boy's in there—my two girls . . .

"Bess—Bert," Linda was saying. She was sick with horror, sick with having watched a small portion of humanity fight for self-preservation. She had herself strangely enough felt no actual fear, only a sickness, a nausea, a helplessness. She remembered most of all Dick's arm about her . . . and one sentence . . . "Darling, you're safe."

There on the street her knees buckled under her. The younger Hopkins boy was crying. The other said nothing, clutching Linda's hand. They had lost all sight of the people with whom they had come. "I must get these boys home," said Linda. "I'll take them to my house—Dick, would you drive them home later? I must telephone their mother. Oh, *where* are Bess and Bert?"

Her voice was a little out of her control. Dick said, "Hush, of course, I'll drive the kids home. . . . Hey, Smith," he yelled suddenly as the face of a man in the watching crowd caught his attention. "You'll have to step back, Mr. Jarvis," one of the policemen was saying, in his ear.

Smith, a bookkeeper at the mills, said, astonished, "Dick?" and Dick said, "Here, my car's parked, way up the street. Get Miss Anthony home, will you, and the boys. . . . I'll stick around here. Leave the car at the house."

"Dick—" Linda began.

"Go along," he told her, suddenly very grave, very mature, with the strained anxious eyes of a complete stranger. "I'll come or phone. I'll wait for Bert and Bess. *My God*——"

The roof was falling; had fallen. A moan, concerted, like the sound of a beast, went up from the crowd. "They're not all out yet," said someone, sobbing. The firemen were playing the hose on the building. Not far from Linda a woman clutched at empty air and fainted.

Linda found herself, with Smith's grasp on her arm, the boys clinging to her, hurried to the car, and driving home. She sat, drawing the God-given cold fresh air into her lungs with great gasps. She saw her mother hurrying out of the house and before the car had slid to a stop she was calling, "I'm all right, dear . . . we're all all right."

Mrs. Anthony said, her lips shaking, "I just heard . . ."

Somehow Linda managed to thank Smith, who parked the car in front of the house and vanished, running down the street. The street was black with people. Mrs. Anthony then asked, "And Dick?"

"He stayed," said Linda.

CHAPTER TEN

LINDA went into the house, her mother hurrying, with little short steps, beside her, asking innumerable questions . . . How did it start? What happened? Did everyone get out? "I heard the bell ringing, saw people start to run . . . someone shouted—'It's the Elite.' . . . I——"

She seemed to see the boys for the first time. "Who are they?" she wanted to know.

"The Hopkins children. I'll have to phone their mother immediately. She may have heard."

Jim, the youngest, was saying proudly. "Once, I got knocked down." He displayed a bruised hand. "Then, Miss Linda came . . ."

"You poor child. I'll fix that for you," Mrs. Anthony said. She took them off to find iodine, witch hazel. Linda went to the telephone, sitting down thankfully by the instrument, taking a long time to get her number. The lines were very busy.

She got Mrs. Hopkins. No, Mrs. Hopkins hadn't heard. Linda explained gently. "I have the boys with me, Mrs. Hopkins. The—a fire started in the motion picture house and they were separated from their friends. I'll bring them out myself, pretty soon."

She answered the startled questions of the older woman as best she could and hung up presently, limp with reaction, and took her head in her hands. She could hear her mother, in the kitchen now, getting out milk and cookies for the boys. She heard her say: "I'll make coffee, too, in case someone needs it."

Linda needed it. But she couldn't move. She sat there. Bert . . . Bess . . . and now—Dick. Had he gone back into the building to find them! But, oh, he mustn't go back! But that was an insane, a disloyal thought. Bess might be in there . . . one of her dearest friends, and Bert . . . He—no, if he went back it would be a wasted gesture.

She sobbed a little under her breath.

Minutes passed. Years. Eternities. The telephone shrilled, there on the table beside her. She lifted her shaking hand and guided it to the instrument and held it to her ear. "Yes?"

"It's Dick, Linda. Bess and Bert are with me, they're all right. Bess wants to stay on here. There's a lot she can do, before the ambulance comes. Bert will stick with me. I'll see you later . . . I haven't forgotten about the kids."

She said faintly: "I can drive them home."

"No, wait for me. As long as their people know they're all right you can wait, can't you?"

"I'll wait," she said. It was like a vow. All their differences had vanished, gone up in the smoke of that living sacrifice. She clung to the edge of the table and whispered into the receiver . . . "Dick, are many people hurt?"

"We don't know yet. Minor injuries, of course, from the crowd. And people fainting . . . hysterical women . . . some," he said, and his voice broke, "some were caught inside . . ."

She hung up and went back to the kitchen. The boys were perched on the table, their eyes round, their small chests sticking out with importance now that they were safe and their fright had passed. They would lord it over the schoolmates who had been safe at home, that night, thought Linda, smiling dimly. She steadied eyes and lips. "Was that Dick on the wire?" her mother asked.

"Yes, he's coming in, presently."

"Has he seen Bess and Bert?"

"They're all right, they're staying to help."

She thought: I ought to go back. But what could I do? Bess, she's a nurse, she can do something.

She loathed her own inactivity and set herself to entertain the boys. "I phoned your mother," she said; and "Gee," asked Jim, "did she think we were burned?"

"Hush, lamb, don't even mention it." She saw her mother's face turn ashen. "Here, sit down," she said gently, "it's all over."

Neighbors were coming in, the house was filling up. Survivors arrived, as the Anthony home was not far from the street on which the motion picture house was located. Mrs. Anthony made pots of coffee, strong black coffee. "Linda, look in the cupboard, there, by your father's desk, we have some brandy, I think."

Presently it was really all over, although how

many had perished would not be known until the smoking, shattered ruins had cooled. But those who had been injured, and rescued, had gone to the hospital or to their homes, as their condition called for. Bess appeared; she was smoke-streaked, and blackened, and pale. She said: "What a night!" and reached thankfully for the coffee. Linda's arms were around her. She found herself crying while the boys looked on in ashamed amazement and the neighbors came closer, all talking at once, dozens of them it seemed to Linda. . . .

"Bess——"

"Brace up, Linda, I'm all right. Bert and Dick stayed to help, if they could. They'll be along. Hello, you boys, how did you get here?"

"Miss Linda brung us," one of them piped up importantly.

"Bess, you were ahead of us, what happened?"

"I went back . . . there was a kid . . . couldn't have been over six—why on earth they allow it—" Bess grumbled.

"Miss Linda came back for us," said Jim proudly.

Bess smiled at him.

The neighbors were dispersing. A taxi came hooting up to take one or two people home. "If the men would only come," said Linda.

They came. Bert's eyebrows were singed, he looked terrible. Bess shrieked, her composure gone. "Bert, I thought you promised . . . !"

"I'm a volunteer," he grinned, "so's Dick, or after tonight. We're O.K."

Dick didn't look much better. He said, in answer to something Mrs. Anthony asked him:

"He arrived just before I left. Hadn't heard before. He's wild, of course. He didn't dream that such a thing—Is that coffee? Give me quarts! Got a doughnut, Mrs. Anthony? I'm starved. Here, Bert, catch."

He sat on the kitchen table and swung his long legs and talked and ate, and entertained the boys. But his eyes were anxious . . . set on Linda, on her pallor, her quiet. Bert and Elizabeth, in a corner, were arguing. Now Bert said, suddenly: "I'll get Bess home. She's all in. There's nothing more we can do tonight."

The elder Jarvis arrived, a very bad color. He stormed in, made temperish through fear and grief. He spoke briefly to Mrs. Anthony and Linda and turned excitedly to Dick. Linda heard scattered words—*insurance—lawyers—investigation*—and set herself to clearing the table, washing up the cups. Jarvis said heavily, at last: "Well, we'll be getting along home. Lord, I wouldn't have had this happen for a million!" He looked at his son. Dick had been in that burning place. *Dick!*

He said so. "That you should have been there, of all nights!" He said it without thinking. Mrs. Anthony remarked: "Linda was there too, Fred."

"Of course, Linda." The older man was silent, looking at his hands. He said presently, as Bert and Elizabeth made their exit: "Got your car, Dick, or will you come home with me?"

He had to have him with him. He said gruffly:

"Your mother doesn't know yet that you—were there."

Dick said: "That's good. No, I can't come with you, dad. I've the car here. I'm going to drive these youngsters home."

"Youngsters?" Jarvis regarded the two boys for the first time, puzzled. He said, "I see," blankly, and rose, walking toward the door with the gait of an old man. "See you later," he told his son, over his shoulder.

There was a flat silence in the kitchen when he had gone. Dick explained, conscious of embarrassment: "He's pretty much upset, you know."

Linda nodded briefly. She asked: "Shall we go along now?"

"You're not going?" her mother said, in amazement.

"I'd better." She tried to smile. "Mrs. Hopkins will want to see me. Besides, the air will do me good. My head aches, a little."

She found her wraps, put them on and herded the sleepy boys toward the porch, the street, the waiting car. Presently they piled in, the boys demanding the chilly exhilaration of the rumble seat. Linda sat beside Dick, huddled into her coat collar, tired, let down after the tension.

They drove as rapidly through the town as the traffic laws and the still milling crowds permitted. People called to them from the street—"Have you come from the Elite?" "Have you seen So-and-So?" "Do you know what started the fire?"

They answered, after a fashion. Presently they

were on the outskirts, taking a quiet back road which Linda advised . . . "The main road will be crowded," she said.

There was constraint between them. It had come about suddenly, at the entrance of Fred Jarvis. The kinship which Linda had felt, the feeling of understanding which had pervaded her fear for Dick, had vanished. She sat there, shivering and silent. Something of this change in her was subtly conveyed to him. He asked anxiously: "Sure you're all right? The shock, you know."

"I'm fine," she answered.

"Sorry Dad was so—brusque," Dick murmured, "but, you understand."

She replied, "Quite," in a constrained voice. Dick stepped on the accelerator. The car bounded forward. "Whoopee!" yelled one little boy in the back and shook his slumbering brother by the shoulder. "Hey, wake up, dumbbell, we're *traveling!*"

They reached the Hopkins farm. Lights burned, the door was ajar. Mrs. Hopkins ran to meet them. Dick lifted the boys from the rumble, and carried in the one who slept, relaxed, his small dirty freckled face touching and innocent in the defenselessness of slumber.

"Here you are," said Dick, and put him in his mother's arms.

She stammered. "I can't say it—" She kissed Linda, crying, rare and difficult tears. She said, conscious of her neighborhood responsibilities, "The folks next door—did they get out all right?"

Jim cried, "Sure, mom, I think I seen 'em."

Linda said soothingly, "Of course." But she didn't know the Smiths by sight; she could only reassure, vaguely, making an effort at a confidence she didn't and couldn't feel.

"They haven't come home," said Mrs. Hopkins.

"Perhaps they stopped with friends in town."

"But they could have telephoned—when they missed the boys—if they were all right," Mrs. Hopkins said with a stubborn logic.

The sound sleeper had awakened. He and his brother ran in circles about the living room, tired, excited, talking. "You boys hush up," ordered their mother with a poor attempt at sharpness. The oldest boy of all came downstairs in shirt and trousers, he'd been waiting up, too. Lottie, Mrs. Hopkins said, was asleep. She hadn't waked her. She'd come home, late, from school; tired, her head hurting her.

Linda said nothing. This was not the time to say it. She looked at Dick. "We'd better go," she told him, "Mother will be worried."

A car rattled into the yard; there was a buzz of excited voices. Mrs. Smith, fat and short, ran in. She cried, "We didn't phone, we was afraid of scaring you . . . someone told us they'd seen the boys with Miss Anthony."

Her husband followed, a leisurely man; and one or two others. Linda and Dick made their escape in the general confusion. "If it hadn't been for her . . ." Mrs. Hopkins was saying, deeply.

Out in the car, "She sure thinks the world of you," Dick said awkwardly.

"She's a client. They're people I've been interested in for some time," Linda explained. She was silent again, too tired, too let down to talk.

But he couldn't keep still; he couldn't wait until another day, when, nerves rested, and judgment prevailing over emotions, they could have talked things out with a degree of logic, of calmness and of fairness. He burst out irrepressibly:

"You *saw* how Dad took it . . . you can't believe now that he knew there was any danger!"

"Oh, must we talk about that?" she asked, stirred to anger. Why couldn't he leave her alone, feeling the wind on her face, the thankfulness in her heart, the temporary peace.

"I think so. You heard him say, he wouldn't have had it happen——"

"Dick, please don't be idiotic. Of course, he wouldn't have had it happen! No man in his senses would! What I complained about—before—before the fire was that people said for ages the place was a fire-trap and would go up like tinder. To talk about it now is like closing the barn door after the horse has been stolen," she explained, in homely metaphor.

"But he had no idea of conditions, I tell you," Dick protested doggedly, "the place was inspected, just as others are, regularly."

Tired, nervous, she found herself laughing. She said scornfully:

"Inspectors wouldn't bother—Fred Jarvis!"

The car took a rut with unnecessary violence. Dick broke out savagely:

"Are you trying to intimate that my father, for the sake of saving a few dollars in repairs, would stoop to grease the palms——"

She said wearily:

"Oh, what's the use of talking about it, Dick. I'm not trying to intimate anything. I'm simply saying that the general awe and regard in which he is held by the various officials in this town enables him to go scot-free—at other people's expense. Perhaps he doesn't pay graft. Perhaps he doesn't have to—possibly not when he owns most of the town and can put people in office and take them out again!"

She could not see his face. But he was white. His voice was a taut thread ready to snap. He said:

"There'll be an investigation of this. If—if he was at fault, he won't be spared. But I'm not afraid for him."

"You needn't be," she said; "the investigation won't amount to much!"

Terribly loyal to his father. Well, she liked that. She admitted it. She felt herself softening toward him. After all, it wasn't his fault. He'd worked hard that night; must be tired, as she was; and a good deal more shaken up, by the things he had heard and seen and which she had been spared. She said pacifically: "I'm sorry, let's not quarrel, Dick."

But quarreling was the only outlet open to him to relieve his frayed nerves. He answered, with complete absurdity:

"We don't seem to be able to do anything else. And you're *not* sorry. You're glad!"

She gasped, unable to believe her ears:

"*Glad?*"

"Glad it happened. So you could think you'd proved yourself right—anything, just so long as you're right!" he told her.

She said, after a minute, in a small clear voice:

"You know that isn't true, Dick, you're only saying it because you're tired—and angry. If I thought for a moment that you meant it——"

They were pulling into town. The first lights showed her his face, drawn and strained, a taut white line about the mouth. He admitted, after a moment:

"I'm sorry. I didn't, of course, mean that you were glad—about what happened but—" the curious hostility between them showed again, for a moment, "it *was* fortuitous, wasn't it?"

She cried, "Perhaps you think I set fire to the place myself——"

They were reaching sheer inanity. Staring at each other, like angry children; shouting ridiculous accusations; but their eyes were perfectly adult.

"Don't be a little fool," he said strongly, "but, it was only the other night . . ."

"What of that? They've had a fire scare there once before," she told him. "I—" She broke off, fighting back the angry nervous tears.

Now they were turning into her street. She wrenched open the door and sprang out, as the car slid to a stop, before he could move to help her. She fled, up the steps, without a word. He sat staring after her. He'd been the fool, of course. Possibly because she had been right . . . about the condition of the place. Anger, fear, self-reproach were so entangled he could not separate one from the other. He started to get out of the car. Hesitated. Slammed it into gear and drove on home. His people would be waiting for him. His mother must have heard now and be half out of her mind with worry, the way women were when nothing had really happened to the person they loved. Women had a way of thinking, But it *might* have happened.

Tomorrow he'd send Linda flowers, and write her a note, and try to see her and tell her he was sorry to have made such an ass of himself, brutal, unkind. But the things she'd said about his father had gotten under his skin.

No tears for Linda until she was alone. She had to see her mother first, to talk, for a little, before going to bed. Once in bed the tears didn't come. She was dry-eyed, she shook with anger. This was the end, then. They couldn't go on, trying to be friends, reaching every now and then a little armed truce, playing at being comfortable and happy together.

She acknowledged the note and flowers which reached her the next day with a few short formal lines. "We were both tired and upset," she wrote. "We'll forget everything," she ended. But when, after several fruitless attempts to reach her he did succeed in talking to her on the telephone she only said wearily, "Oh, Dick, what's the use? We only quarrel and say wretched things to each other when we do meet. After all, there are certain things upon which we'll never agree, not in a million years. Let's not try to be friends.''

That was one thing to which he couldn't agree. But she was adamant. He hung up, baffled, having done no more than to extract a vague promise of "some time . . ."

CHAPTER ELEVEN

When they next encountered it was at Elizabeth's, then again at the Country Club and now and then on the street. He found it impossible for him to get her off by herself. She was perfectly amiable and courteous but there was a barrier about her which he was unable to crash. And the investigation of the Elite fire died, as she had prophesied, aborning. He spoke of it to his father in an eager, embarrassed sort of way, stammering his wonder. Jarvis shrugged. "I'll build the finest picture house in this part of the state," he said merely; "the other's over and done with, the legal exigencies met."

Through the insurance company and the lawyers the damage to property and to persons was settled, and life went on as usual in Lawrenceton. And the builders and carpenters and architects arrived to discuss the erection of a new theater. The fire was forgotten in an amazingly short space of time, save by those who had had an intimate and terrifying knowledge of it. But Bert, at the meetings of his small but growing club, was not among those who forgot. "Jarvis has to learn some time," he told them, "that he can't get away with things much longer. Building a New York theater in what he has determined to keep a hick town won't mend matters, nor will paying damages . . . out of court, to the people who were hurt or the survivors of those killed."

Eight people had perished in that fire.

Mrs. Hopkins, talking of Linda at parish meetings, at grange meetings and at the homes of neighbors, was bringing Linda business. Most of it small but not all. There were several exceptionally prosperous farmers in the district, hard-headed gentlemen who, once persuaded that Linda could put them in the way of making their money, wrested from a treacherous soil, work for them, were not averse to letting her do it. "You'll make the Quota Club," Pearson congratulated her when she was talking to him in his office one day, "the first woman to have done so in the entire history of the house!"

But there were other things on her mind than business. Lottie, for instance. Lottie was, according to Helen Carter, attending school less and less, Lottie who, according to her mother, was staying out nights "with friends."

A little way out of town there was a dance hall. A garish "modern" sort of place with an orchestra and plenty of the usual "makings." Lottie's older brother had brought her home from there, not once but twice. Lottie was threatening to leave home. "She can't," said Linda, "she's not of age." "If you'd talk to her," Mrs. Hopkins suggested, at her wits' end and sick with fear.

Talking did no good. Linda soon found that out. Lottie asked sullenly: "What's wrong with the Blue

Heaven? Sure, the fellows bring flasks. *Your* boy
friends bring flasks to the Country Club, don't they?
What's the difference? We can't join clubs and
travel with your crowd, but we like a bit of fun and
dancing now and then. I don't see any difference,''
said Lottie. "Sometimes your gang comes to the
Blue Heaven. I've seen 'em. They think they're
slumming, most likely,'' Lottie remarked bitterly.

Well, what *was* the difference? Linda pondered
that. None, she supposed. A difference in price, in
setting, in social standing. She left the Hopkins
place that day very much troubled and drove
straight back to town and to Bert's office. He was
in, dictating to his one elderly stenographer, and
shouted to her as she paused at the door, to come in
and watch the legal wheels go round . . . what was
on her mind, if anything?

She sat down by his desk and when they were
alone she told him. She didn't, she said, like Lottie's
attitude or the sound of the place. Why hadn't it
been raided? She caught herself up. The Country
Club had never been raided. What was the difference? She said aloud, "Something's awfully
wrong!" She told him what Lottie had said. "Mrs
Hopkins said,'' she went on, "that the people who
go there for the most part are youngsters of high
school age. Something has to be done. Who owns
it?"

"It's on Homer Manton's property,'' he told her
thoughtfully.

She commented, "It would be!"

"No one has any influence with Manton, unless

it's Fred Jarvis," he said. "Look here, Linda, I'll go out there and look around. I'll take some of the boys along for an evening of inspection. How about it?"

"Bess and I——?"

"No, you'll stay home, where you belong."

He reported to her a day or so later. It was worse than he'd thought. A big barn-like shack. "I believe there's liquor on the place," he said, "and that they sell it. But we haven't any proof. They didn't sell *us* any. There are rooms, upstairs," he said uncomfortably.

"Can't we do something?"

"I don't know, Linda."

"The newspapers——"

"The newspapers?" He laughed. "You know who backs the principal one. That's out. The others wouldn't dare, either."

He frowned, looking at the carpet on the Anthony living room floor. "Three of my gang are trying to buy the *Comet*," he admitted; "if they succeed, things will start humming in this neck of the woods."

The *Comet* was a weekly sheet. "They want to run it as a daily, a morning paper," he explained, "they've got almost all the money they need, together. They're a thousand short."

She said: "I can get the thousand. I've got it, as it happens."

"*You*—? Linda?" He stared at her. "It's a risk," he told her definitely. "Sure"—at her accusation—"I kicked in. Not much. Couldn't afford it, marrying and all." He grinned. "But I don't like to have you put up your dough," he told her.

"Can't I do it through you, so no one will know, except the owners? If your crowd could get control of a paper and make it go . . . really go? It would be an enormous help in elections, Bert, you know that. It couldn't be bought, or frightened, could it?"

"It could not. But, Linda, a thousand—that's a lot of money for a little tyke." He grinned at her again, but hopefully. She said: "I've made quite a lot, and saved some. And had a nice fat bonus. I can afford it, Bert, it's worth it."

Later, when the details had been arranged, she returned to the subject of Blue Heaven.

"Something's got to be done," she declared.

"Sure, but Manton can't be got at. There's just one way," he told her, "and that is through Fred Jarvis. Want to tackle him? I'm not exactly *persona grata*," he confessed.

Then he said, diffidently, looking at the carpet again, "He owns the District property himself, Jarvis does."

The District property was down by the railroad yards. One didn't speak of it as a rule to decent women. There were women there, however, raddled, bedraggled creatures, whom someone had so erroneously named daughters of joy; and there were drunken men, at all hours of the day and night.

"*Fred Jarvis* owns that property?"

"Yes. I don't think it's generally known. He's holding it, he says, for an expansion of the railway

WHITE COLLAR GIRL

there. But that won't come, as long as he can keep it out."

After a moment, he added: "The man who runs Blue Heaven—he isn't a native here, you know—has some sort of an interest in the District, Linda. He looks like bad company for those darned fool kids." He sighed and added, "If this were fiction we could work a reform through Dick."

"What do you mean—Dick?" she wanted to know.

"Oh, we'd shanghai him and take him to the Blue Heaven and stage a rowdy party and a fake raid and Fred would get all wrought up over his ewe lamb and request Homer Manton to kick the lessee out. But, unfortunately, Dick's grown up and quite able to take care of himself and would probably be too bored for words to go near the joint."

"Well, work it the practical way," she suggested suddenly.

"Now you tell one!"

"This way. Get Dick to your office, tell him all about it, take him on a tour of inspection if possible, ask him to use his influence with his father and suggest that if he does it may help Mr. Jarvis at election time . . . that he can play it up."

"For heaven's sake, Linda, I thought you were going to root for me at election!"

She regarded him shrewdly, gray eyes sparkling.

"Then it's sure you're going to run?"

"Lady, you said it. It looks that way. Also run, probably," he added glumly.

"Nonsense, you'll make it. But now, about Jarvis——"

"I'm to help him spike my guns by a little early reform?" asked Bert in mock amazement. "Perhaps you've happened in on my dark secret, Linda, perhaps I was saving a slice of Blue Heaven for celestial fireworks in the *Comet*—*if* we get it—and *if* I'm nominated!"

"There's a lot of other cleaning up you can do." She leaned toward him, tense. She could hear her mother moving about upstairs and could hear, too, the old clock ticking noisily in the dining room. "Begin on this now. Never mind if it does react to Jarvis' advantage. I tell you, Bert, this can't wait. It's too important. It may mean—you don't know what it may mean to Lottie Hopkins and to girls like her. Get at Dick. He's the only one who can reach his father. I want that place closed up!"

And while he whistled and then nodded, silently, she added: "There's still the District. That must be closed up too. The *Comet* can start talking about that as soon as the new owners take it over——"

"Soft pedal stuff, Linda. There are such things as libel suits!"

"You can let it be known without calling names. If you ride to any victory, Bert, it's going to be on a double ticket—Reform and Progress, isn't it?"

"You're right. Come around and sell me a bond when I'm feeling better." He looked at his watch. "Gosh, I've got to go pick up Bess. She's around at the house of one of her school kids over on the Flats. Kid's sick or something. Speaking of reform, Bess is hot on the trail. She's talking on sanitary conditions over in the Flats district, says

WHITE COLLAR GIRL

we're headed for another epidemic like we had in 'twenty-nine and she's on the warpath after some of the city fathers who own that property, too.''

He paused a moment in his headlong rush to the door.

"Linda, women can do a lot. Sob stuff and for-my-sake, you know. Why don't you tackle Dick yourself?"

"I'd rather not," she said briefly.

"I see."

He didn't, however. He went to fetch Elizabeth, wondering. Dick and Linda amused and puzzled him. He was certain they "were keen" about each other but in an armed, blow-hot blow-cold sort of way. Darned if he'd like a love affair like that! It was different with him and Bess. Kid sweethearts, growing up together, faithful, all the way, caring a lot. Linda was a great girl; pretty as paint, and smart as the crack of a whip. But Bess. . . . He quickened his pace. Bess was waiting for him.

Ten days later Dick Jarvis went to New York. He went after an interview with Bert, and a longer one with his father. He went on mill business for his father and also to call on Mr. Manton in the Park Avenue apartment in which Manton spent his winters. He returned with a letter to Manton's agent. On the first of the following month, the Blue Heaven closed its portals.

Bert reported to Linda.

"Great work," she said happily. "How—how did Dick take it?"

"Oh, he shrugged a lot at first. said those places

weren't as bad as they were painted. I told him he was crazy. This isn't Chicago nor yet New York but we can get gangsters in here yet, in a small way. There's one crowd started already—been trying to work, of all things, a window-cleaning racket." He paused and laughed aloud. "In a town where the women clean their own windows and like it! However, the point is, there are a good many idle boys and men in Lawrenceton and a good many floaters . . . drifting population, hoboes, what have you. In just such a place as the Blue Heaven you've got a grand layout for the formation of gangs—composed of half-baked kids and men limited in intelligence who are disaffected and full of bad liquor. And in addition you've the usual quota of boys and girls who go there because they think it's smart. Dick didn't think much of the scheme though till I told him that it wouldn't hurt his old man any to be a prime mover in a real reform. So he spoke to him about it from that angle, and then went to see Manton. Manton's not a bad cuss, you know. Just not very bright. He didn't make his money himself, he inherited it and it was invested before the war in things that went over big. Steel, for one. Manton is like Jarvis in that he doesn't want to see the town change any. He likes it as a sort of private summer resort even if he doesn't live here all the year around, see; but on the other hand, if it were pointed out to him that this dubious joint was bringing an undesirable element into Lawrenceton, one which might disregard property and all that sort of thing, if encouraged, he would see reason. Dick and I doped that out together. Well, he did see reason. The guy that ran the place has disappeared off the face of the earth, and it's shut down tighter than a clam. One for us. Or rather, a feather in Jarvis' cap, indirectly."

"That's grand," said Linda.

"The nut element among the younger generation will have to go back to Ye Goodie Shoppe for their excitement," said Bert. "The tough crowd will find another place, or drift back to their own holes in the ground. Great work, Linda."

"Me?"

"Sure, you! You've a way of inspiring candidates—on both sides—with a passion for reform!"

That was that. But there was Lottie to consider. Linda went to see her again and had a long talk with her. She told her finally:

"I don't like to threaten you, Lottie, but I know all about—you're staying away from school——"

"You told me that before."

"Yes, but I didn't tell your mother. As for—Blue Heaven . . ."

"That's been closed!"

"I know. Look here, it doesn't pay, the way you're headed. You won't get anywhere with it. No job, no money for the sort of things you want."

"I don't know who meddled, getting the hall closed up," Lottie said. But she had a good idea. Her blue eyes were black with anger. She was a pretty girl, blue eyes, red hair, a sparkle to her, a snap, or, when her mood changed, a definite sullenness. "It was the only fun we had. I could have got a job there too, next summer. Pete—he's the fellow who ran it—said he'd let me try out with something—dancing maybe or singing, in the summer, when people began coming out there nights. Easy money, he said."

"Pete said that, did he?" asked Linda.

Lottie looked at her defiantly. Linda rose. She said: "I have to go on now, I've some work to do. I'll pick you up after school tomorrow, Lottie. I want to take you somewhere. Then, I'll bring you home."

Lottie muttered something. But she was a little afraid not to go to school. She went, the next day, and at the close of the session found Linda waiting for her. No chance to slip away.

Linda drove the Ford to a certain corner and parked it. "Get out, Lottie," she said, "we're going walking."

Linda had never been in the District before. She had from early childhood been taught to avoid it and if by any chance she visited the residential section which lay behind that part of town, she took the long route, over the bridge. Now, she went, her hand on Lottie's arm, through the narrow twisting streets.

She was a little frightened although it was broad daylight. Lottie, who had heard enough about the District, shrank away, and looked about her. "We—we shouldn't have come here," she said, "what's the big idea, Miss Anthony?"

The houses were ramshackle and dark, with dirty lace curtains. The streets were filthy. Linda's heart was stung with pity when she saw children playing there, in the gutters. Now and then they saw an expensive car parked. There were faces at windows, men lounging in dark doorways stepped forward and spoke, shouted a word or two, or laughed There was a drunken man asleep on a doorstep. And not far off an impervious policeman.

He might be blind to the District, but he wasn't blind to Linda. His eyes opened in amazement as he saw her coming toward him. He'd gone to school with her, had Jim McCarthy. He hurried off his corner and approached her. "Linda, you shouldn't be here. The saints forbid!" he said, in horror.

"With you to protect me?" she asked, smiling a little. "Don't be silly, Jim!"

She walked on, Lottie beside her, casting curious and frightened glances about her. A woman stumbled from a passageway, and swore at them savagely. At the next turn a green roadster was parked.

"That looks like Pete's car, the fellow up to the Blue Heaven," gasped Lottie.

The breaks were with her, thought Linda. She took Lottie's arm and hurried her through the unsavory streets back to the place where she had parked her own car. And then, without a word of explanation, she drove the girl to her own home where Mrs. Anthony, incurious and gentle, had tea ready for them.

"Gee," said Lottie, "this is a swell house." She stroked the fine texture of the porcelain cup she held as if she loved it. "I *do* like pretty things," she said.

"You'll get them, if you work for them," Linda told her. She told herself: That sounds preachy. I wish I could get her confidence. She said suddenly: "That *was* Pete's car, I imagine, Lottie. He—has business in that quarter. You know about the District, don't you?"

"Sure," Lottie flushed and looked away, "all of us know. The boys talk, some of them."

"It's men like your friend Pete and places like your Blue Heaven that make districts like that one possible," Linda told her quickly. "Lottie, your mother works pretty hard, for you, for the boys. She has her heart set on you, she wants you to make something of yourself."

"But I don't *want* to teach," wailed Lottie suddenly, tears in the blue eyes, childish tears.

"You don't have to. I know your mother well enough to know she won't insist upon it; there are other ways of earning a living. Lottie, if you will finish school and cut out this nonsense—for that's all it is—I'll see that you get a good job. I'll stake you to a business course, if that's what you want."

Lottie said, surprisingly:

"It's not. If I can't go on the stage or in the movies, I want to be a beauty parlor operator!"

"Well, why not?" Linda mused. "There's good money in it, it must be pleasant work. But it *is* work, Lottie, and it takes knowledge and tact." She considered a moment. "I've a friend who runs a beauty parlor, a very successful one over in Ben-

WHITE COLLAR GIRL

ville. You finish school and then, if you want to, we'll get you in there. Or, if you want to start learning before you're through school, perhaps I could persuade her to take you, this summer, and teach you something. There wouldn't be much money in it while you're learning, summers, and you'd have to spend most of it on lunches and in getting over and back by the bus. But it would keep you busy—and you'd get ahead. Madame Leona is rushed, summers, she has lots of summer residents and tourists for clients."

"Oh, gee!" Lottie was ecstatic. "Do you think she'd take me? I'd work awful hard. Summers are pretty bad," she said, "just hanging around the farm."

"I'll see, Lottie. I'll have to talk to your mother first. She may not be willing, you know, she needs your help around the house."

"I've never helped—much," Lottie admitted. "Of course, if she says so, I can't—" but her face brightened. "If *you* tell her it would be good for me, Miss Anthony, I know she'll let me go."

"Very well. No more playing hookey or grieving over Blue Heavens?" asked Linda.

"I promise."

Linda drove her home and went in, to talk, satisfactorily, with Mrs. Hopkins, who agreed that occupation for idle hands was the best of all possible preventives, and moreover, occupation that was congenial. As Linda was leaving Lottie called her and caught her hand in a hot tight grasp of gratitude and spoke, so low that Mrs. Hopkins could not hear:

"Thank you for taking me—you know where. I mean, you didn't say anything—not much—but I—well, I understood," Lottie stammered.

Linda, driving home, thought that she, too, understood, for the first time. It had cost her a good deal to set her fastidious feet on those appalling streets. She thought of the glimpses they had had of the women who lived there, women who rarely went out by daylight. There was an immense pity in her heart pervading the disgust and shrinking. Couldn't something be done for them? Oh, she supposed that was sentimental and mawkish. Of course not. But something could be done with the District, which would make it impossible for girls who had been as young and as thoughtless as, say, Lottie Hopkins, to take up their dwelling on that street of mean and shattered houses, and, behind those shutters, to grow into the sort of women for whom "nothing could be done."

She thought: I don't suppose Fred Jarvis has ever walked or driven through those streets. If he has he couldn't let the place stay as it is, he'd raze it, tear it down . . . he couldn't, and sleep peacefully at night. . . .

When election time came, he'd have to inspect—the District, she thought further in determination.

The northern spring, reticent and sweet, scented with flowers while the ground still lay frosted with snow, was upon them. The snow melted, the great thaws set in, the ice in the rivers broke and rushed, crashing, toward the sea, and there was a pale cloud of green on the trees. And before May came tumbling in with flowers in her cool pink hands, Linda had received notice that she had made the coveted Quota Club and would be expected to attend its meeting in Atlantic City, one woman in a group of over two hundred men.

Susanna wrote . . . "Think I'd let you be there all by yourself among those ravening wolves. . . . I'll be seeing you, angel . . ."

In May, with her mother, Bess and Bert to see her off, she went, colors flying, with a new suitcase and some new spring clothes to Atlantic City, taking with her the first issue of the *Comet*, the new daily, of which she was a part and secret owner.

CHAPTER TWELVE

ATLANTIC CITY was delightful. It was Linda's first experience of the springtime sea and, although she insisted to Susanna, who met her at the station, that she would never be able to sleep because of the incessant clamor of the ocean, and that a river was "more restful to live by," she soon discovered that salt air and sunshine produced an appetite like a stevedore's and the unconquerable drowsiness of one of the Seven Sleepers.

She and Susanna shared a great sunny room and bath at one of the biggest boardwalk hotels. Susanna had friends living in Ventnor, so, while Linda was busy with luncheons, conferences and dinners—at one of which she was forced to rise to her feet, wondering if her knees would give way under her, and listen to Mr. Pearson's charming and congratulatory speech about her progress—Susanna played golf and walked miles on the boardwalk and otherwise amused herself. But they managed to do a good deal of talking during the starry nights and the salty stimulating mornings.

Susanna had changed. She was a little thinner, and while by no means subdued, less, as Linda put it, "grasshopperish." She had brought with her a large packet of Happy's letters and read parts of them aloud to her friend; but only parts. In the midst of a thoroughly Happy-like description of work, play or scenery, Susanna would break off, flushing to the roots of her curly yellow hair. "That's all, here," she would say and hastily turn the sheet, but her eyes would linger on the censored sentences and she would be in no hurry to continue her reading. Linda observed these deletions with a smile, but it was a smile compounded partly of envy. For Susanna, although she offered the information that waiting, on probation, for your best beloved to make good was "not so hot" nor pleasant, seemed otherwise perfectly content and more sure of herself with every week which passed. "How on earth you have managed to stay faithful—you who counted the day lost which did not bring you a new scalp!" commented Linda in amazed amusement, early in their short holiday.

They were wheel-chairing down the boardwalk. Susanna cocked an eyebrow at the white-crested blue waves rolling in ceaselessly, to shatter on the wide stretch of beach. She replied, seriously enough: "It was just because I did fritter away a lot of perfectly good emotion that I knew, for keeps, when my hour had struck."

" 'The half gods go—' " murmured Linda.

"Exactly. You'll know when . . . or, do you know already?"

Linda's gray eyes rested on the horizon. Susanna's question was delivered with a magnificent unconcern and as a bolt from the literal blue. Linda answered lightly:

"Certainly not. I was probably intended to be a superb and meddlesome old maid, and in another twenty years I'll have an office and a secretary and deal nonchalantly in tens of thousands of shares without turning one gray hair."

Susanna giggled.

"It's a pretty picture, darling," she observed, sweetly and then, without a change of tone, "How's Dick?"

Linda scorned the obvious "Dick, who?" She answered, after due thought: "Perfectly all right, I fancy. He is endowed with invincible health, you know."

Susanna gave it up. She asked Linda a question or two about the Elite fire. "Angel, when I had your letter I had a bad case of the jitters . . . suppose—suppose . . . ! How on earth did you keep your head? I would have lost mine and run screaming through the aisles."

She wanted to know all about Bert and Elizabeth. "When are they going to get married?" she asked, and "Do you think she'd like linen or silver or something uselessly costly and frivolous?"

"Bess would like anything. They're to be married the first of June," Linda advised her.

"I'll be there." Susanna hugged her own knees and cuddled her chin into the soft, dark depths of an entirely superfluous sable scarf.

"You will! Susanna, that will be grand!"

"I've been holding out on you. Expect a young

visitor, and pretty darned soon. Happy's coming home!"

"Wretch! Why didn't you tell me?"

"Saved it. He's done pretty well, out in the Painted Desert. Dad's giving him a leave of absence. He'll make tracks for Lawrenceton, so will I. Dad's going to put him into the new Luxor Hotel, in New York. It opens this summer. And—I think we'll be married at Christmas. I've been working on the Cruel Parent and he's gotten so he can't stand the sight of me, sighing around the house, like the deserted bride. So that's that!"

She added: "Happy's been saving. He wants me to have a 'real' ring. I don't want it. I've lots of rings. I'd rather he took a vacation at home and— well, when the simpler things pall, we'll talk about diamonds. He'll be able to afford them, by then."

"So you expect things to pall?"

"No, I don't!" The little chin emerged from the sable. "But common sense tells me we can't live at concert pitch always. There are ways to prolong it, though. Good healthy rows, for instance. Happy and I have never had a serious one. I'm saving that for the day, after we're married, when he forgets to kiss me good-bye. Or surrenders to the marital peck!"

Four days at Atlantic City passed swiftly. Susanna and Linda took train for New York and Linda stayed a day or two with the Hudsons in the much publicized penthouse. She found Mr. Hudson perfectly reconciled to Susanna's plans. "The boy's good, really, Linda, all he needed was to get out on his own. I must say Susanna has better judgment than I gave her credit for." And Mrs. Hudson, if not reconciled then at least resigned. "If she wants to throw away her life!" sighed Mrs. Hudson, with a metaphorical shrug of her slim shoulders.

Linda returned to Lawrenceton filled with a new enthusiasm for her work and a new incentive. Listening to the two hundred-odd salesmen and sales managers, listening to the speeches delivered by the heads of her house had acted as a very real spur to ambition. She was not yet so immunized by business life that she could become cynical or bored by bigger sales talk. It was still new to her; still exciting; still a daily adventure.

On her return she settled back into her usual round of existence, enlivened by the newspaper clippings her mother showed her. The Lawrenceton evening paper had rather outdone itself in praise and glory. Bert, who came with Elizabeth to see her the evening she returned, reported that the sale of the *Comet* had caused a good deal of excitement, and that the subscriptions and public interest were gratifying. Advertising, too. It would be a question, however, when the election campaign started, how much of their advertising they would hold.

"The fireworks have started already," he admitted, "if rather sub-rosa. We're getting committees together. You're to head the women's. Hope you don't mind."

"What about Bess?"

"Bess will subordinate herself to your leadership," he answered, grinning. "After all, as she'll be Mrs. Albert Warren then, wife of the brilliant young candidate, she feels that she had better hide her light under your bushel.''

They listened to the news of Susanna and Happy with appreciative grins. ''I wish I had her on my committee,'' Bert acknowledged, ''I've an idea she could get plenty votes. Those she couldn't win by sheer sex appeal, she'd talk out of the bewildered voters. She's all right,'' he said hastily, as Linda raised a dark eyebrow. ''No offense meant!''

He reported further that Pete, recently of Blue Heaven, had left town.

''Are you sure? I saw his car, before I went to Atlantic City—oh, a good time before.''

''Where did you see it?''

She told him.

''For the love of Mike, Linda, what were you doing there?'' he asked with strong disapproval, while Bess exclaimed in horror.

''A tour of inspection,'' Linda said gravely, ''or, an object lesson. Never mind, Bert, it was ages ago. So he really has left, has he?''

''A delegation saw him off on the train,'' Bert said soberly, ''and a little, oh, perfectly friendly, persuasion was used. So that's that. Good riddance, we say.''

After a time he remarked:

''About the Jarvis mill group. They are not all entirely happy, you know. Benevolent employers don't make up for fat pay envelopes, and all Dick's personal popularity doesn't hold water with some of the younger men. I've half a dozen enlisted in my group. Wonder if you'd be willing to address some of the wives and mothers informally some time, Linda?"

"I've never made a speech in my life! Are you out of your mind?"

"You'll learn. Bess has learned from talking herself blue in the face about weighing babies and boiling bottles and paying attention to sniffles. She has promised to take over the practically house-to-house canvassing of the parents of her ewe lambs. It's up to you to snitch as many of Jarvis' people away from him as you can, for the cause."

"Bert, we'll never do it! After all, they've their jobs to consider. Once Fred Jarvis learns that any of them are voting against him out they'll go, without further notice."

"Check, my child. But if I get the reins of this man's town into my hands we'll have jobs for everyone, and new ones. We'll have business, and business galore. This bridge project looks like a pretty sure thing. Build the bridge in our territory and this town will hum. Not only with the tourist business, although that will be a big item, as it will be the shortest of all possible cuts to Canada, but with all-year-round business. People travel, even in the North, in winter. Some of the hands at the mill are pretty fed up with old-fashioned methods and a paternal sort of tyranny. Dick, I admit, has brought new blood and new ideas into the mill with him, but he can't remake the place in a day and he can't proceed under his own steam. Jarvis gets his throttling moments, you know, and no doubt feels, along with

WHITE COLLAR GIRL 171

some of his higher-up old fogies, that methods which were good enough for his father should be good enough for his father's grandson.''

"That sounds like one of the old puzzles," Elizabeth remarked, "you know . . . 'father and brother have I none,' or whatever it is."

Bert laughed. "Never mind that. Look here, Linda, are you on? If you can make sales speeches and sell stocks and bonds in this day and age you ought to be able to sell *me*. Think of it in that light. See it as selling, not only one able-bodied young man to the town but progress and business along with him; one hundred percent prosperity."

"He isn't," explained Elizabeth hastily, "as conceited as he sounds."

Linda pondered. She had made some rash statements to Dick Jarvis not so long ago. It looked very much as if she were now being called upon to prove them. Very well, she would. She lifted her head. "That's the ticket," said Bert approvingly. "The light of battle in the maiden's eyes. Good stuff, Linda. If we're all ridden out of town on a rail, I promise you'll have the best tar made *and* ostrich feathers!"

She said slowly:

"I've a little influence, here and there. You know I'll use it, Bert."

"Sure, I know. I've got every up and coming progressive under thirty, in this town, on my side. *And* the *Comet*. We'll make the grade yet, Linda, I'm not worrying."

Susanna arrived, in time for the wedding, and in

time, too, to meet Happy's train and to display him at the church. It was a simple and pretty wedding, and although Elizabeth's fancy was for intimate friends only, Bert had reminded her that, after all, "you're in politics, now." With the result that everyone came, from all walks of life, and the small church overflowed with its audience.

The Albert Warrens went to Canada for a weekend but that was all the honeymoon they allowed themselves. On their return they moved into the small house Bert had rented, and which their friends put in apple-pie order for them during their brief absence. Elizabeth was resigning from her job but not until her contract ran out, which would be the following autumn, so, the day after their arrival home saw Bert going to his office as usual and his wife stepping into her small car to make her ordinary rounds. "I think," said Susanna radiantly, "they're too awfully prosaic for words!"

But Happy, whose husky arm was about her shoulder at that moment, contradicted. "No, they're not, honey . . . I tell you that's a partnership, and a romantic one, too."

"What about us?" she demanded.

"Oh, we're just a little different from everyone else in the world," he admitted cheerfully, "and just a little bit happier. But Bess and Bert will do!"

He was to have a month at home, and his progress through the familiar streets was triumphal. Every three steps people stopped to shout at him, to wring his hand, to say "Happy, the old place hasn't looked the same since you went away!" He didn't look quite the same either. He had put on weight, becomingly, he carried himself better, his blue eyes were keener, less casual and lazy, and according to Susanna, he had acquired a "manner." "Well," Happy defended himself, "you know the hotel business, Susanna, you were brought up in it."

"I was born in a hotel," she admitted.

"And you'll go on living in one, I suppose," he said.

He was at peace with all the world. He had work that he liked, that was eminently suited to him. He had the personality for the job, and his judgment was growing daily. Mr. Hudson's long chance had turned out one of the best bets he had ever made.

He spent his nights at his mother's house and his days with Susanna. His mother, once compelled to face reality, had surrendered. She was still a little tearful when surrounded by the innumerable members of her enormous family connection, but she and Susanna had managed to become, if not friends, at least amiable acquaintances. Naturally, Mrs. Anderson took upon herself all the credit for Happy's success. "I always knew," she said, "he had it in him!"

Dick gave them, and the young Warrens, a dinner at the Country Club. It was the first time Linda had seen him since her return from Atlantic City, save, casually, on the street. She dressed for the party with even more than her usual care, making a business trip to Benville during the morning an excuse for a prolonged visit to Madame Leona. The visit had reason as well as rhyme, however, as school would be out the end of June and Linda was anxious to place Lottie in the beauty shop, if possible. Leona, a shrewd, dark-skinned little woman with beautiful eyes and gorgeous white hair, said instantly that she could use a willing girl and would be glad to train one. Her two trained operators had taken courses in Syracuse. But her own methods differed slightly and, even with the basic knowledge they had acquired, she had been forced to train them, too. If Linda's candidate was quick and anxious to learn Madame Leona thought that two summers would give her the knowledge she needed. "I can't pay her much, Miss Anthony, you understand, and I'll use her for odd jobs about the shop, appointment desk and so forth, for a long time. She is willing?"

"Yes, of course. I don't want you to pay her much. Enough to cover her bus fares and her lunches, that's all. Both her mother and I are anxious to have her learn a trade and be occupied over the summer. Next year is her last in school. She's very bright, you know, just turned seventeen, but has been lazy about book learning. I think *you'll* find she'll learn like a shot once she is interested. It's awfully kind of you, Leona."

But the little woman waved that aside. "After all you've done for me," she said, "it would be a pity if I couldn't do something for you. But it isn't all gratitude on my part. I could do very nicely with just such a girl. I hope," she said anxiously, "that she's good-looking? A homely girl in a beauty parlor is no advertisement!"

WHITE COLLAR GIRL

"She's quite pretty," Linda assured her, laughing, "and I'll bring her over as soon as school closes and let you judge for yourself."

That day she herself had a very special facial, a manicure, a shampoo and finger wave. "You look perfectly sweet," Leona murmured, standing off to regard her handiwork with justified pride.

"Who wouldn't," Linda asked her, "with you to beautify 'em?"

"That's all very well, but even an artist has to have material to work on," Madame Leona told her gravely.

CHAPTER THIRTEEN

The dinner party was a great success. Bess, in her wedding gown, Susanna in the blue which Happy loved, "Any color, as long as it's blue, suits me," and Linda in a very pale, cool green, a printed chiffon frock that was spring itself. "I must say," murmured Dick, looking around the table, "that as a group we are a credit to the club."

Good food, laughter, light talk, dancing. Happy and Susanna holding hands, unabashed, under the table and Bert and Elizabeth discovered, now and again, indulging in some intimate little dream of their own. Dick, swinging Linda out to the dance floor, asked her gravely:

"Don't you feel rather envious and out of place surrounded by so much young love?"

"No—I think it's grand," she told him; "aren't they awfully dear?"

"Who, for heaven's sake . . . and do you mean costly?"

"No, I do not. All four of them."

He said: "They make me feel lonely." He said further, holding her closer: "Ah, Linda, if only we weren't enemies . . . !"

She made no reply, humming a little to the lilt of

the music. But her heart beat quickly, rather near his hand. She thought, I'm all right, as long as I stay away from him. . . .

He said: "You might be nicer to me. I'm leaving for California next week."

She almost stumbled, almost missed a step, accomplished dancer though she was. "California?" she repeated blankly.

"Yes. There's very little doubt that the mill can carry on without me," he admitted, a little ruefully, "and something has come up about my father's California property—he has oil leases there, you know—which makes it imperative for one of us to go out. So I'm elected."

"You'll have," she said, "a very nice trip."

"Is that all you have to say?" He very deftly swung her through the open French windows and halted her there in the dusk of the veranda. There were Japanese lanterns in the trees beyond but they shed only a small and glamorous light. "Linda, why do you hate me so? Linda, won't you miss me at all?"

"I don't hate you, Dick," she replied soberly.

"But—you couldn't—*love* me?"

Her lips shook, she twisted her hands together. He made no effort to touch her; merely stood there, close, trying to read her face in the scented gloom.

She said: "Why do you ask that?"

"Because—you know why, Linda. No matter how much we quarrel, no matter how much I fight against it, I—you know I care, so much," he said very humbly.

She thrust her hands out to him; drew them back. Her heart cried, Oh, what do the differences matter, Dick, I can't fight against this any longer, either! But she was committed to Bert. She had to fight on Bert's side. Perhaps it sounded foolish, perhaps small town political ambitions and affiliations had nothing to do with love. But even if Dick forgave her, and understood, his father would not. His people would loathe her. She couldn't come between them and Dick. She said, after a moment:

"I'm sorry——"

"I suppose that means you can't stick me at any price? I might have known it." He said, with a change of tone, "Bert's really going to run next fall . . . with you to help him!" He laughed a little and Linda said swiftly: "You think I can't?"

"My dear, I think you can do anything your mind is set on. I suppose I shouldn't be giving dinners for my father's political rival. However, it's a long way to election." He caught her hands in his. He said, this time without humility:

"Well, we might as well go back. I've done what, I suppose, you've always wanted me to do."

"Just what do you mean?" she asked, without stirring.

"I've made a highly colored fool of myself, isn't that obvious?" he asked her. "Well, that's that."

He touched her arm, and indicated the wide windows. Other couples were coming out on the veranda now, laughing, talking. And a scent of French perfume synthetically sweetened air already fresh and fragrant with June.

She thought, What has happened to me . . . to us? She thought further, I can't go back in that room, and face lights, and people . . .

But she did.

"Where on earth did you disappear to?" Susanna wanted to know.

"We were out looking at stars," Dick replied lightly, for them both, "falling stars, for the most part."

Long afterwards when they were at home again and Susanna had finally chattered herself to sleep, Linda, in a jade-green robe, sat on the cedar chest under her bedroom window and regarded the lovely darkness outside with wide, dry eyes.

He—cared; had said so. But that kind of caring was a mockery. Everything he said to her was a mockery. He "cared" because—because she was difficult, because she had opposed him at every turn, because, as he had said they were, in a deeper than surface sense, enemies.

He was going to California. Let him go, thought Linda, her hands linked under her chin. He'd forget about her there; perhaps she'd forget about him. Why not?

She contemplated in retrospect the two romances which had touched her life most closely: Susanna's sudden and obstinate, gay and tender romance with Happy; and the romance of Bert and Elizabeth which had flowered, sweetly and quietly, in their very youthful days and had grown surely, steadily and to real depths and heights.

It wasn't possible that Dick's attraction toward

her and hers toward him was really love. It couldn't be. Love didn't come to you with a sword in one hand, love wasn't composed, half of a longing to surrender, and half of a determination to be free. . . .

Susanna's visit drew to a close. She would be going to Long Island this season with her parents. They couldn't spare her for long, now that they had yielded and victory would be, ultimately, hers. She promised to return, in the fall, before her contemplated marriage. Perhaps Happy could get a little time off, too, she said. He was going back to New York with her, to start in upon his new duties at the Luxor. "Better come down," he invited all his friends, "and try and get a hall bedroom in the new palace. I'll sell you a suite, before you know it." He could, too, persuasive creature, they decided, a little astonished at his new keenness and ambition.

Dick Jarvis left for California. Linda read of his departure but did not see him before he left. The summer fled by on wings of fleetness. She had her own work, she had the satisfaction of seeing Lottie happily placed with Madame Leona, and she had her work for and with Bert Warren.

Wherever she went, wherever there was a possible vote, she spoke of Bert, his ambition for the town, his integrity, his progressive, active mind, his perfect fitness for a rather thankless position; a position which would bring with it very little in salary and which would curtail, as it happened, his own professional earnings. But Bert was willing; and so was Elizabeth. Bert didn't mean, Linda knew, to stop at being Mayor of Lawrenceton. There were other jobs, other rungs to the ladder.

People listened to her. They had become accustomed to listening to Linda and to finding that she had something honest and worth while to say. Many said: "Well, I never liked Fred Jarvis anyway and this young fellow seems like a good bet. I'll think it over, Miss Anthony."

She selected her Women's Committee with forethought and care. Elizabeth of course, Helen Carter, and several of the older women, the women active in club attempts at town reform, and progress. There was very little wealth back of her committee but a great deal of willingness to work and whole-hearted coöperation.

The *Comet* started its campaign. Jarvis, reading, was both grieved and amazed. He had never thought of himself as a hard and selfish man, ready to sacrifice the welfare of a community to his own Lord-of-the-Manor attitude. Mrs. Jarvis was horrified. "Can't something be done about it?" she wanted to know.

Pressure was put to bear on certain advertisers; the advertising of the *Comet* dropped off. But the Civic Club, and the Women's committees raised a small sum from among their own groups and took space in which they set forth Bert's qualifications as well as his picture. Two or three rather independent merchants, who had long regretted the unprogressive atmosphere of the town, and regretted even more that the majority of its buying power bought in New York, rather than at home, took the leap and started advertising exclusively in the *Comet*. So, as far as loss and gain was concerned, the paper found itself breaking even, to the delight of the inky and determined young men who ran it.

The American Legion group, after due consideration, ranged itself solidly on Bert's side. Bert had done a good deal for the Legion, in a quiet way, over a span of several years. He had helped various legionnaires, had seen them through certain legal difficulties and had procured jobs for them.

Linda, addressing her first audience from the mill, in Bert's crowded office, one evening, was as terrified as she had ever been in all her life. But with her first low words spoken, she took heart and soon found herself free of panic, talking directly to the men and women who listened to her, urging them for their own sakes to support Bert. "What about our jobs?" growled one man in the front row.

She admitted the risk. But with Warren in power there would be more jobs, she told them; he would encourage industry to come to the city. He had won over the small, struggling chamber of commerce, they would see a change in the town before very long, if they would support her candidate.

The tenor of her first speech and of subsequent ones was printed in the *Comet*. Jarvis, unbelieving, read, and stormed his way to the Anthony home one day and demanded of Mrs. Anthony: "What's got into your girl? Has she gone crazy?"

Mrs. Anthony replied that she did not believe so. Jarvis prowled up and down the cool, dark living room, his hands in his pockets.

"If her father were alive," he said explosively, "he'd put a stop to such nonsense."

Mrs. Anthony remarked mildly:

"Linda is of age, and can do as she pleases. Personally, I have never thought mixing in politics a proper occupation for young girls and women. But girls have changed since my day!"

"More's the pity!"

"I'm not quite sure of that. Linda has been very successful in business. As far as Bert Warren is concerned, he is an old friend, she believes in him, she wants him to win out, Fred."

"*I've* known her since she was knee-high to a hop toad," Mr. Jarvis argued.

"You're not of her generation," Mrs. Anthony reminded him.

"Are you against me, too, Mary?" he asked, in astonishment.

Mrs. Anthony smiled at her husband's old friend. She said gently:

"Linda's converting me, Fred. Oh, I know how you feel about Lawrenceton. How you want it protected against an invasion of industry, how you'd like to keep it just as it has been for years, placid and picturesque. I know that if Bert has his way and, as he says, puts it on the industrial map, much of the atmosphere, the charm peculiarly its own, will be gone. But—we can't mark time always, Fred, we and our generation. Youth must be served, I suppose, and it is youth that is getting stimulation from the machine age. We may despise and deplore it but I don't believe we can stop it, indefinitely."

He stamped out again, a little later, entirely baffled by the longest speech he had ever heard from her, in his knowledge of her. She told Linda afterwards: "Linda, he's hurt. Not as angry as hurt. He's held this town in the hollow of his hand so long. He can't understand why anyone would turn against him!"

Dick, in California, received annoyed bulletins from his father. Dick sent postcards to Bert. "How's the campaign?" he wrote. "I'll be back soon and spike your guns, you old fox. Just at the moment I'm taking a holiday in Hollywood. Boy, you don't know the half of it. Met Dorine Dunne at dinner last night. Print that in the *Comet*."

Bert passed the cards around. Elizabeth laughed a little. "The democracy of the camera," she remarked. "If Dorine Dunne had stayed home, where, after seeing her on the screen, I firmly believe she belongs, do you think for a moment she would have broken bread with the Ward McAllister of Lawrenceton?"

"Maybe he'll fall for her," said Bert glumly.

"That would please his father," commented Linda, sitting there in Bert's office with her carefully typewritten reports.

But her heart shook. Not because of Dorine Dunne, blond, sugar melting a little at the edges; but because of Dick, very far away, in a community where beauty was a drug on the market. They'd like him out there. Not alone for his money, she thought, but because he was a likable person. Or so people seemed to think.

WHITE COLLAR GIRL 185

"If he gets a camera test," grinned Bert, "they'll have him running for office instead of his pop-eyed old man. And I'll lose."

The young men on the *Comet* were working furiously. They were making a good thing of their paper. The editorials were snappy and to the point and very much in the vernacular, that he who ran might read. There was plenty of local news, even gossip. There were items from all over the world, state and country politics, foreign policies, disasters. And school and athletic news, with a column devoted to the American Legion doings and those of the fraternal organizations and chamber of commerce. And paragraphs from the outlying towns. Another couple of years, people said proudly, and the paper would be known all over the state and further than the state.

One of the owners, Frank Hayes, was an Albany man, the son of a prosperous blanket manufacturer, who had given him his original stake, but with his tongue in his cheek. He, however, found himself becoming interested in the venture and before autumn had pledged a sum which would serve amply to expand the scope of the paper. He believed it was worth it. Mr. Hayes came to Lawrenceton and met Bert and Bert's committees. He decided these young people would bear watching. Frank took him out on the river, showed him various properties. The blanket mills had been talking expansion. "Here's the site for your branch factory," Frank told him, "if Bert Warren gets in. If Jarvis does, you haven't a Chinaman's chance."

Mr. Hayes would talk things over with his directors, he promised. He gave his son and his partners a dinner at the Lawrenceton House. The men and women serving on Bert's committees were there. Hayes met Linda, whose small contribution had helped, materially. He held her hand a long time. He said to his son: "If you ever have to fire your staff, here's someone who could run the works." He knew all about her, from Frank, from Bert. He said: "Young woman, if you ever want a job——?"

"I have a job——"

"What's that?"

"Investment securities," she told him, laughing.

She looked very charming. He regarded her with appreciation. "Is that so! Gilt-Edge Girl?" he inquired. "Well, suppose you come see me, tomorrow morning."

He gave her, on the following day, an order for twenty-five thousand dollars, the largest lump sum she'd ever handled. She was almost speechlessly grateful. Here was a man who dealt in real money through New York brokers, who had a fortune in stocks, in bonds . . . not a small investor but a big one. He said, smiling:

"The thousand you put into my kid's paper meant a lot more to you than twenty-five times that. I'll remember you, Miss Linda. We'll do business again, some day."

The *Comet* had no more worries. Advertising losses didn't bother it at all. It went on its way serenely, and Jarvis grew nervous. He undertook quiet negotiations and inquiries. No, not a chance.

The *Comet* wasn't for sale, his scouts reported, and, as far as they could see, no possible measure would be able to put the upstart sheet out of business.

Jarvis started looking for items which might be interpreted as libelous. But Bert Warren was the legal adviser-in-chief to the *Comet's* editors and owners and Bert was very clever.

Forced to hold his hand, Mr. Jarvis received a delegation of the men sent to Lawrenceton on the Bridge Commission, dined them, and took them in his speed cruiser for a trip up the river, and in two of his cars for a trip along the riverside. The commission was made up of other residents of the town, among them the rival candidate for mayor. On their departure, Bert was inclined to be hopeful. "I talked myself blue in the face," he informed his eager listeners, "trying to persuade them that this was the place for the bridge to cross. I don't know if I succeeded. They've gone to inspect Benville and one or two of the other towns. However, this is the logical site, anyone with two eyes in his head should see that. Boy, how it would boom us! The mills of the gods grind slowly, of course, and the commission will have to present its findings at the capital and all that. Still, fortune may favor us— and common sense."

Linda listened, much interested. She had heard through Elizabeth of trouble in the families of the workers in Jarvis' mill. Elizabeth had been begging for clothes for the school-children. Linda was a well-known mendicant by now and went about her job of collecting shoes and underwear, coats and dresses, with her usual enthusiasm, and stopping by the shabby Larson house to deliver her booty, sat for some time in the little living room, listening to Mrs. Larson complain of conditions. One or two casual sentences made Linda prick up her ears. She left the house with an entirely new stock of ammunition, determined to keep it to herself until the last battle of the campaign was on. "Fireworks," thought Linda. "I'll save them for then!"

CHAPTER FOURTEEN

But she could not risk everything by placing too much faith in a random remark. She must find out more accurately, if possible, if what Mrs. Larson had conjectured was, indeed, truth. She made guarded inquiries at home and at Benville. Madame Leona was a perfect repository of contemporary history and events. Women, in beauty salons, talk more than they realize. Women who will not confide in their closest friends will, under the soothing hands of an experienced operator, divulge their most intimate secrets and those of their dearest acquaintances. Therefore, Linda, bent on sifting rumor from fact, asked Madame Leona a careless question or two. "Everyone thinks," said Leona, "that the bridge will be built at Benville. I hope it will be, it will increase business about a thousand percent. It means a good tourist hotel—they are talking sites already—and tourist hotels mean tourists and tourists mean business for the shop."

One of her most regular and valued clients was the woman whose husband, a real estate man, was interested in the hotel project, and had entertained and argued with the Bridge Commission.

"Lawrenceton always has seemed to me the most

feasible place," Linda remarked, smiling at Lottie who hurried from appointment desk to booth to greet her and back again. Lottie, very trim in a pale pink uniform, and looking happier than Linda had ever seen her, and, by the same token, prettier. "How's Lottie coming along?"

"Smart as a steel trap, that one," Leona told her. "I'm grateful to you for sending her to me. She'll be valuable to me some day. What were we talking about?—Oh, the bridge! But Mrs. Carruthers tells me that the older men in Lawrenceton are inclined to be against it, and advise Benville as the logical site."

She mentioned names. "I see," said Linda, relaxing under Leona's soothing hands.

It was clear to her now that, with his hatred of change and alteration, Fred Jarvis was working, more or less secretly, against bringing the bridge to Lawrenceton. She reflected that he, personally, would lose very little by deflecting it to Benville. If she was not mistaken, he owned considerable property there. She must find out. If the progressive people in her town ever learned that their candidate for mayor was stubbornly and willfully blocking the bridge, a symbol of progress if ever there was one, they would make short shrift of him at election. But now was not the hour in which to speak.

She kept her knowledge to herself, waiting. The *Comet* startled and amazed its readers by beginning a series of articles devoted to the "Blemishes" on the fair Face of the town. They ran a week's "roving reporter's" comments on the condition of the

Flats, and another week's reporting was devoted to the District.

Jarvis, filled with foreboding and horror, hurried to see lawyers and advisers. Impossible to say that he had been wholly blind to the uses to which his attacked property had been put. Yet he had not been deliberately callous. In common with many men of his generation, property owners, men who had never known the pinch of poverty or the stigma of degradation, he had thought—if he thought at all —that such conditions were bound to exist in a "civilized" world and that while he might deplore it, theoretically, his hands were clean enough. The property had been leased by him to an agent, and the agent had in his turn re-leased it. He was one jump removed from touching pitch, or so he thought.

Dick returned, pretty much upset. He faced his father across the big flat desk in the elder Jarvis' private office.

"I never knew this," Dick accused him; "surely, *you* must have known!"

Jarvis looked uncomfortable. "The property had been ours for years," he explained. "I leased it, twenty years ago, to Abner Howard. I never inquired what he had done with it."

Dick stared, unbelieving.

"But you must have known" he repeated helplessly. "In a town of this size—you couldn't help but know!"

"That there were speakeasies there, I knew," Jarvis admitted, "and that the place had a bad reputation. That's all. I didn't," he said honestly, "concern myself with it, to any extent. Howard has offered to buy several times; but I've held on, because of the railroad yards. The *Comet* is simply out to muck-rake and make things look a good deal worse than they are. They are employing all the yellow journalistic methods, scare-headlines and all the rest, playing up the human interest and drama. Too damned silly. Did you see yesterday's headlines?" He threw the despised paper on the desk. "Shall Lawrenceton Expose Its Youth To Such Dangers?" "I'd like to wring their necks!" he muttered.

Dick said seriously:

"Wringing their necks won't help. You'll have to clean that place up. You can break Howard's lease. See your lawyers. There must be a legal way to do it, now that you are aware—for the first time, we'll say, although nobody will believe it—of conditions there. Threaten him. I'll see him, if you like. We'll run him out of town, and we'll pull the place down, every shack in it. Something has to be done. And not entirely because of your candidacy, either!" Dick told him point-blank.

His father looked old and worried. After a moment's apoplectic stuttering and swearing he calmed down. "Very well," he said, "if you think it can be done."

He had a lawyer come up from Albany. The terms of the leases were consulted. Howard was, in a remarkably short space of time, dispossessed and with entire legality. The *Comet's* teeth—if comets have teeth—were pulled. But the *Comet* was able to recover and take the credit to itself. However, people following the news, said, to one another: "Jarvis is all right. As soon as he realized what has been going on there in the last few years he took drastic steps to remedy it."

But others said, "To save his neck, and give him a look-in, this fall!"

"Dick's work," Bert commented to Linda and Elizabeth. "There's another weapon we've managed to put in his hands."

Linda said thoughtfully: "The articles in the *Comet* broke too soon. They had time to remedy the situation." She was determined that what she knew would not break—too soon.

"It can't be helped," Bert said, after a moment. "Personally, I'm glad. Even if it did wake Jarvis up. For the good of the majority, you know——"

They saw very little of Dick. He was starting his campaigning. Going among the people of the mill, canvassing from house to house and succeeding where others could not have forced a foot inside the door. He was holding rallies, making speeches, working hard. And he had, he thought, the older element solidly back of him.

Bert was not idle; nor were his committees. Linda, coming from a conference at Bert's office one evening, and declining Bert's offer to walk home with her, heard herself hailed. Dick's car slid up beside her and stopped. He said, smiling: "Little girls shouldn't be out so late at night. Shall I drive you home?"

"It's only a step."

"Get in, I'll drive you somewhere else then . . . just to make it worth your while." And, as she hesitated, "Afraid of me?"

"Well, no." She got into the car and slammed the door. "Why should I be?"

He set the car into motion. "Hope some of your roving reporters see us," he chuckled, "it will make headlines, all right. 'Rival boosters for rival candidates observed hobnobbing in roadster late one evening!'"

She laughed, in spite of herself.

"Nevertheless," said Dick, soberly, "the *Comet* did me one good turn. You know what I mean. Will you believe me if I tell you I had no idea—and I don't believe my father had either?"

"That's absurd," she said abruptly, "not about you, of course. You have spent the greater part of your life away from the town. But your father has always lived here."

He said seriously:

"I, too, hold him responsible. But not as you do. You question his motives. I don't. I say he was—blind——"

"Deliberately."

"No, not deliberately. His generation has always lived behind drawn shades, Linda. Not deliberately, and not with an idea of making money out of evil conditions."

After a moment, she said:

"Perhaps you're right. But I hold him responsible just the same. There is such a thing as criminal negligence."

"He remedied it, as far as he could," Dick told her.

"Can these things ever be remedied?" she asked him.

He was silent. Then he said:

"Everywhere I go I hear of you. You—you've been poaching on my preserves, you know, Linda."

"All's fair in war and politics," she told him lightly.

"Haven't you left something out?"

They were riding along the River Road, through the cool dusk of a late summer night. Autumn was chill in the wind, and the stars were bright and remote. He slowed the car's swift even pace and leaned toward her to repeat his question insistently. "Haven't you left something out, Linda?"

"I think not," she told him. She clenched her hands in the pockets of her tweed coat. Her hair blew in curling tendrils about her face. Her lips felt dry.

"I wish we had you on our side," he told her, "or, perhaps I wish you were on *my* side. You're a darned good little fighter, you know that, don't you? Loyal. Bert's lucky. I'd tell you I wish I were Bert only that isn't true. I'd rather be myself . . . under certain conditions."

She said abruptly:

"Did you have a marvelous time on the Coast? Tell me about it."

The car gathered speed again. He replied evenly:

"Nice of you to be so interested. Yes, and no. Part of it was hard work; part of it was exhausting play; part was adventure. You know, or perhaps you don't, that I was around when one of the oil wells blew up and covered a whole town with oil and terror for several days, till they got the lid on it, so to speak."

In answer to her startled questions, he went on:

"No, it wasn't a Jarvis well. I had to come back home to find the lid blowing off as far as we are concerned." He laughed shortly. "Hollywood. Aren't you interested in Hollywood?"

"Of course, I am. Did you meet everybody?"

"Not quite. Not, at least, Garbo. But there were others. It's an amazing place. I had a heady sense of unreality all the time. Did you know I met Dorine Dunne?"

"Bert told us. What's she like?"

"Prettier than she is on the screen. I can't make out if she's an affected little piece or if her affectations have become such second nature that she really believes them to be natural. She was a little shy of meeting me at first. I gather she doesn't care for old home folks. But we got along very well. She's taking her three months' leave of absence in October and I've persuaded her that she can relax and rest, up here, better than by going to the South of France. Change of climate is everything," he remarked solemnly, "and she'll give the town something to talk about."

"She might," suggested Linda almost too demurely, "make a good assistant campaign manager for your father. Hadn't we better turn back? It's pretty late."

Dick complied.

"I hadn't thought of that," he said gravely, "but it's an interesting idea. Would you suggest a float, with a model of the old homestead on one end and a Hollywood horn of plenty on the other, and Miss Dunne in the middle in the grass costume of her last successful picture, *Only a Hula Maiden,* waving a banner inscribed 'Home Town's Only Screen Star Says Vote for Jarvis.' "

"Dick, you're an absurd person!"

She wished that he might always be absurd—laughing, boyish, friendly; that they might drive for uncounted eternities through the cool, sweet air, angers and enmities forgotten. . . .

But now he said, with a change of tone:

"Yes, I've always known you thought so."

He went on speaking of Hollywood, of the people who had entertained him; but now she thought he might have been talking to anyone. She sat quietly beside him, listening, and only half hearing. They were coming into town now, they were turning in at her street.

"What do you hear from Susanna and Happy?" he wanted to know.

"Not much. Susanna's usually a ready letter writer but I imagine when she isn't interrupting Happy's work by telephones from Southampton to New York she's writing to him, which uses up her surplus energy. They may come back up here in the fall, however."

"That's great," he said, as they stopped in front of her door.

She thanked him, said good night, and went on up the steps. She thought, ascending them slowly, that meeting him like that, talking to him, made it harder for her to go on. It should make it easier; but, perversely, it did not.

This was September. October came in vocal with the torch song of the trees. The last very active campaigns for the elections were under way. "I'll have to charge you," Linda told Bert, "I'm neglecting business!"

But business was miraculously coming to her, through the people she was learning to know, was meeting all over. She had become a poised public speaker, realizing the value of a little humor, of an intimate personal touch, and forgetting her normal panic in her seriousness to impress her audiences with her basic sincerity. "That girl ought to be muzzled!" growled Jarvis to his son.

Dick said nothing, thrusting his hands in his pockets and walking about the parental living room where his father sat over an after-dinner cigar.

"Can't you do it?" the elder Jarvis suggested.

Dick whirled on a hasty heel.

"I—what do you mean?"

"You're good friends."

"I wouldn't call it that, exactly," Dick said judicially, while his mother looked up from her survey of solitaire cards, quickly.

"You see a lot of her, or used to. I should think her friendship for you, to say nothing of my once intimate relations with her father, would have made her reconsider throwing her weight on Warren's side. Warren. Who is he, anyway, a little hick lawyer, half shyster!"

"Bert's not that," Dick said, loyally and angrily, "he's a hundred percent honest. And about the most progressive young man in this town."

"Do you want to see him mayor of it?" inquired his father.

"I want to see you mayor," Dick told him smiling, "as your heart's set on it."

"Stuff and nonsense! I don't care! It will mean a lot of responsibility," his father said, with an overdone indifference. "If it weren't for the sentiment of the town which has forced me to run, I wouldn't consider it."

That was not true. Dick had a half smile, wholly affectionate, for the older man's vanity. He said to himself in some wonderment. Can't they *see* how much he really cares for Lawrenceton . . . how his fight against what they think of as progress is really a battle for old traditions and old, serene ways of living?

He had said that once to Linda. And she had replied shortly, as he recalled now: "Only people with money and no need to worry over jobs and the next meal can afford to talk about traditions and serene living. And they are very much in the minority."

CHAPTER FIFTEEN

EARLY in October Dorine Dunne arrived with a fanfare of trumpets. She had come to Lawrenceton, she told the assembled press at the station, to rest and forget. It was not quite clear what she proposed to forget. She took an entire floor of the hotel, and brought with her a small entourage. A personal maid, the first French maid ever seen in the town as even Mrs. Jarvis preferred a native variety, a male "personal representative," and a sour-faced, smartly dressed female secretary.

Dick met her at the train; and gave her the first dinner, at his father's home. Mr. Jarvis was annoyed. He didn't like showfolk. Dick persisted. But when Linda's name came up Jarvis was adamant. "I won't have that girl set foot in this house!" he said. Even Mrs. Jarvis found that ultimatum ridiculous.

"Very well, I'll give the dinner at the Country Club," Dick compromised coolly.

Mr. Jarvis ceased to be adamant. "Give it where you damned please but don't expect me to be present!"

Linda, however, declined the invitation. Bert and Elizabeth had been included, as Mr. Jarvis decided that to invite his rival to a formal dinner showed a magnanimity that would reflect favorably upon him. Why, therefore, he had attempted to draw the line at Linda, no one could say, save perhaps that the mere fact that she was a woman and a young one and had attempted to defy him and all his works grated upon his very masculine nerves. But the Warrens declined also and the dinner, which was long and lively and entirely dominated by Dorine, went on merrily without them, the guests including most of the gayer younger and married set in the town; and the papers, even the metropolitan papers, had long notices. But the *Comet* confined itself to a terse little paragraph:

"Richard Jarvis, son of the candidate for mayor, entertained last night at his father's home for Miss Dorine Dunne, screen star, formerly of this city."

There was something a little bit snooty about that bald and brief item. People when they read it chuckled for no good reason.

The *Comet* had been mysteriously promising fireworks . . . The *Comet* was saving itself for the final battle, or so the *Comet* said. Jarvis grew uneasy. And made certain inquiries on his own behalf.

The result of these was summed up one night, shortly after the dinner party.

"This bridge business——"

"What about it?" Dick asked, unwarned.

"Nothing. Only if it gets out that I've been blocking it, quietly, there will be trouble. I mean if it gets out before election. There are a lot of fool people in this town who believe that the building of the bridge at Lawrenceton will mean everything to the city: factories, tourists, bigger and better business. They can't see it will mean a town of trippers, half the undesirable element in the state flocking up here to make a little money on the side. If the bridge goes through, I'll go out. It's unthinkable. Benville's the place for it, it's a commercial town already. It's just as near the main route of travel as Lawrenceton . . ."

"You mean to tell me you have actually thrown your influence to the Benville side?" Dick asked.

"Yes, to a degree, but, while I'm not ashamed of my standpoint and am willing to go to the mat for it, it wouldn't help me at election, thanks to Warren's campaign among the townspeople, and his platform of new business and progress. Progress! Corruption!"

"I think you're wrong," said Dick baldly.

"You do? Well, time will prove it. I've got it on pretty good authority that your little friend Linda Anthony has this information and is going to hold it till the right time. One of my men came to me recently. His wife had made an unconsidered remark—women are fools—and he learned about it, weeks after. He's loyal enough. And she's been seen a lot over in Benville, hobnobbing with some woman who keeps a beauty shop——"

"Who are you talking about?"

"Linda, of course!"

"I see. You think she hasn't said anything of her knowledge?"

"Not yet. If she had, the *Comet* would have had

it by now. No, she's saving it for the final campaign. Look here, Dick, she's got to be out of town before Election Day—and she's got to stay out!"

Dick said, laughing, although his eyes were grave:
"What do you want me to do, kidnap her?"

"Exactly," his father replied, in some relief, "get her away from here; keep her away until it's too late."

"You'll lose my vote," Dick suggested, "if I have to do the keeping."

"Your vote won't count. Your work's done. We can manage the last few days without you. Look here, don't laugh. I—you've got to get that meddlesome girl out of the way, do you hear me?"

"You're not *serious?*"

"Never more so in my life."

Dick thought rapidly. He was not at all in sympathy with his father's views. He thought, however, If Lawrenceton is the right place for the bridge he can't stop it, he's too sure of himself and his influence. But, to kidnap Linda!

The idiotic, the melodramatic plan had its possibilities. To take Linda away somewhere, to have her all to himself, to make her forget bridges and politics, enmities and quarrels, to tell her that all these things didn't matter, that he loved her, and wanted her; that he would always love her and that love was a bigger thing than the barriers she had willfully erected, the misunderstandings she had permitted, even encouraged, to grow up between them . . .

"I don't suppose it can be done," his father said. "I mean, so it would look unpremeditated."

"Leave it to me," said Dick.

A day or so later he came to his father.

"Is the Lodge in shape for visitors?"

"Well, it usually is. I've Jenkins up there, all year round. Why?" asked Jarvis, puzzled.

"I thought I'd like to throw a party there, a house-party, a week before Election Day," Dick explained, not a feature altering its composure. "I think it would amuse Miss Dunne. I'd get the Nortons, and as I understand Susanna Hudson and Happy Anderson are due in town about then, I'd ask them; and, of course, Linda, and another man."

His father looked at him. His father said, his face alight with something that was pure mischief, "You're bound to run into dirty weather, this time of year."

"That will be just too bad!" Dick agreed.

"I'll wire Jenkins and have the Lodge stocked," Jarvis said. Then he smote his son soundly between the shoulder blades. "You're a great boy," he admitted.

Dick wired Susanna and Happy. The wires were materially the same. "Hustle on up here," they read, "going to give you a party at the Lodge, big whoopee and a good time had by all."

"What Lodge?" demanded Susanna, returned to town, of her fiancé.

"His father's. It's over in Canada, a swell little place. I was up there with Dick, hunting, once when we were kids."

"Let's do it. You planned to take a week off. We'll go up together, by train."

Dick came to see Linda.

"Don't you think it would be fun?" he asked. "Dorine says she'll go. She's getting fed up with Main Street, I think, and this promises to be something different. The Nortons are game. Here's a wire from Susanna and Happy."

"When would we be back?" asked Linda.

He made a swift calculation.

"Sunday night."

"That's pretty close to Election Day," she pondered aloud.

"Not too close. I have to go back too, Linda, you know," he said.

"That's so." She considered him gravely. Of course, he had to be back. But she hesitated. "I don't know——" she said doubtfully, "I'm not at all sure . . ."

"Oh, do come. Bert can get along without you for a few days," he said carelessly; "think it over . . ."

He did not urge her. She saw him again that same afternoon, driving Dorine Dunne to the club. Dorine's fair hair was close to his shoulder. He was driving rather carelessly, looking down into the pretty sparkling small face so near him.

He doesn't, said Linda to herself, care if I go.

Susanna and Happy arrived, and Linda was still undecided. "I shouldn't leave—if anything should happen," she began.

"What can happen?"

"Weather for one thing," Linda answered, "people have been storm-bound before."

"What of it?"

"It's very near Election Day."

"Well," said Susanna logically, "if you lose your vote, so will Dick; you'll cancel each other. I can't see that it's so important. Do be a sport, Linda. I don't want to go without you. It might be heaps of fun. And what about this movie queen anyway? My in-laws-to-be tell me that Dick is giving her something of a whirl."

"I haven't met her yet," Linda replied shortly.

She consulted Bert. He looked her over and nodded.

"Go to it. You rate a rest. You're looking awfully tired, Linda," he said affectionately. "You've certainly been our right-hand man. You can afford to let down."

"But suppose we get stuck up there?" She laughed and told him Susanna's solution of the canceled votes.

"Well, that's right," Bert agreed, "everything is lined up now, Linda. Even if anything should happen—and nothing will—we're all set."

But Linda still had her card up her sleeve. Returning home she removed it, metaphorically speaking, and regarded it gravely.

She telephoned Dick. "I'll go," she told him.

But the night before they were to start she spent an hour at her portable typewriter, and very early the next morning appeared at the Warrens' modest door before Bert was up. Elizabeth was in the kitchen and greeted her caller with astonishment and a frying pan. "Linda, for heaven's sake, has anything gone wrong?"

"No, but it may. Is Bert sleeping?"

"Yes, lazy brute! But I'll have him up in a minute. Did you want to see him?"

"No. Here." Linda gave her a long envelope decorated with blobs of red sealing wax. "If I don't get back to town Sunday night give this to Bert. He'll know what to do with it. I think he'll take it right to the *Comet* office—it's important, Bess."

Elizabeth regarded her with amusement, and the envelope with curiosity.

"He's not to have it now?"

"No. It's by nature of a parting shot," Linda explained. "The *Comet*—well, the boys are all right but they get a bit previous. This is something that should not break until just before election; until it's too late for Fred Jarvis to do anything about it. Gosh, there's Bert, yelling his head off for you. Do you have to stand for that? Thank heaven I elected to be an old maid." She grabbed Elizabeth and kissed her. "Put that away," she warned in a whisper, "in a safe, if you have one."

"I have a safe deposit box," said Bert's wife.

"Good girl. Good-bye," and Linda departed, smiling and fleet, for home and breakfast.

The party got under way in two cars. They ferried to Canada and drove to the city seventy-five miles away, leaving the cars garaged there. Then they took a train, and later buckboards; and so arrived finally at their destination.

The Lodge lay by a small and frozen lake. There were many trees, great old trees through which the untainted wind sighed by day and night. The house itself was comfortable, with dormitory bunks for the men in a great sleeping room and smaller rooms for the women, two in a room. Susanna and Linda roomed together while Dolly Norton, somewhat to her consternation, was paired with Dorine. Dorine was pleasant enough to the women in the party but her attention was fixed upon their host. She called him "Dicky-boy."

"Sounds like a canary," said Happy, grinning.

The main living room of the Lodge was very big. The bark had been left on the trees which composed it and there was the usual plenitude of antlers, rough, hand-made furniture, fur rugs, Indian blankets and the like. There were the oil lamps, at which Dorine exclaimed. She hadn't seen an oil lamp since her picture *The Trail of Forty-Nine,* she explained. Which only went to prove that she had forgotten the old homestead, Happy commented, despite the fact that, now she had returned, she ran out to see her grandparents now and then and had even presented them with a radio and a Scotch terrier!

There was also a bathroom, which was a luxury, if rather primitive in its fittings.

Jenkins was maid of all work and an excellent cook. And the party was well supplied with provender for hunger and thirst. Dorine had brought "camping" clothes with her . . . breeches and silk shirts and gay handsome sweaters. She was very small and looked charming, if synthetic, and knew it.

They had for the first day or so gorgeous weather. Then it clouded and the first heavy flakes of snow began to fall. "Oh," said Dorine, shivering, catching Dick's arm and pulling it around her in an "unstudied" gesture which revolted the other feminine members of the party. "Oh, Dorine's *so* afraid of a blizzard!"

Dorine's original schooling, if any, had been gained through walking into Lawrenceton through blizzards and winds, rainstorms and sleet. Dolly grinned wickedly.

"This won't amount to anything," Dick soothed her.

But it snowed harder and it kept on snowing. Susanna and Happy were perfectly oblivious. They tramped out in the white whirling world—"Don't, for heaven's sake, go too far," Dick besought them— or spent their hours in the living room over a checker or backgammon board, not caring, as long as they were together. Norton, a keen woodsman and a wizard on snowshoes, began to hope for what he called a "real" one. And Dorine grew bored, languishing, demanding every moment of Dick's attention.

Linda said to Susanna, looking out the windows:

"We'll never get out of here in time, unless we make a start now."

Happy, looking up from the checkerboard, said:

"Dick had storm warnings before we started. He got a bulletin, by wire. I saw him put it in his pocket."

"Why didn't you tell me?" Linda stamped her foot at him, and looked out on the blinding world with eyes dim with angry tears.

"I don't think I realized it then. It comes back to me now. I'm pretty sure."

She said frantically: "I've got to get out of this!"

"Oh," said Susanna, "don't be a crab, Linda. Dick didn't make the storm, you know. Even if he did get a warning, he couldn't know it would be so bad. Besides, what can you do at home? You've done your bit, and your vote won't count one way or the other . . ."

"I suppose not."

No, there was nothing she could do. Besides, Bess and Bert—and the *Comet*—would have her information in time to use it. No, it wasn't necessary for her to return, as far as that went. But she loathed the feeling of being trapped.

Nevertheless, the party would have come out of the woods safely enough had not all means of communication and transportation mysteriously broken down. On Saturday morning the skies cleared to an even, lowering gray and the snow was thick and white underfoot. "I'm afraid," said Dick lightly, "that I won't be able to get you back in time. Sorry . . . but something seems to have happened to the buckboards . . . they're way overdue. If they don't show up there's nothing to do but wait."

"Buckboards!" said Linda scornfully.

"Sleighs, I mean. They're to send sleighs from Hawes," he explained hastily, "but something's the matter. Perhaps last night's storm . . . trees down or the bridge at Great Creek. As soon as we can we'll send Jenkins out to see. Can any of you girls cook?"

Mrs. Norton admitted, unblushing, to culinary knowledge. Dorine shirked. "I wouldn't know how to boil water!" she said. Susanna said, with a dire look at her blond competitor, "I'm learning."

"Heaven help me," sighed Happy.

"There's nothing to do but unpack and reconcile yourselves to a few more days of simple life," Dick said easily, "I'm awfully sorry——"

They weren't, they assured him in chorus.

All but Linda, her voice was conspicuous by its absence. She disappeared a moment later, and missing her, he went out, to find her standing, in a pair of oversize men's boots, a short wool skirt and a man's sweater, looking out over the frozen waste of the lake.

She turned at his approach.

"You never ordered buckboards—or sleighs—or whatever they are," she said furiously. "You've done this on purpose, Dick Jarvis!"

"Now, why should I do that?" he inquired mildly.

"To keep me away from Lawrenceton." She was so angry that the tears choked her throat and roughened her voice, to her own horror.

"But I'm keeping myself away," he reminded her, "and so there's two votes gone, yours and mine.

Happy, Susanna and Dorine can't vote, of course. And I've never asked how the Nortons stand—or Jack Manton.''

Young Manton, grandson of the Park Avenue Homer, was the even man on the party. A harmless person, rather amusing.

"You can't keep me here," Linda told him. "I don't know what your motives are but I fancy that they're just so you'll be able to laugh at me, that's all."

"Linda, you are being childish."

She said:

"I shouldn't have come. I knew it all along. I— I despise you for this, I always shall. After we get out of here, I never want to see you again."

He took a step toward her, flushing. Then he shrugged his broad shoulders in the heavy mackinaw and tramped the short distance to the Lodge, slamming the door behind him, causing the game players to jump. Susanna whispered, "He's had another row with Linda." And Happy agreed glumly. "Love," said Happy, "in its most primitive state. I'm not having any, here. So watch your step, woman! I'm too comfortable to fight with anyone!"

Linda stood where Dick had left her, staring out over the lake. Then she looked up at the sky. It was the first real snowfall, Jenkins had told her. It might not amount to anything, after all. It had stopped snowing.

That afternoon she went out into the lean-to shed and found there a pair of snowshoes which fitted her. She found breeches too, which had evidently been Dick's in his younger days. Then she waited her opportunity.

It couldn't be more than two hours' trek into the village of Hawes. She'd get a train from there. Then a plane from the city, if necessary. She'd make it, she told herself.

That it was no longer necessary for her to be on the scene of action, so far as elections were concerned, she understood clearly. But that didn't matter. Nothing mattered except to get away from under Dick's quiet, amused eyes, from the sound of his voice, from the sickening sight of Dorine Dunne setting her cocksure cap for him, from the stifling atmosphere, and from what she still fancied to be a mere practical joke on Dick's part.

Her chance came when Susanna and Happy were out in the kitchen with Jenkins. Dorine was taking her beauty nap in her bedroom, the others were playing cards. Linda dropped her snowshoes out of her bedroom window and followed them, wearing the breeches, a flannel shirt, a heavy sweater and a Canadian toque. Once outside, she put the snow shoes on and started off.

The first going was swift and exhilarating, over the deep piled snow. The small winding trail through the woods was an unbroken path of white. She looked for fallen trees. There were none. She'd see, if she got to the creek, if the bridge was down.

It was not. She crossed it, laughing in the face of a wind which had risen, after the ominous calm, and which now blew the snow from branches and path into her cold rosy face. Her eyes and eyelids stung. Now the snow was falling, as well as drifting. In another half hour she was making desperate going against a wall of shattered white, and a cutting wind.

The storm had returned with redoubled force and she had not yet reached Hawes and safety.

CHAPTER SIXTEEN

IT WAS some time before they missed her.

Susanna and Happy staggered in from the kitchen bearing a strange afternoon "tea" concoction of welsh rarebit, cinnamon toast and coffee. The card players greeted them with shrieks of hunger. "This place is death on the girlish figure," Dolly Norton remarked, "I've never had such an appetite. Assault and battery on the schoolgirl complexion, too," she added, one side of her round face nicely crimsoned from the big log fire.

Dick rose and put another log on the flames. He looked out of the window and said casually: "It's snowing again." He grinned a little, and Susanna looked at him sharply. She said reproachfully: "I take it, you're glad of it?"

"Why shouldn't I be . . . when it gives me the pleasure of your company for another twenty-four hours or so?" he replied, with what was intended for a courtly bow.

Happy, his mouth full of rarebit, gesticulated with a piece of toast.

"Lay off my gal," he ordered, "don't spoil her with pretty speeches. She doesn't rate 'em from me!"

"No, but seriously," Susanna said, planting herself beside Dick on the big stone hearth, "of course, it's nothing to me how long I stay up here, provided you get me home for the Big Ceremony at Christmas. But it's pretty hard on Linda. You know she wanted to get back—by the way, where the heck *is* Linda?" she asked in some astonishment.

"I thought she was taking a nap," Dick said, astonished in his turn.

"Who, Linda? She never takes naps. She doesn't need to. She leaves that to our playmate from Hollywood. Ouch—speaking of angels . . ."

Dorine had arrived in their midst. She was rosy and smiling, her big eyes drowsy. She wore, to the sartorial confusion of the ladies, and the æsthetic delight of the gentlemen, elaborate lounging pyjamas, wide black velvet trousers, a wrap-around blouse of jade green embroidered in peacock blues, and a little velvet jacket. She also wore entrancing mules; and as she had gone to bed determined to sleep, with tonic pads on her eyelids and a nourishing cream mask on her face, she made the two other girls in the room feel about forty, haggard and worn. They looked at her with loathing.

"Cheerio," cried Dorine, very British. "Oh, am I in time for tea?"

"It's coffee," said Susanna.

"But I can't drink coffee, at this time of day!"

"Have a highball?" suggested young Manton, holding out his own glass.

"I mustn't drink highballs. Can't I have some tea?" She sidled up to Dick and slid an arm through his own. "Come, Dicky-boy, make me some nice tea," she implored.

Susanna looked nauseated and Happy choked.

"Linda—" began Dick, looking at Susanna.

"I want my tea," said Dorine.

"Oh, all right, come along," Dick yielded; "better get Linda up," he said, over his shoulder to Susanna.

"She's asleep, isn't she?" Dorine asked. "I heard her opening her window, oh, ages ago."

"You did?" Susanna stared. Dick fell back a step, detaching himself from Dorine. "Better let her alone, then," he advised Susanna, "maybe she'll sleep it off."

"Sleep what off?" Susanna demanded.

"I'm not," explained Dick, "in very high favor." He disappeared into the kitchen and was heard soothing the saturnine Jenkins. Susanna looked at Happy. "They've been fighting again!" she said tragically.

"Don't you and Happy ever fight?" asked Dolly, laughing.

"Not much. Anyway, that's different," Susanna declared.

"Sure, it's different," Norton agreed. "Wait till you're married, you'll see the difference then."

His wife threw something at him; he dodged expertly. "There, you see?" he warned Happy gloomily. "When you're married you have to be a bank balance, an expert accountant, a lawyer, an actor, a doctor, a mechanic, a carpenter, a juggler and a contortionist!"

Dorine and her tea returned presently. She usurped the built-in divan and swung her trousered legs, regarding her slim ankles fondly. She had tea and dry toast, heroically disregarding the appeal of the sugary-cinnamony-buttery sort which Susanna, a bit maliciously, urged upon her.

Another bridge game started. The phonograph, set in motion, offered more or less musical accompaniment. Dorine rose and held out her arms to Dick. "Come dance with Dorine," she commanded.

And in this way another hour passed.

"I'm going to wake Linda," Susanna exclaimed finally, rising. "She can't hide away any longer. Besides, there's a draught from her window. She's a fiend for fresh air. Golly," she paused by Happy's chair and fiercely tweaked a lock of his blond hair, "look at it snow!"

She went on through the living room avoiding the dormitory-sleeping quarters, made her way up the small, narrow hall, and burst unceremoniously into her bedroom. "Hey, Linda, for Pete's sake, snap out of it, will——"

Her voice died away.

A moment later she was back in the living room.

"She's not there! Her room's empty! The window's open, and it's snowed great guns on the floor!" she announced dramatically.

"Not there?" repeated Dick blankly. "Then where on earth can she be?"

"She hasn't gone far, in this storm," Norton began.

Happy said soothingly: "She's always been

WHITE COLLAR GIRL

crazy about nature in the rough. You'll probably find her tramping around outside. Maybe she got up and decided to have a breath of nice fresh air.''

"Well, I'm going out and find her. She ought to be spanked!" said Dick. He dropped Dorine with an uncomplimentary suddenness. The fox trot on the phonograph went on monotonously—with vocal chorus; and finally whirred to a stop. It was some time before someone remembered to rise and shut off the machine.

Dick was getting into high boots and heavy outer clothing, pulling a fur cap down about his ears. "I'll go with you," offered Happy, and the other men chorused, "Me, too."

"No, stay here. No use all of us getting soaked. She's not far off; probably, as Happy says, she only slipped out a moment ago——"

"She couldn't slip out without our seeing her," Susanna objected.

"That's right," Dick agreed, frowning. Then his face cleared. "Sure she could. There's a porch off the dormitory, she could have gone through there and gotten out."

"Well, what of it? I mean, why on earth should she?" asked Susanna logically. "If she wanted to go for a walk, no one would have stopped her, most likely—I mean, she's free, white and twenty-one. I can't understand it."

Dick was at the door. He opened it. A great gust of wind blew in, scattered the cards, and left some snow on the floor, in that brief moment.

"Lord, it's thick," Dick muttered.

"Hey, Dick!" Happy shouted, rising. But the door slammed. Dick had gone. Dorine stood in the middle of the floor, her mouth drooped childishly. "Well, I must say . . . !" She murmured. But no one was interested in what she said, or thought, if anything.

A buzz of voices rose. Susanna, paling, slipped her hand into Happy's. "I'm worried about her," she said.

"He should have taken Jenkins with him," Norton declared. "He's an old timer in these parts."

"Nonsense," said Happy, repeating a confidence which he did not feel, "she can't have gone far." He was seized with an illogical anger against Linda, because he, too, was worried. He turned on Susanna. "You women are all crazy!" he said savagely. "Just because she gets sore at Dick, she pulls a fool stunt like this and . . ."

"Hush," warned Susanna with an almost imperceptible gesture toward Dorine, who had returned to the haven of the divan and was sitting, curled up, one hand caressing her slender silken ankle, and her enormous eyes fixed with extreme curiosity upon Happy.

Dick, out in the storm, his head bent, was struggling around to the lake side. He called, at intervals. No, she was not there, nor was she under the comparative shelter of the trees.

Halfway to Great Creek there was a cabin built for the hunters. Perhaps she had gone that way, and surprised by the storm, had found harbor there. He struck off in the direction of the trail and floundered at every step. Swearing, he returned to the lean-to shed where extra equipment was kept and pulled off his gloves to strike a match and set the swinging oil lamp alight. He routed out his snowshoes, and discovered, at the same moment, that a small pair, kept there for women guests, were gone. This set him to searching. Hadn't he had a pair of old breeches here and a flannel shirt? If so, they were gone too.

He hesitated a moment. Better call Jenkins . . . or Happy . . . or Norton. No, he'd be damned if he would! He'd find her himself and tell her, without an audience, just what he thought of her for running off in this idiotic, dangerous and cavalier fashion.

The snowshoes made his going much easier. The storm was lessening, a little, at least here, under the trees, the force of the wind was broken. He reached the little cabin, which was unlocked, wrenched the door open, and called. No one was there.

Doggedly he kept on.

His anger was dying within him. Fear, which he had fought frantically and with every common-sense natural explanation available, returned and tortured him. If anything happened to her—it was his fault. He'd find her, make a clean breast of it, ask her to forgive him. But first of all he would tell her that he loved her . . . so much . . . so much with every day that passed. Surely their stupid quarrels and their groundless hostilities would vanish when he had made her see that he loved her, that he wanted her, that for so much love she must have compassion and, perhaps, tenderness in return.

He had loved her ever since the night he had looked into stormy gray eyes, disturbing eyes, and listened to the cool, indifferent inflections of her enchanting voice.

He would find her. He *must* find her.

He set his teeth and carried on, dodging snow-laden, dangerous branches. If she had come this way . . . But she must have come this way. There was no other way out, and he had by now made up his mind that, headstrong and willful, making a gesture of pure defiance, she had determined to make her way out—to Hawes and thence back to Lawrenceton.

Yes, this was the only way. On the other side of the Lodge lay wilderness; back of it lay mere wilderness, while straight ahead of it was the lake, and the woods beyond the lake.

Once, he almost lost trail. He recovered it and kept on, sickened. If she, too, had lost it . . .

He thought of her, small, gallant and obstinate, fighting the storm with her girl's slight strength and her resolution. Thinking, he groaned aloud. "Linda," he said. "*Linda* . . ."

He called her, time and time again. Now and then he took from his pocket the electric torch he had picked up in the cabin and flashed its small yellow circle ahead. But the light made no headway against the swirling dance of the heavy flakes, blown into insane and unending patterns by the wind.

He crossed the bridge of Great Creek. "Linda," he called. "Linda?"

A mile or so beyond he thought he heard a faint answering shout, from the left of the trail. Here, the going was more open but the wind blew all the more furiously. He set his teeth against it, he was half blind with wind and snow. The tears the cold wind forced from his straining eyes froze on his lashes.

"Linda!"

Surely, he had heard something . . . surely there had been an answer? Or was it the maunderings of his imagination? Was it the echo of his own anxiety? If he didn't find her . . . He must find her. She would perish . . . in the storm. Night was approaching, it had approached, the heavy dusk, black, a sinister background for dancing white, had started to close down before he crossed the bridge. Had she reached Hawes? Was she safe?

"Linda——"

"Here!"

This time he heard it clearly, definitely. It came again, the answer, from the left of the trail. The wind aided it. He stumbled off the trail, and half beside himself, made in the direction of the sound. He crashed into trees here and there, floundering on his snowshoes.

"Linda!"

Now she spoke almost at his side. He saw her then, half incredulously. A small blur in a darker blur. He seized her arms, took her into his own, into a soaking wet embrace. "Linda—for God's sake!" he said; and it was like a prayer.

Her teeth were chattering.

"I got off the trail," she told him in the wisp of a voice worn with shouting. "I've been stumbling around in here, I don't know how long. I'm—Dick, I'm so *cold*."

"Here, we'll get back, at once," he said briefly. Time enough for explanations later. He led her back on the trail. To his horror, she began to laugh. "I was so near it all the time!" she explained hysterically.

He remembered that men had been lost, had wandered in circles but a stone's throw from the lifesaving trail, and there, in their own futile tracks, had died. A shuddering seized him; not of cold. He wished, too late, that he had brought the other men with him to expedite their return. If he could get her to the cabin, there was a fireplace there, and logs, cut and ready; light and warmth and a change of clothing.

He had her arm, was helping her. He said encouragingly, "Stick it out for a little longer, Linda, we'll make the halfway cabin and rest there first."

"I was afraid," she began.

She had been afraid. The storm had closed in on her; once she had stumbled and fallen. Then, somehow, she had lost the narrow trail and had made the circuit of the wind-bowed, snow-covered trees, feeling them with her numbed gloved hands, even crying a little, calling. Surely they would have missed her and come to look for her by now. Calling; thinking herself a fool, knowing herself for one. To embark, out of anger, out of pride, on so mad an expedition; to find herself, her ardor for escape gone, alone in a white and whirling world, a world of snow, of wind, of massive tree trunks, of drowsy cold. . . .

"Don't try to talk now," he ordered shortly.

She subsided, more docile than he had ever seen her. Back along the trail they went, in single file. Then the bridge; and some distance beyond the bridge, the cabin.

"I can't go on," she said finally.

"You must."

"I'm so tired, Dick . . . so—sleepy——"

"Stop a minute."

He knelt beside her in the snow, bracing the electric torch against a fallen limb and, by its light, taking from her heavy feet the snowshoes. He said, "You can hold these, can't you?" and picked her up, and went with what strength and swiftness he could muster the final distance between trail and cabin, setting her down at the doorstep . . . shaking the snow from his broad shoulders. He took off his own snowshoes, and opened the door. "Get inside," he said briefly.

She went in, staggering a little, the door swung shut and they were left in the thick darkness. She saw the spurt of a match, and then the lamp swung, casting its circles of light over the small room. "Where—where is this?" she asked him.

"Halfway Cabin, we use it when we hunt," he replied. He was kneeling by the hearth, digging out the newspapers from the wood basket, breaking up kindling wood, building his fire. "I'll have a fire here in a moment," he said cheerily; "we don't dare keep an oil stove in here, you know."

There were bunks along the wall, a table and some chairs. "Come closer to the fire," he said, as he got the wood to burning, and then, looking anxiously at her small face, blue with cold, he turned from his task and went to the cupboard on the far side of the wall, opened it and pulled out various hunting gear. He said, assembling shirts, sweaters, breeches and socks: "Afraid we haven't any boots to fit. Get out of your wet things, Linda, and into some of these . . . then when you're warmer and dry, we'll get back to the Lodge. There must be," he told himself aloud, "a flask of brandy here, somewhere . . . I remember Jenkins saying—unless someone's happened on it earlier."

He found it and handed it to her. "Get outside of some of that," he ordered, "and into fresh clothes."

"But, Dick——"

"I'll keep my back turned," he told her testily.

"I didn't mean that. I mean—you're wet through——"

"No. I'll last till we get back. Here, hurry up."

His fire was going beautifully. He stood before it, his face turned toward the wall, whistling between his teeth. He hadn't had time to be thankful. Now there was time. He asked, without looking around, "Did you drink that brandy?"

"Some of it," she told him, and gasped, "it was pretty dreadful."

"It's a hundred proof!" he told her reproachfully.

He heard rustlings, heard clothes dropping on the floor, heard her say "All right," and then turned to see her, eclipsed in sweater and shirt, in breeches and socks, many sizes too large for her. Color was coming back into her face. Her hair, damp with melted snow, curled riotously. "I'm all right," she said nervously, laughing a little. "Dick, hadn't you better have some of the brandy?"

She held out the flask. He shook his head. "I'm fine," he said, "now come over nearer the fire. You're warmer now, thawing out won't hurt half as much."

He pulled up a chair for her and stood beside it in front of the blaze. Steam rose from his sodden clothes. "Oh," she told him, "we ought to get back . . . they'll worry—I——"

"Wait a minute. Worry! You don't know the half of it. I was nearly out of my mind. Linda . . ." He moved closer to her chair and dropped on his knees beside it. "Linda, why did you do it? Why did you run away? You might have—you might have—" He couldn't go on; he stopped, looking up at her, imploringly, his dark, good-looking face shadowed with a dreadful possibility.

"I was a fool," she admitted. "But I was angry. I got it into my head that you were keeping me there, at the Lodge, for—for a practical joke. I was determined to get back home, in spite of you. I found the clothes, and the snowshoes, and waited till you all were busy and out of the way and then I climbed out through my window. I thought you'd miss me sooner. But I had figured on getting a good long start, even at that. I hadn't realized the storm was so bad.''

He explained briefly why they had not looked for her earlier. He said, his hands on hers: "Linda, you must forgive me, for everything. You know that I—love you. You couldn't help but know. I've told you, a dozen times. Ever since that night you came up to dinner—remember? It didn't matter how much we quarreled or what stupid, unkind, unfair things we said to each other. I mean the things I said . . . I love you, so much. You can't . . . *not* love me, Linda. There'd be no rhyme or reason in it. You must care for me . . . a little . . ."

She was trembling again, but not from cold. She said, "Dick," and he went on unheeding, prepared to make a clean breast of the whole situation.

"I did keep you up here on purpose. I admit it. Dad—well, he found out that you knew he had taken a certain stand on the bridge situation. He was sure that you knew, and were waiting until just before election. So I—swore you shouldn't use it as a plank in Bert's platform. That's all. You were right, we could have pulled out of here, before the storm got under way; we could have reached Hawes, and managed to get home. But—as you suspected, I hadn't ordered any transportation. Linda—say you forgive me? It wasn't all on Dad's account that I did it. It was . . . oh—an extremely childish desire to prove to you that I was the stronger, that I could set my will against yours. And a desire, not at all childish, to have you up here—with me. Not alone. I knew we couldn't come alone. But, Linda, some day we will come alone, just you and I—together, for better, for worse . . . won't we?"

He was smiling at her now. But his eyes remained grave and ardent. And now they were very much alone, in the leaping firelight, in the shut-in, isolated comfort of the small cabin. The dancing flames and the circle of light from the lamp threw wavering shadows. Linda drew back a little in her chair. She thought, There's no use fighting—it's a lot bigger than I am, than we are. She thought, I'll tell him—that I've loved him all along; that of course these other things don't matter, can't matter and never have.

And now, sure of her own surrendering, shaking a little with the anticipation of rapture, she cried out at him, light-hearted, miraculously happy in the certitude that she would, in a moment, feel his arms around her, his lips against her own.

"But you didn't keep me here! Not really. Before I left I put all the information in Bert's hands. In a sealed envelope. If I didn't return by Sunday night he was to use it. I—One up!" said Linda, her eyes dancing.

He felt as if he had been struck in the face. He rose to his feet slowly and towered over her. At his expression, her hands which were ready for the clasp of his hands drew back . . . her lips, which were forming words of tenderness, of yielding, were mute. He said—and laughed:

"So you outwitted me, after all? What a fool you must think me! What a fool I've been!"

He walked away a step or two. She cried out, her eyes following him in amazement:

"But, Dick—you didn't think I'd come up here, at this time, with all the chances of bad weather against me and not leave the information? I didn't dream you'd try to keep me here——"

"I think you did," he said stubbornly. "You never have trusted me!"

In the face of what he had done, or tried to do, that was the most absurd thing that he had said as yet. She got to her feet, hampered by her clumsy clothes and her knowledge of them. Her face flamed, her eyes were clear gray wells of anger. She said, low:

"You're angry now. *Because* I outwitted you. Because you think you've been made a fool of! Well, you have! As long as you thought you had me here with my hands tied, where I could do no damage to your father and his ridiculous campaign, you were willing to be magnanimous, to forgive me, to ask to be forgiven. But as soon as you found out that, after all, all your elaborate preparations had gone for nothing, you turn around and sulk like a schoolboy! Well, by now everyone in Lawrenceton knows what your father stands for—stagnation—selfishness, at the expense of other people. As fast as the presses can print it, it will be known. And it will defeat him, Dick, and you know it!"

"I don't care about that," he said wearily.

"Then, what *do* you care about?" Her face grew

rosier, but she said steadily: "You said—you cared about me. Was that part of it too, to keep me here, flattered into a sort of stupor of the intelligence, until you were ready to take me home and deliver me, with my teeth drawn!"

He said heavily:

"All that doesn't matter now. If you'd cared for me at all, in return, this wouldn't have happened. I would have had your loyalty. Not Bert."

"No matter what side I'm on?"

"You would have been on my side."

"Your side is despicable," she cried out, fighting back the tears, the angry and wounded tears, hating herself for her impulse of surrender, grateful with every breath her body drew that she had been spared the irrevocable word and gesture.

There were voices, outside, coming nearer.

"Search party," said Dick grimly. He went to the door and threw it open. Happy and Jenkins struggled in, shaking the snow from their heavy clothes.

"Good Lord . . . we were going crazy, waiting. Linda, you little idiot, what have you been up to?" demanded Happy. "Susanna's in hysterics with Dolly to console her, and Dorine finds the party so dull she wants to go right home! We saw smoke—or rather Jenkins smelled it when we got this far along the trail . . . it's as black as your hat outside," he added.

They had brought plenty of equipment. "Everything but the stretchers!" Dick remarked. He explained, as Happy, advancing upon Linda, shook her soundly, and then went to the fire, "I found her beyond the bridge and brought her back here to get warm and dry. We were just about to start back to the Lodge."

"Well, snap into it then," suggested Happy, "or Susanna will be a nervous wreck and it's not in my contract to marry a lunatic."

He dropped a big paw on Linda's shoulder. "Linda, what possessed you to do it?"

"Ask Dick," she said abruptly. She found her way to her wet boots and managed to get them on, and then took up her snowshoes. "I'm ready," she announced.

Happy looked at Dick. Then he whistled softly. Sparks were flying, he thought, and not from the fireplace.

Jenkins intimated dourly that he would remain behind in the cabin and wait till the fire burned down, after which he would stamp out the embers and join them. Dick, ready in his turn, flung open the door. It was night, thick, and black, and alive with falling snow. But the wind had abated.

They left Jenkins and tramped the remaining distance to the Lodge. It was late when they got there, and the going had not been conversational. Linda was terribly tired. She was warm now, she was no longer afraid, but she was sick with weariness, sick with the weight of her own emotions, with the sense of having been let down.

What had they quarreled about and why? If he

was so petty that the discovery of her stratagem had turned him from lover into enemy ... She flung up her head and felt the cool kiss of the snow against her hot cheeks. He ... he had thought himself the holder of all the trumps, he felt he could afford to be generous ...

It didn't matter why they had quarreled. Nothing mattered. It was over, this time for good. It had proven to her that enmity was stronger than love.

They reached the Lodge. Susanna, detaching herself from Dolly's comforting arms, flung herself upon Happy, Linda and Dick indiscriminately. "I thought I'd lost all of you," she sobbed. She said, her small and elfin face puckered up with the sorrow of a forlorn child, "Oh, Linda, how could you do it!"

Linda kissed her. "I didn't do it," she said.

There were questions and explanations. Not many. Linda said merely: "I wanted to get back. I was an idiot to try it. Thanks to Dick I didn't, however, perish in the night."

"Of course, you didn't," said Dorine, with an adoring look at her host, "not with Dick to look out for you."

"It was nice of him," Linda said lightly, "but consider the headlines the alternative would have made. 'Son of candidate makes away with chairman of rival's Women's Committee in the Canadian woods.' I must," she said, "get out of these clothes. They are cramping my style."

She vanished into the bedroom, Susanna in hot pursuit. Linda sat down on the bed, put her face in her hands and cried . . . violently, hopelessly. Susanna, very much frightened, cast herself down beside her. "Linda, were you hurt? Linda, when I think of you out there——"

"No, I'm all right. Please, Sue, there's a darling —please—go—way——"

More desolate than ever, Susanna returned to the living room. Dick was out in the kitchen. "Heaven knows when Jenkins will be back . . . did you people get anything to eat? I'm starved—" he was shouting. "Happy," whispered Susanna, "she's crying her head off."

"Who?" asked Happy stupidly.

"Linda . . . who else?"

"It's reaction probably," said Happy.

"Probably. And it's probably Dick, too. Oh, I could shake them both," said Susanna. "If your father were alive and running for President of the United States——"

"A pretty picture," commented Happy, astonished, "and so damned likely!"

"And mine were the rival candidate, do you think it would make any difference?" demanded Susanna, unheeding the interruption.

"That sounds all right. But mine is not; and yours is not; and you don't know what difference it *would* make," Happy argued seriously. "Besides, I've a notion this goes deeper than family loyalties. I mean—Oh, hell," he said—disregarding Susanna's indignant, "Well, you needn't swear at me, darling, it isn't my fault."—"I can't explain it. But Linda's pretty self-willed. So's Dick. Each wants to prove to the other that he—I mean she—is the stronger. Do you get me, by any chance?"

"I think so. You're as clear as mud. But go on," Susanna urged him.

"It's like a tug of war. In the first place, they seem to have gotten off on the wrong foot from the time they met. I mean since they grew up. Since then it's been battle. Anything that came up, like mayors or what not, has only been a sort of good excuse. Now, *we're* different," explained Happy complacently.

"And how, pray?"

"Oh, I always was the stronger and you knew it. You may make a lot of wisecracks and appear to be the modern flapper personified and all that, but you are not really."

Dolly and her husband strolled up at this juncture and listened with deep interest. "Get this," Dolly murmured to Norton, "it may teach us a thing or two."

"Oh, I'm not, am I?" demanded Susanna. "Then what am I, if you'll be good enough to carry on?"

"Well, underneath," replied Happy, stretching his long legs and greatly enjoying himself, "underneath, you are nothing but the primitive submissive female——"

"I won't be called a female!"

"But you are, aren't you?" he asked mildly, "or else I've been sadly misled."

"Happy Anderson!"

"In person. I mean to say, that's what you are and always were. Waiting for a real he-man to come along and tell you where you got off. All your feminine wiles and strategies led up to that . . . and to my capture. And when you had effected it you were proud as a flock of peacocks. But as far as that goes, being captured is not exactly the term. I mean to say, I was not taken unawares, you know."

"Happy, if you don't shut up!"

Norton and Dolly were laughing. Susanna slapped Happy's hard cheek with a swift motion and then, with a swifter, leaned forward and kissed the mark of her hand. "It's all right with me," she whispered, "you certainly explain it beautifully. You are goofy. So am I. Gee, I'm hungry."

Jenkins returned presently and they had supper, which supper had been started by Dick. Linda didn't appear. Susanna, vanishing in the direction of their bedroom, came back again to report:

"She's pretty much all in. I'll take some coffee in to her, she says she doesn't want anything else."

Dorine brightened. She had very much resented losing the limelight for the duration of Linda's absence and rescue.

When Susanna finally went to bed Linda was asleep. Or so she thought, shivering, undressing carefully in the dark. But Linda was not asleep.

Morning dawned, that familiar gray. But when they went outdoors to "smell" the weather they found that a pale yellow sun was forcing its way through, a sun they could look at directly, the shape and color of a seashell. And the wind had dropped, but it still snowed, at intervals.

By the following noon there were indications of steady clearing and of fine weather. "We'll get out of here tomorrow," said Dick. "I'll send Jenkins in ahead to Hawes."

He had not spoken to Linda, save when forced to, since their return to the Lodge. Nor she to him.

CHAPTER SEVENTEEN

They reached Lawrenceton late the night of Election Day. The polls had closed, the votes were still being counted. Linda and Susanna sat up, waiting for telephone calls, while Happy prowled about the living room. "They say it's close," said Mrs. Anthony. "Linda, I was so worried about you—when you didn't return. Bert kept telephoning, of course."

The *Comet* lay scattered in sheets on the tables and chairs . . . there were special editions. There were headlines . . . *Jarvis, candidate for the Mayoralty, secretly blocks bridge project*——

"That has fixed him," Happy said, reading. "Linda," he looked at her severely, "Linda, do I see your fine Irish hand in this?"

She said nothing, but smiled faintly. All the triumph had gone somehow.

Before midnight she had persuaded Happy and Susanna to go with her to Bert's office. Bess sat there with him, her composure breaking; the men from the *Comet*, others. By midnight, or a little after, they knew.

Bert had won, by a narrow majority, but he had won.

WHITE COLLAR GIRL

"Due," Bert said, tired, drawn and happy, "in a large measure to you, Linda."

He was speaking of his victory. Linda answered slowly: "I didn't do much, Bert. Just dug up a few facts and talked to a lot of people."

"It was the bridge business that clinched it," Bert told her. "I had a hankering notion of dirty work at the crossroads . . . but I hadn't any facts, actual proof, to go on."

"Neither had I," Linda admitted; "a sentence here, and a phrase there. That was all. Call it a hunch if you like; or woman's intuition," she added, smiling.

"Woman's indiscretion," Bert retorted. "Women are strange people—they are people. Talk about rushing in, taking the bull by the horns, or what have you. Men, I find, myself included, are infernally cautious. Part of my caution is, of course, legal training. I heard Jarvis almost burst a blood vessel when he picked up the paper . . . well, that's that. He hasn't denied it, however. Couldn't very well. Now, I've my job cut out for me. The commission hasn't handed in its findings as yet so I'm going to Albany as soon as possible, with a petition signed by practically everyone in this town. All the business men of any account . . . except, of course, Sir Frederick! Hayes' father has promised his support. He's well known in Albany, has a lot of influence."

Elizabeth had occasion to speak to Linda alone.

"I hope this hasn't made a lot of difference between you and Dick," she said anxiously, and a little shyly.

"There was plenty of difference between us already," Linda told her, twisting the phrase to her own account.

Now that it was over, now that a nine days' wonder had died, Lawrenceton had settled to the new régime, and people who had not voted for Bert Warren were congratulating themselves, and others, audibly upon their "choice of a splendid, progressive young man ... what we need, what I've always said we needed is youth—new blood—vigor—get-at-iveness—" Linda settled back into her routine, conscious of the tired ache at her heart, the completely let-down feeling.

Susanna and Happy returned to New York, directly after they came back from the Lodge. "I'll be seeing you," Susanna promised, hugging Linda soundly. "Maid of honor and all that sort of thing."

She added, as Linda hesitated a moment: "Don't say you can't afford the time! Of course, you can. You have to. It isn't every day in the year that Susanna gets herself a husband!"

"Naturally. I can take time off," Linda retorted, "but a Park Avenue church wedding frightens me. To say nothing of clothes. I suppose you'll have me tricked out in solid diamonds and platinum, with an edging of priceless rose point."

"*You're* priceless, darling. Father will pay all the damage. Look here—send me your measurements, I'll order your frock and hat. You can trust

WHITE COLLAR GIRL

me that far, can't you? Then, you'll come down, ahead, in time for final fittings. I'm going to have Gerry Peters for a bridesmaid, she's about your height and weight, I think. We'll use her for the preliminary fittings, just like a screen star's stand-in. Now that's all settled, and, speaking of screen stars, how long is Dorine going to stay up there and addle the natives? Of all the washouts!"

"Three months, all told," Linda answered. "She has to be back on the Coast at the end of that time for a new picture."

"Well, if I never see her again it will be years too soon," Susanna declared, "and as far as her art is concerned, she doesn't spell box office to me. Give me *Rango* any day in the week! Linda . . ." her voice dropped and she looked through her curling lashes at her friend, "Linda, you and Dick had a battle up at the Lodge, didn't you?"

Linda nodded. "It doesn't matter," she said briefly; "don't worry your little head about it. He wasn't awfully pleased, you know, at the part I played in his father's defeat."

"He's pretty dumb," was Susanna's only comment.

"I haven't seen him since our return. I don't expect to," Linda told her.

"All men—except Happy—are idiots," Susanna said hotly, "and even Happy has his weaker moments. That's why I keep such a tight rein on him!"

Dick was having his own troubles. His mother desired to go South. In all the long Jarvis history no Jarvis had been exposed to the public ignominy of defeat. She wanted, she said, without giving her reasons, to go to Virginia and thence to Florida.

Mr. Jarvis, not at all subdued by his disaster, made annoyed and negative noises.

"South? Such nonsense. But if you insist, Jessie, go along. Dick and I will carry on here."

"I don't want to go without you, Fred," she told him.

"If you think I'm going to run away from my own home because I've been made a laughing-stock of by that whipper-snapper Warren and a minx of a girl—!" He blew his prominent nose with unnecessary vigor and continued—"you're very much mistaken."

He added something to the effect that he hoped his friends were satisfied; he hadn't, he added, really wanted the job, at all, he'd been persuaded against his better judgment.

Jessie said nothing. She had become an adept in this art, over a long life of marital discretion. Dick's impulse toward his father was all a pitying and tender understanding. His defeat had hurt him deeply, hurt, his son judged, and judged rightly, more than his vanity, even more than his pride in himself as Leading Citizen.

"I might as well," Jarvis continued, "get what pleasure I can now, before Warren and his pack of so-called progressives ruin the town and make it into some sort of an infernal machine. As for Linda Anthony!" He turned on Dick with an unexpected and astonishing violence, "I forbid you to see her any more, do you hear me?"

Dick heard him. Anyone else within half a mile could have heard him also. Mrs. Jarvis shuddered and set the pearl hoops at her ears to swinging. "For heaven's sake, Fred, must you shout?" she asked plaintively.

"Sorry, Jessie. But what I said stands."

Dick raised a dark eyebrow.

"Forbid?" he asked quietly.

Mr. Jarvis, whose rages were short, if not sweet, cooled a trifle. He remembered that Dick was no longer in prep school, nor yet in college. He replied, with a faint approach toward a compromise and apology:

"Perhaps I used too strong a word. I'd rather you didn't see her, Dick. She—" He was silent, speechless before the contemplation of Linda's misdeeds.

"Don't worry," Dick told him with a short laugh, "she wouldn't see me if I were half a yard away. In other words, she *can't* see me. She has a blind spot where I'm concerned."

"Do you mean to tell me—" began Jarvis, in another rage, and stopped, torn between the implications of Dick's remark and his own opinion of Linda. But Dick had left the room. Jarvis stared at his wife.

"Now, just what did *that* mean?" he demanded heavily.

Mrs. Jarvis sighed.

"I don't know. I can't understand him . . . or

Linda either, quite apart from this nonsense of the election. He's been attracted by her ever since he came home, Fred. Hadn't you seen that? But apparently she won't have anything to do with him."

"She won't!" Jarvis set his jaw. "What's the matter with my son?" he inquired stormily.

"I'm sure I don't know. You know I had hoped that he and Susanna Hudson . . . Well, that came to nothing. Why on earth Susanna with all her background and opportunities chose to throw herself away on Radford Anderson—" She made a gesture of helpless incomprehension. "However, that's neither here nor there. It's been Linda, all the time, with Dick. I can't see how you failed to see it. I even spoke of it to Mary Anthony one day casually, of course, and in a joking way. But she was very noncommittal."

Jarvis' emotions still conflicted. The mere thought of a girl, any girl, refusing to be interested in his son was incredible and incomprehensible, yet on the other hand, the thought of this particular girl regarding Dick with coolness should be gratifying. But it wasn't. This was an entirely parental reasoning.

He said tentatively:

"Perhaps after all Dick would go South with you."

But Dick declined. He replied, when consulted: "I suppose I am more or less of a figurehead at the mills. But I don't intend to be. If I thought you wanted me to be ornamental and not useful there for the rest of my life, I'd pull out and get another job.

I took the position, I mean to hold it, and not just because I was born Jarvis instead of Smith. And I've no idea of running away—from anything."

"Anything" was elastic enough. "Anything" was Linda, as it happened. He added with a rather wry little grin: "Besides, it wouldn't be fair to Dorine. After all, I coaxed her up here, didn't I? I have to show her the town."

That was a poser. Later, Mr. Jarvis indulged in another session of sputtering to his wife. "Dorine indeed! Of all the cheap little anglers! Don't deny it!" (She hadn't intended to.) "I've seen the way she makes sheep's eyes at Dick! Not that I have anything against screen actresses—" he added, magnanimously, and not quite truthfully—"but this one!" His tone was sufficient. This one was a local product. He had "known her when." She had, for him, no especial glamour. On the contrary.

Mrs. Jarvis replied fretfully:

"Fred, for goodness' sake stop fretting about Dick. You don't like Linda. Now, you don't like Dora Dunne. But it doesn't matter. It won't ever matter whom you or I like or don't like. Dick's grown up, he's not a child, he'll do as he pleases. I'd just as soon he didn't marry for a long time yet but when he does I'm not going to worry myself sick about it. It's his own life," said Mrs. Jarvis, with a surprising wisdom and one which astonished even herself. But that wisdom deserted her, being perhaps a theoretical sagacity only, when she—among others—was forced to the unhappy conclusion that Dick and the delectable Dorine were becoming, or had become, practically inseparable. Not that Dick deserted business. During his business hours, Dorine amused herself. She spent hours with her grandparents—and a photographer. The entourage yawned and was as satisfied as it could be in the circumstances. At least, it had had some slight personal freedom, during the week when Dorine, unaccompanied by her bodyguard, was in Canada. But back again in the routine, the personal representative arranged for photographs of Dorine, in the home surroundings, or sent snappy little items to the press, or, off duty, worked with more or less success upon the Great American Novel he had always intended to write. The French maid was frankly bored and the secretary occupied with little else than forwarded fan mail.

Dorine, of course, did her duty by the home town. Made an appearance at a Legion dinner, at a Chamber of Commerce luncheon, and presented a new silk banner to the Girl Scouts, and hastily, another to the Boy Scouts. But for the most part, she was "resting"; lunching with Dick, dining with Dick, driving with Dick, flaunting him not only in his own car but in hers, which was of an even more expensive make, so inevitably little rumors crept into metropolitan columns and the fan magazines which carried last minute flashes on their front pages. "We hear that little Dorine Dunne, blond menace of Ultima Picture Corporation is that way about a certain rich, young nonprofessional in her home town, where Dorine is resting at the moment."

In the course of her expeditions in and about

WHITE COLLAR GIRL 247

Lawrenceton Dorine discovered Benville and Madame Leona, and decided that after all life in the sticks had compensations. After a period of urging and commanding she engaged the exclusive services of Leona herself for one day every week and sent the car and chauffeur to bring her from Benville and to return her to her shop, turning her improvised suite at the hotel into a temporary beauty parlor, and ordering facials, body massage, shampoos, manicures and finger waves with a total disregard for Leona's by no means moderate charges for these services. During the rest of the week Dorine managed to get along with the ministrations of her maid, who, perfectly trained in the obligations to, and demands of, beauty, was Gallically scornful of Leona and all her works. But it was, of course, through Leona as well as through other interested people that Linda was obliged to hear of Dick Jarvis' assiduous attentions.

"The girl is a fool," said Leona frankly, "but a pretty fool. She has a lovely body and the most beautiful skin I have ever seen. Overtended, however. By the time she is forty she will either sag or start having plastic work done. It is a hothouse sort of beauty, originally an accident of nature, which she has enhanced. But I am wondering if she will be content to give up her work and live in Lawrenceton. I doubt it very much. They say at the hotel that old Mr. Jarvis is frantic and is using every excuse to get his son away, somewhere, until he gets over this infatuation."

Linda listened perforce. She could not believe it.

Yet what else was there to believe? She had, with some frequency, the evidence of her own eyes.

With Hayes' influence in Albany and Bert's consistent work, it looked certain that the Bridge Commission, approaching its final deliberations, would settle upon Lawrenceton as the site for the bridge. Their conclusion reached, Mr. Hayes, forewarned, telephoned the new mayor of this added victory. The result had not yet been made public. But it wouldn't hurt Bert to know in advance.

His Honor, therefore, indulged himself in hospitality and gave a large dinner at the Country Club, early in December. His committees attended, the owners and editors of the flourishing *Comet*, while Hayes came up from Albany to talk seriously to certain property owners about the site for the proposed branch of the blanket concern. He had talked, with stunning effect, to his directors. Linda, at the table, was next to him. He beamed upon her, having heard, through his son, a highly colored account of her campaigning.

"Of course," he said indulgently, "a pretty girl —such as you are, Miss Anthony—shouldn't really meddle in politics. You've done a lot of good, I'll admit, but think of the harm you *could* do."

"For instance?" she asked, smiling at him.

"Suppose our friend Bert had been unmarried . . . suppose our quondam friend Jarvis had been young and likewise unmarried. Think of the extra rivalry you would have caused. By the way, I am very much pleased with the little investment you made for me. I'd like to make one for Mrs. Hayes, for a Christmas present."

"That would be awfully nice," Linda told him gratefully.

"Christmas presents at our time of life—" he mused. "In our early days I managed something, silk stockings, a purse, perfume. Later, checks, when I found that my choice of jewelry did not meet with her fancy or that she had all she could use. She goes out very little, she has not been in good health for years, I am sorry to say. On one occasion she insisted that I buy for her something personally —she didn't care, she said, if it were only a box of candy. At the time I was very much occupied, and the assignment, as Frank would say, slipped my mind. And I had neglected to have my secretary make a note of it. On Christmas Eve, we were trimming the tree; suddenly I remembered. I made some wild excuse, rushed to the corner drug store and bought a box of candy, which I presented to her on the following morning. You should have seen her face. But she was game; and thanked me. But when January first came around and the drug store bill arrived—a bill she always paid—and the candy was on it, she was not as pleased. Since then she has not objected to checks or a bond or two. But we'll talk business later. I'm not much of a dancer, Miss Linda, but I would be very honored . . ."

She danced with him. She looked, one man thought who watched her, like a slender flame, in her bright chiffon frock. Mr. Hayes thought her charming also and paid her compliments, of, it must be confessed, the blanket variety as far as lightness and subtleness went. "I'm not the only one who thinks so," he told her, "there's a young man over in the corner who hasn't been able to take his eyes off you and then he looks at me with the bitterest envy in his glance. He's a good-looking boy, by the way. But in an unfortunate position."

She glanced in the direction her partner indicated. Dorine and Dick, dining alone in the corner, appeared very much engrossed with one another. She turned her eyes aside and answered with as much indifference as she could muster:

"Oh, I think you're mistaken. About not only the envy and interest but the unfortunate position. That's Dick Jarvis, son of the famous Fred. And with him, Dorine Dunne, our one local celebrity."

"You don't mean it . . . not the screen star?" asked Hayes, an inveterate motion picture goer.

"But I do. She's up here on a long vacation. She was born here, you know."

"You were, too, were you not?"

"I certainly was."

"It is almost too much for one town to produce," he mused gallantly, "but I was right—about young Jarvis, I mean. What a situation to be in—torn between charmers . . . the brunette and the blonde."

"Gentlemen prefer the latter," she murmured.

"Not all of us. Myself, for instance, and my son are not in the class you quote. I'd like very much to have you for a daughter-in-law, do you know that?"

"Have you spoken to Frank?" she asked him seriously.

"Well, not exactly. I've intimated it was time for him to settle down. His heart was broken, you know, some years ago, by something small and Spanish. It occurred on the trip around the world which I gave him as a graduation present. It always does, somehow. I remember my own Grand Tour. My fate was a Welsh girl. It took me a month or two to recover. I recall that her name was Blodwen and that she was dark and stormy and afterwards married a dour Scotch doctor and sent me photographs of her first-born. Twins, to add to the insult! However Frank seems to believe he isn't the marrying kind. I can't understand it. I think with a little persuasion from you——"

"I'm a business woman," she declared as they returned to their table, "and not interested in mere gambles."

"Such as . . . ?" Frank Hayes asked her, rising to draw out her chair.

His father explained, to Linda's confusion.

Young Hayes sighed.

"She won't even look at me, Dad. I can't get a date with her, that's a fact."

"You've not tried very hard," Linda said, smiling. She liked Frank Hayes, an alert person, intelligent, enthusiastic and attractive.

"I'm shy," he announced solemnly. "I need a lot of encouragement."

He danced with her later. He said: "You know my father's taken a tremendous fancy to you."

"I'm glad. I like him, too. All the nicest men are married," she said, sighing.

"Thanks a lot, and me a bachelor! Mean Bert, I suppose?"

"Bert, and others."

"Speaking of married men or men about to be married, what do you know about the Jarvis-Hollywood entanglement?"

"Nothing," she said.

"If you hear anything, remember your loyalty to your paper and see that the *Comet* scoops it for the society column. Or should it come under News of the Silver Screen?" he asked gravely. "It would be dreadful to make a social error!"

As they were leaving Linda caught another glimpse of Dick and Dorine; in his car, parked up the driveway, under the trees. He struck a match, and cupped it in his palms. She saw its brief light waver over his face. She saw him hold it to Dorine's cigarette, and imagined she heard her intimate murmur of thanks. A jealousy, alive and vivid and entirely unexpected, swept over her. She clenched her teeth against it, and literally. Why should she care? Because he had once, very long ago, kissed her; because he had once, not so long ago, knelt by her side in an isolated cabin and told her that he loved her? But he hadn't loved her, he'd loved conquest merely; loved getting his own way, proving himself the stronger.

Why should she care if Dorine flaunted him about town with the careless possessiveness with which she wore handkerchiefs laced through a bracelet or real precious stones in her high dancing heels? Let him jump through the Hollywood hoops, she didn't care.

But not a day passed without the remembrance of that moment in the cabin coming back to her, to set her heart to beating with a sickening pace, to flush her cheeks and burn in her eyes and in the palms of her hands. Another word, and she would have——

Go on and say it, she told herself scornfully— would have fallen on his neck like a love-sick schoolgirl and told him you didn't care how long you were snow bound as long as he was with you; you didn't care, down deep, what happened to elections, or to anybody, so long as he loved you——

Now and then she woke from disturbing dreams and found herself weeping.

CHAPTER EIGHTEEN

AFTER all, the *Comet* did not scoop the Dunne-Jarvis engagement. A New York columnist did; and other papers picked it up. Wires came from the Coast.

"It's too absurd," said Dorine to Dick, in a magnificently simulated confusion, "a girl in my position has no privacy, can't even be permitted friends—Goldberg, of Ultima, is wild. There's a clause in my contract, you know. I'll have Dave deny it at once . . . ?"

But she used, vocally speaking, no exclamation point at the end of her sentence, nor yet a full stop. Her voice trailed off into the prettiest interrogation mark.

Dick, who had been summoned to the royal suite, said "You'd better" with unflattering alacrity. He had known, and perfectly, whither he was drifting. Dances, lunches, dinners, and of late very un-Rumpelmayer teas served in the private living room by extraordinarily friendly waitresses, who burst in upon the sight of Dorine, *en négligé*, chaperoned, from a considerable distance, by her secretary. Yes, he had known. There had been banter, and a kiss or two. Oh, a meringue variety of kisses. And, of course, Dorine called everyone "darling," from her grandmother to Dave, the personal representative, from Dick to her Persian cat, Toto, who traveled with her in an especially designed basket, and who was fed pure cream, to the detriment of the feline figure, and whose paws and fur were dusted daintily after meals with a lace-edged serviette. . . .

Dorine had been rather fun. Restful in a sense, for all her insensate preoccupation with herself and with a, from Dick's standpoint, nonexistent career. Part of her stock in trade, of course, to coo and make great eyes and talk an infernal sort of boop-a-doop baby talk . . . "big strong mans," and all the idiotic rest. She talked like that to Toto—and, probably to the mythical Mr. Goldberg, who in an office composed mostly of secretaries and suits of armor, signed contracts and advised "Watch your diet, baby, watch your diet!"

No, he hadn't taken her seriously.

But Linda . . . Linda had hurt damnably. Still hurt. It had been sheer torture to watch her revolving about the room in the arms of that stuffed-shirt Hayes, to watch her flirting—he knew flirting when he saw it, outmoded though the expression might be—with Hayes' smart-aleck son.

Dorine had taken his mind off Linda. Or, had she?

But he hadn't intended to involve himself seriously. He had a sudden mental vision of hitching his matrimonial wagon to this little star and groaned aloud at the thought. A touch of neuralgia, he told Dorine hastily in reply to her almost maternal anxiety.

He agreed with her, heatedly, that it was nonsense. She mustn't jeopardize her contract and Mr. Goldberg's wrath by permitting rumor to go undenied. He added something sufficiently gallant. But which left no unguarded opening.

A day or two later he had occasion to speak to the indispensable Dave privately, while waiting for Dorine to dress.

"How about this rumor business? Dorine's denying it, of course."

Dave, red-headed, small, cocky as a city sparrow, twisted an eyebrow at him.

"She hasn't denied it," he said calmly.

"But—" Dick's vaunted poise deserted him, he found himself stuttering. "But she said—Goldberg . . ."

"She hasn't confirmed it, either," Dave added without haste, "and she's used to Goldberg and he to her. She lets him stew. He stews beautifully, with sound effects and lights." He grinned. He liked Dick, a lot. He said soothingly: "It won't hurt her romantic publicity, you know. It's all in the day's work, to her. She got quite a bit of unpleasant publicity—I assure you I had no hand in it—about two years ago, when that osteopath's wife sued her for alienation. Goldberg was pretty wild. But this is the sort of thing the public eats up. 'Screen Star Returns to Schoolgirl Love in Small Town, Spurning Dukes.'"

"Dukes?" asked Dick, aghast. He added: "I never laid eyes on her, to my knowledge, until I met her on the Coast."

"What's a little thing like that between fans?" Dave retorted. "Sure, dukes. At least, it had a title, Russian, I think. Extra, in a war epic. The affair lasted long enough to make headlines. Then it died a natural death."

"We're not engaged, you know, Dave."

"Aren't you? That's odd." Dave eyed him, still grinning. He then said, very offhand, but by way of masculine warning, his loyalty to his sex, in the circumstances, outpacing his loyalty to his salary check. "You know, recently Dorine's been slipping. Not so hot at the box office. And it's a toss that she might like to quit . . . 'at the height of her career,'" he quoted.

"Oh!" commented Dick very thoughtfully.

Dorine appeared, a vision. She said: "I've got to have some clothes. Dick, why don't we all go down to New York for a shopping session?"

"Love to, but," hastily, "I can't get away."

"Darling, your stupid mills will run without you!" she told him.

Dave departed, still grinning, to work some more upon his novel . . . *Press Agent Tells All*. If and when it was published he would lose his job. But he wouldn't care about jobs, if he got a book over.

The rumor was not denied; neither was it confirmed. It reached the ears of Mr. Jarvis. He walked into his son's office one morning a few days later and dismissed the secretary and sat himself down at Dick's desk.

"I won't have it!" he announced.

"What?"

But Dick knew.

"I won't have you frittering your time with this peroxide moron and causing a lot of gossip."

"Her hair's her own," submitted Dick gently, implying that his time was his own as well.

"Peroxide or not, I won't have it! You'll cut it out!" roared his affectionate parent.

"Why?" asked Dick, but mildly interested.

"I won't have you marrying——"

"Hey, hold on, wait a moment. Who said I was thinking of marrying anybody?"

"There's been plenty of talk," his father told him.

Dick replied gravely, but his eyes danced.

"You can't, you know, dictate to me, Dad. Not in matters of the heart."

Jarvis stamped out, slamming the door. He made his way home and burst in upon his wife with the startling information "Dick's made up his mind to marry that—that——"

"Linda?" asked Mrs. Jarvis. "You don't mean Linda?"

"Of course, I don't mean Linda. I mean—this Dunne girl. He as much as said so."

He muttered something. His wife wailed suddenly and honestly: "But, Fred, I don't *like* her. Spoiled, affected little thing!"

He agreed very strongly.

"I don't care about her being a motion picture actress," said Mrs. Jarvis. "I'd rather she weren't, she'd make Dick a better wife if she weren't—I'm getting all mixed up. I mean, I don't care how she earns her living, it isn't that. I just don't like her. She—she *patronizes* me," said Mrs. Jarvis, letting, if not a cat, then at least a kitten, out of the bag.

"She does, eh?" Mr. Jarvis inquired glumly.

"If it—were only Linda!"

"You like Linda, don't you?" His wife nodded. He said, somewhat to his own astonishment, "Well, I liked her too. She was a pretty sweet kid, only now, you know how I feel about her now."

"You shouldn't. After all, she was only acting according to principle. She—she felt Bert Warren would make a good mayor——"

"And I wouldn't."

"Possibly. But, what has that to do with her and Dick if they are really in love with each other?"

"What in tunket makes you think that they are?" her husband inquired with sincere astonishment.

"Dick. Linda, too. But most of all Susanna."

"Susanna!"

"She came to say good-bye, before she left. She —said something. Not much, but enough. I admit she didn't say it until I had pumped her a little. Fred, just what was back of that Lodge house-party?" she asked him suddenly.

He had the grace to look ashamed. But he answered hastily, if mendaciously: "Nothing, that I know of. What should be back of it? So Susanna said, did she——?"

"Very little. But it set me thinking, and remembering things I hadn't noticed at the time. Linda's a fine girl, Fred. She comes of as good stock as there is in the country. Her father was your friend, her mother has been mine, for many years; we've watched Linda grow up. She's pretty and intelligent and sweet; she's straightforward; and she has courage. I think they care for one another. I've always thought Dick did, I wasn't sure about Linda. I am sure now. You shouldn't have made that ridiculous scene about her, forbidding him to have anything to do with her and all . . ."

"What of that?" demanded Mr. Jarvis. "If he really cared for her, do you think he'd let a little thing like a father's interference stand in the way? If he would, he's no son of mine!"

His wife laughed. She said, "Fred, at times you are perfectly precious!" She ruffled his hair. She said, rather wistfully: "It hurt you, didn't it, losing the election? Oh, you needn't growl and shake your head. You've been used to running the town, unofficially, so long. I have too. Sometimes I think we've been pretty pompous about it. I haven't," she admitted, "as much authority as I had. The charity work, for instance. Elizabeth Warren and her younger crowd have pretty well taken it out of the hands of me and my generation. Oh, they're courteous, but they make us oldsters feel like—last year's hats. I want to see Dick happy, and settled." She paused and looked at Dick's father with misty eyes. In that moment her years and her rather imperious aura slipped from her and he saw the small, rosy-cheeked eager country schoolm'am he had loved and married. "Fred, do you remember how your father and mine quarreled, how they forbade us——?"

"Do I?" He rose. He said: "I'll talk to Dick."

"You'll do nothing of the kind," she warned him, "unless you want to spoil everything. If you go to him and say, 'All right, as far as I am concerned, the ban on Linda Anthony is off,' he'll say, 'What of it?' Things won't work out as easily as that, you know."

"You're right." After a moment he added: "But I think I know a way——"

"Fred, what are you up to?"

"Never mind." He chuckled and kissed her. "Forget it."

She didn't, of course, cudgeling her brain to distraction.

He had his plan, half formulated. But he had no idea how to go about it. This should be handled pretty carefully; yet it couldn't, he realized, be handled carefully at all.

His chance came when, one afternoon a few days later, Mrs. Jarvis, ill with a miserable headache, asked him to have his chauffeur stop off at the Anthony house with some books for Mrs. Anthony. "Mary sprained her ankle yesterday," she explained, "I only heard this morning. I telephoned to see if there was anything we could do, and Myra came back with the message that she'd be glad to have something to read."

"All right," he said, "I'll tell Jim."

But he took the books himself, dismissing his car when he reached the house. Linda opened the door. He asked gruffly:

"How's your mother? Jessie sent these books——"

He thrust them into her arms. She thanked him. "She's all right," she told him.

"Linda, look here, may I come in a moment?"

He looked at her sheepishly. For the first time she noticed a resemblance to Dick, something in his eyes, his half smile. She answered, without warmth, "Certainly, if you wish."

He followed her into the living room, where a fire of coals burned in the grate. Coals of fire were appropriate, somehow. He let himself sink into a shabby chair, sighing with comfort. "Your dad and I spent many long evenings over pipes and good talk in this room," he said.

She was silent. He burst out testily:

"Sit down, there's a good girl. You make me nervous."

After a moment, she asked him:

"What did you want to see me about, Mr. Jarvis?"

"It used to be Uncle Fred," he reminded her.

She had no reply to that. He said, determined to have it over with:

"Look here, Linda, I've been pretty sore at you. Wanted you on my side, that was natural, wasn't it? This bridge business . . ."

"Obviously you didn't like that," she replied with a coolness which took his breath away, "or you wouldn't have taken steps to keep me out of the city at election time."

"Did Dick tell——?"

"I knew, soon enough."

"You hate me for it, don't you? And Dick? Linda, it was a sort of a joke."

"Was it?"

"No, of course, it wasn't. I—well, I was mad, clean through. I'm sorry. I ask your pardon. You're a darned good opponent, better than Warren even. Will you accept my apology?"

He looked concerned; as sheepish as a boy caught in the jam closet. Linda laughed outright. She'd liked him so much, at one time. She was liking him again, against her will. He had charm. . . .

But she remembered a locked small box, upstairs in her bedroom.

Jarvis said:

"Look here, my boy's in love with you. This idiotic business about Dorine Dunne is your fault!" Actually he was reproaching her! She felt herself go scarlet. "I don't know what's happened between you and Dick. I suppose it's as much my fault as yours," he admitted, "but—well, there it is. He isn't in love with that film-flam flapper. He's in love with you!"

She couldn't be angry. She tried to be. To her extreme horror she felt her eyes brim over. She said simply, brokenly:

"We've quarreled."

"I thought so. Lost him, have you?" he asked, putting the masculine construction on the situation. "Do you think you can get him back? I'll bet you," he said slowly, "ten thousand dollars that you can't. If you win, it's in addition to a wedding present!"

CHAPTER NINETEEN

"TEN THOUSAND DOLLARS!" Jarvis repeated slowly.

Linda looked at him in amazement. She was too astonished to be angry. She said swiftly: "You can't *mean* that!"

"But I do——!"

His insincerely casual manner left him. He leaned forward and touched her hand. He said: "Linda?" interrogatively. He said: "You're pretty angry, aren't you? You're thinking . . . I'm a crude and vulgar old man. High-handed, too, used to having my own way . . ."

She answered, as he paused for a moment:

"I don't know. I'm thinking what—what Dick would say if he knew. . . . I'm thinking how very much you must dislike Dorine if—if——"

She couldn't go on. He said hastily:

"Forget all that. Look here, Linda, when you were just a kid we used to be great friends. Remember how I stole you one afternoon and took you up on the hill and we went belly-whopping? I—I was very fond of you then; wished I had a daughter just like you. Dick's fine, he's been a satisfactory son as sons go. But sons trek off to school and college and grow up, pretty suddenly. You lose 'em, early.

Daughters are different, I guess. I've had a spell of hard feeling against you, couldn't understand why you wanted to work against me, why you went out of your way to—Oh, I know, I'm not your generation. You youngsters hang together."

"It wasn't that," she interrupted. "Bert Warren is what we've needed here, for a long time. I know how you feel about Lawrenceton, Mr. Jarvis. But it's selfish. You can't keep it for your own little footstool, forever. It costs other people too much——"

"You say you know how I feel about Lawrenceton," he repeated. "I wonder if you really do? I've lived here all my life, and my father and grandfather before me. Perhaps I'm a back number. Reactionary, you kids might call it. I love this town, every stone and stick in it. I have liked it the way it's always been, hill and valley, farm land, river . . . quiet, somehow, and peaceful. I've hated the thought of commerce coming in, I've hated the idea that it must be Americanized in the new sense. In the less usual sense of the word it has stood for older American traditions of peace and leisure. But nowadays people don't want peace or leisure. They want noise, confusion, business, money pouring in, foreigners, bigger buildings, traffic, machines. . . . That's what they want."

She argued, her steady gray eyes on his own:

"But don't you see *you* can afford all this because you've made your money? You're safe . . . you're secure. Nothing can happen. Of course, you feel you've earned peace and leisure. But other people aren't as fortunate as you are. They have to make their way. You've been standing in their path. So they couldn't make it. You've sewed the town up, tight. They hadn't a chance. Why should it belong to you, because you were lucky, and live in a well-conducted household, the wheels all oiled for you? I know you feel you've done a lot for us, charity, parks, giving people employment, but it isn't enough. They don't want charity. They want progress, room to expand, room and a chance to work out their own destinies. Perhaps Lawrenceton will change from now on. Perhaps even some of us will regret it, in a sense. But it will only be in a sentimental sense. Practically, we can't regret it. And you haven't been as benevolent as you think you've been, have you? You've given employment, yes, and provided doctors and Christmas baskets. But you've employed cheaper labor everywhere you could, you've set your foot down on higher wages . . ."

"That's merely good business," he interrupted.

"Well, suppose it is good business. Then you admit that you conduct your business along the lines of the most profit. Why shouldn't other people? You'll have to step aside and give them their opportunity, Mr. Jarvis. Dick—Dick's loyal to you, yet he, too, has done what he could to modernize things, with the insurance he put through and all the rest. He'd do a lot more, if you'd let him. I think he's always been on our side, from the standpoint of judgment. But from a standpoint of family loyalty and affection he had to be on yours. Bert hasn't been in office long. But he's making a difference already. You know that. We've a live newspaper in the town now, it looks as if we'd get a branch of the Hayes Blanket Concern, the bridge will go through, you can't stop it now; business will come to Lawrenceton, and with it new blood, new ideas. . . . You have to sacrifice for everything—everything worth while. Some of the old landmarks will go; but new ones will rise in their stead. You must see that."

She was flushed; her eyes shone. He said slowly: "Yes, I suppose I do see it." He laughed uncomfortably. "Will you believe me, Linda, when I tell you that I wanted to be mayor just to—to——"

"To be officially benevolent?" She laughed with him. She said: "You should have been born a British duke, with villages and livings and farms and heaven knows what. But you would have had to be born a long time ago. Britain is changing too, since the war."

"I fancy you're right. Yet it's hard to see the old order changing." He made certain admissions, grudgingly. "Warren's done well, after his fashion. Will do better, I dare say. I can always move, I know. But I won't. My roots are here. Linda, tell me, about Dick——"

"Must we?" she asked, low. "I thought—you were joking, weren't you? In pretty bad taste . . ."

"No, I was not joking. Just one question, honestly asked. You'll answer me as honestly, I am sure of that. Do you love my boy, Linda?"

She replied, raising her eyes to his, unheeding of what it cost her to do so.

"I suppose I must love him. I've fought against it. It—it's so unreasonable. We quarrel," she laughed shakily, "like bad-tempered children. I've fought against it. I——"

"Has he told you he loves you?"

She said, "Yes." She said: "He didn't mean it. He was—piqued, I think. He's used to easy conquests."

"No. He did mean it. But he's stubborn, as stubborn as you are, Linda. One of you will have to give in; one of you must relinquish pride and all the rest of it. Pride isn't worth unhappiness. And I have something further to confess. It was I, of course, as you know, who told him that you must be disarmed, over election. Not only because of elections but because, in my heart, I was not very proud of my action on the bridge question. I—I didn't want it known," he told her very humbly. "But that isn't what I started out to say. When you returned from Canada I told Dick he must stop seeing you——"

"You did? By what right—?" She stopped, flushing. She said scornfully: "If he had cared for me, at all, do you think that would have stood in his way? It only proves my point!"

Jarvis laughed outright, delightedly. She had plenty of spirit. Her eyes were stormy and her mouth a straight red line. He said mildly:

"Of course it wouldn't. He as much as told me so. He also told me you couldn't see him—for dust. Or something like that. That I needn't worry, you'd settled the matter yourself."

"He said that?" She was silent, thinking this over. Jarvis said gently: "I want to ask you, with all my heart, to be Dick's wife."

Her mouth relaxed and she smiled at him, slowly. He caught his breath. She was lovely, *lovely*. . . .

"But Dick hasn't asked me," she reminded him.

"He will. But that's up to you." He rose and stood over her. "Linda, before I go . . . one more question . . . have you any personal animosity toward me or has your attitude been actuated by impersonal motives only—leaving Dick out of the question entirely?"

She rose also, and stood there facing him, small, determined, young. She thought, I can't tell him. She thought, I must . . . She said, aloud: "I've tried to think I haven't. But—will you wait here, a moment?"

She turned and left the room. He stood there, astonished, impatient. What now?

He heard her quick step on the stairs in a moment or two. She came quickly into the living room again. She carried something in her hands. A small black box, the lacquer peeling. Jarvis frowned at it. There was a little key, now she turned it, in the lock. The box opened. In the bottom were a few letters, an elastic band about them. She slipped the band off, and held out the letters, mutely.

He took them into his big hands and turned them over. His writing! Letters written—from Detroit, from Washington, from California—to Allan Anthony. He pulled one from an envelope and read the brief lines. His brows contracted. He looked at Linda, still standing there. "What does this mean?" he asked her quietly.

She set the empty box on a table. "You mean you don't know?" she asked. "You can't remember even now advising him to put his money into——?"

The hand holding the letters shook. He laid them down on the table beside the box and without apology sat down heavily in the nearest chair, still staring at her.

"Yes, of course, I remember. I was advised, in my turn. I invested, a good deal, and pulled out, with a loss," he said slowly.

"He did, too. A good deal for him. Relying on your judgment. He—he'd always been cautious, conservative—But he trusted you. He saw a chance to double his savings, I suppose. Sold his bonds, invested. When the crash came *he* couldn't pull out, he could only hold on, hoping for the upward swing. It never came . . ."

"Allan!" said Jarvis. "Then, all along you've thought . . . Linda, it wasn't deliberate on my part. How could it have been? I thought—I'll do Allan a good turn. I swear to heaven I never dreamed—I asked him, once, if he'd taken a flier. He said, yes, he had, and thanked me. We didn't speak of it again. I was away when the bottom fell out of things, I never thought of it again . . ."

"You could afford not to think," she said bitterly; "he couldn't."

"Linda, if it was money . . . I would have made good. . . . Why, good God, child, he was my closest friend. I—loved him. I wouldn't have had this happen——"

"Money? You think it was the loss of the money I minded, for myself, for my mother?" She stared at him incredulously. "Can't you see it killed him?"

"Killed him!"

"He'd been a banker all his life. People trusted him, came to him for advice. Perhaps he advised others to—do what he did. I don't know. But he'd always played safe—and then, this. The thousands you lost didn't matter to you one way or another. The thousands he lost made all the difference to him. He'd—let himself down; and us. It killed him, I tell you, knowing what he'd done. Oh, if he'd only told us!" she cried, and found herself sobbing harshly. "If he'd only told us! But he didn't. He carried this knowledge around with him, brooded on it, knew it irretrievable; thought of us, and died . . . Heart, they said. They were right."

"Linda—*Linda* . . . !"

He put his arm about her and was grateful that she did not try to draw away. She was crying, because of the relief of telling, of exposing the knowledge, that had festered and cankered in her mind, to the sunlight and open air of confession. She said brokenly: "I tried to hate you for it. Sometimes I persuaded myself that I did. I don't know. It seemed so unfair. It *was* so unfair. I didn't know you didn't realize. But you should have. That's like you," she said, "and the things you've stood for, not realizing . . ."

His eyes were wet. He said, "Linda, if I could go down on my knees to you—if I could make it up to you . . ."

"You can't bring him back!" she told him.

"If you had said something to me——"

"Too late! I didn't know, myself, till I went through his papers. We didn't understand. None of us understood."

He said heavily: "Your mother knows?"

"No one knows. Why should they? It couldn't help matters any."

"There aren't any words——" he told her. She drew away from him, a little. He wore the face of a man stricken. Gray, old, haggard. She thought, He does care, he *does*. She saw the unashamed tears on his face. Something broke down in her. She cried out, *"Uncle Fred—"* and turned her face to his shoulder and wept, like a desolate child.

"Linda, can you forgive me? No, of course, you can't. It goes too deep for that. But believe that I didn't know. If he had come to me——"

"He wouldn't," she told him, muffled, "he would stand by his own mistakes. He wouldn't blame you."

She was silent, thinking, He wouldn't want me to blame you, either. She said, controlling herself, "I'm glad I told you. Somehow, telling you has taken all the sting out of it——"

"My fault," he said absently, incredulously, "my fault."

"Perhaps not. You didn't think, you couldn't understand . . ."

WHITE COLLAR GIRL 273

He said gently: "Now, you're making excuses for me. That's sweet of you, Linda."

He added, after a long moment:

"Your father was fond of me, you know. He'd want me to look after you. When you and Dick were youngsters he used to say to me 'We'll make a match there, Fred.' Linda, try not to think bitterly of me."

She said: "I don't any more. I don't know why, but I don't."

He brushed his lips across her hair. He said: "Dry your eyes, youngster. I think I hear your mother calling you. Look here, you're big enough to—to—" He stopped, and said low: "But I'll never forgive myself."

Somehow their positions were reversed. All the fight, all the arrogance had gone from him. She looked at him with eyes which were very clear, despite, or perhaps because of, her weeping. She said: "I shouldn't have told you. But I'm glad. I— No, it wasn't your fault, Uncle Fred, you couldn't possibly have realized."

"There's only one way you can prove to me that I'm forgiven."

"How?"

"Dick."

She smiled at that, a wavering and misty smile.

"If I could be sure——"

"Child, you can be sure. In your heart, you are sure. We want you——"

"But—Dick——"

"Don't you *know* that he wants you? You're not

the girl I take you for if you don't find out—in your own way."

"Linda!" called Mrs. Anthony.

Linda slipped from the circle of Jarvis' arm and fled to the doorway. She answered: "Coming, in just a moment, Mother."

Now she was back again. He watched her pick up the letters and put them in the grate, watched her set a match to them. Gone now. But there would be always, in his heart, an ache of consuming regret, for his blindness, his unconcern. He said: "Thank you" very gravely as she rose from her knees.

He walked toward the door, with Linda beside him. At the door she halted him, a hand on his arm. "Uncle Fred?"

"Well?"

"Did you mean that . . . about the bet?"

He looked at her; and laughed loudly, happily.

"Of course, I meant it!"

"Well," she mused aloud, with demureness, "if you'd make it really worth my while——"

"Worth your while!" He stared at her.

"I'm a business woman. If I have to quit, I may as well go out in a blaze of glory. Ten thousand dollars. And . . . an equal sum, invested for you," said Linda glibly, "in your name, at seven percent, with safety!"

"Racketeer! Done," said Jarvis; "and like all women, you're betting on a sure thing."

"If Dick finds out——!"

"He never shall. Not through me."

"But women tell," she mocked him, "and he'll say I married him to win a bet."

"You haven't married him yet," he warned her.

"But I shall," she assured him, and turning ran up the stairs to her mother, lighter of heart than she had been in many months.

Now, having just recovered from one stimulating campaign, she must plan another.

She thought: It's insane. I have no certainty . . .

Yet, since seeing Dick's father, she had. She remembered the surge of jealousy that had swept over her at the sight of Dick and Dorine, together, engrossed, lost apparently to the world. Yet only apparently. For had he not watched her, dancing with the older Hayes? She had Hayes' word for that, and the evidence of her own swift glancing eyes, eyes which had looked away again, as swiftly. . . .

She couldn't telephone him, couldn't corner him when next they casually encountered, couldn't say, in the words of the ballad, "Can't we be friends?" No, that was impossible. Jarvis had said, "One of you must yield." But there were other ways, ways which had no obvious appearance of yielding. . . .

Other men . . .

She began seeing Frank Hayes, now and then, and with him, his confrères on the *Comet*. Twice she saw Dick at the club. Once he was with some other men, a rather noisy stag party. Once with the Nortons and Dorine. On each occasion she nodded to him, smiling, perfectly friendly, but no more. Yet it was all he needed to come over and ask her to dance and she watched him fighting with himself every step of the way.

He thought, she amused herself by pondering, that he was breaking a paternal edict. She asked lightly: "How have you been? One never sees you any more."

"I'm forgiven then?" he inquired.

"For what?" she wanted to know.

"For Election Day."

"But that's over and done with," she replied, in wide-eyed astonishment, "and besides, *we won* . . . !"

"Yes, you won," he admitted gloomily and added: "Dad has taken it better than I thought he would—in some ways."

But on each occasion after they had danced he left her, with an almost absurdly formal word of thanks; and returned to Dorine who invariably waved at her and smiled . . .

He thought, She thinks she can afford to be magnanimous. And watched her laughing up into Frank Hayes' animated face, with such marked resentment that Dorine, displeased, touched his arm with her small hand. "You're not being very entertaining," she told him, stifling a synthetic yawn.

"Sorry, all play and no work is making Dick a dull boy," he retorted.

Dorine was getting bored. She had been attracted to Dick Jarvis because of his money, because, too, to be fair, of his own obvious charms. She had toyed a little with the idea of making a romantic

WHITE COLLAR GIRL

marriage and retiring from the screen. But she'd never live in Lawrenceton, settle down among people who had known her since threadbare days, and to whom, the glamour of her profession having passed, she would become once more, the "little Dunne girl from down on the Willton Road . . ."

Still the romantic rumor kept cropping up persistently enough. She had withheld her hand. She must return to the Coast, very soon, and things would have to be settled one way or another. She sounded Dick on the subject of Lawrenceton.

"You surely don't expect to live here the rest of your life?"

"My business is here. Why not?"

"But you could go to New York . . . and start in business there. Be," suggested Dorine brilliantly, "a broker. Brokers make lots of money."

"And lose a lot. No, thanks, I'll stick around here. You see, I like it. I haven't outgrown it as you have, Dorine."

"But suppose—but suppose you marry, and your wife doesn't want to bury herself, up here in the wilds."

"I wouldn't marry the sort of girl who would think it was burying, you know," he told her, laughing. But his eyes were grave enough. She understood; and played for a few minutes with the idea of "sacrifice for love's sake."

She spoke of returning to the Coast; and the grinding of cameras. "I'm so tired of it," she told him, sighing.

But Dave had his own opinion on the subject. "If she gets a good picture and thinks she can stage a comeback she'll be off like a shot," he said.

He said it, not to Dick but to the elder Jarvis whom he had met of recent date and who amused him hugely. "I'd buy the blamed company and give it to her if it would get her away," Jarvis told him with dour frankness.

"There's a lot of stock on the market," Dave said casually, "and big stockholders have something to say . . . and if they want a particular star shoved to the front——"

Mr. Jarvis thought that over. Then he excused himself and put a long distance call through to New York. In due time Mr. Goldberg received a report that a new stockholder in Ultima Pictures was strongly interested in the career of Miss Dunne. "Now why?" asked Mr. Goldberg; and was told that the new stockholder was a power in Miss Dunne's home town. "What publicity!" cried Goldberg and was crushed to learn that publicity wasn't wanted.

Things moved swiftly. A high-priced novelist was satisfactorily sold down the river, staff continuity and dialogue people pricked up their ears and oiled up their typewriters. A visiting couturière from Paris was pressed into service at a pleasant sum and asked to design Miss Dunne's new gowns for her newest picture. Messages flew, on electric wings, between Hollywood and Lawrenceton. "It's your big chance," said Dave to Dorine, "the biggest chance you've ever had."

Dorine decided in favor of a career. "I hate to

leave," she told Dick, "but I owe it to my public." She couldn't cry, except to music. There wasn't any music. She remained dry of eye. "And my time's up and now that they've this wonderful picture—it's being written especially for me and it's in my contract that I'm to be in on the story conferences."

"Great stuff," said Dick sincerely, oh, very sincerely. "We'll miss you, though."

"Sure?"

She flew at him, kissed him enthusiastically. "You'll see me off?" she asked.

She was going as she came, by train. The car would follow, with the less important luggage, as it had on her triumphal entry. Her departure would be no less triumphal.

After Dick had left the hotel . . . "By the way," she said to Dave, "I hope you're sending out notices . . ."

"Sure. But about this rumored engagement? A call came through this morning from a fan magazine."

"Deny it," said Dorine dramatically; "didn't I tell you to before? As if I'd consider——!"

She was breathless, watching other people pack.

So the papers had the denial; and Dorine had her career; and Mr. Jarvis had his stock, which, in the long run, happened to pay him surprisingly well. Ultima Pictures had other stars beside Dorine, most of them box office.

Just before Christmas, therefore, Dorine left Lawrenceton and her grandparents settled down to their usual routine, the props removed from their living room, the camera men vanished. Lawrenceton recovered swiftly from the pang of the local celebrity's going. She had stayed too long to be news. Moreover, things were humming, now that the word of the bridge had been officially broadcast. New business was coming in, slowly, but inevitably. Bert was tremendously busy. Susanna wrote Elizabeth: "But you and Bert *must* come to the wedding. Didn't I come to yours?"

"I'm afraid we can't," Elizabeth told Linda. "Bert won't leave, he feels he mustn't."

But Dick was going down. Dick was to be Happy's best man. Mrs. Jarvis would go too, with her husband. If she couldn't go South she could at least spend a week in New York.

The wedding was to be on the thirty-first day of December. Susanna had set the date a little ahead, on consideration. "So we'll be sure to start the New Year off right," she had written Linda, in the letter announcing the exact day. "You come down right after Christmas, angel. I'll expect you on the twenty-seventh."

On Christmas Eve Linda encountered Dick on the street. He said "Merry Christmas," and relieved her of bundles, wreaths of ground pine and sprays of holly.

Walking along toward her house in a world beautifully blanketed with white, he looked at the lighted trees in the windows they passed. "Looks jolly, doesn't it?" he commented.

She agreed. She lifted her rosy face to the clean cold air. "It smells like Christmas!" she told him.

"I know. I suppose you heard that Happy's throwing a bachelor dinner on the thirtieth. It ought to be a good one!"

"You'll be there, of course?"

"Naturally. But I hate weddings," he said gloomily, "they are worse than funerals."

Very cheap cynicism, she told him mildly, and very immature. Old stuff.

Conversation languished. Reaching her house, he said: "I'll be seeing you on the train?"

"No, I'm going down on the twenty-seventh," she told him. "Wish your family Merry Christmas for me. Good-bye."

She was going into the house. Something, as she passed him, fell at his feet. The door closed. He rapped on it. "Hey, you dropped something," he shouted.

"Did I—? It doesn't matter," she called, through the door. But he heard her laughing. "Keep it, for Christmas."

It was dark there, on the porch. He picked up the little piece of house trimming. Holly, most likely.

Down the steps, out on the street and under the light, he regarded it, at first casually, then with a quickened interest.

It was a sprig of mistletoe.

CHAPTER TWENTY

The atmosphere of the Hudson penthouse was one of excitement, tears, laughter, hurry. There was a fragrance to the days Linda spent there which she never forgot . . . it was compounded of the odor of French perfumes, of cosmetics, and bath salts; of fresh flowers; of furs and tweeds, satins and silks, chiffons and linens; of packages; and of the raw warm smell of packing cases being ripped open by Happy's impatient hammer.

"Packages," said Susanna when Linda tried to explain, "don't smell. Unless they are delicatessen." She was regarding something square from Tiffany's. "If this is another candlestick, I'll scream. We've twenty-six already. It doesn't save light. Candles cost like the dickens."

"Open it," suggested Linda, "it may be a fish fork!"

Silver, china, crystal; checks, jewelry, furniture, lingerie, linen. "For heaven's sake," Susanna commented, sitting back on her heels, "did you ever realize, Happy, that most of these people have children and that their children will get married and that we'll spend the rest of our lives, and bank balances, returning presents in the polite, expensive sense?"

"Judging by the rate you've been returning or exchanging them in the not so polite sense," Happy responded, "you'll lose track of the donors. And that's no hardship."

The penthouse was in a state of flutter. Doorbells ringing, telephones shrilling, photographers calling, messengers running. The place was never quiet. Mrs. Hudson had succumbed. She spent her time giving excited orders and countermanding them between sobs and smiles. She regarded Susanna alternately as something too precious and fragile for mere words and as something stronger than a span of oxen, and thus able to stand for hours, while frocks and suits were fitted to her slim body, or to sit for other hours while hats were molded on her curly head and shoes upon her tiny feet. Mrs. Hudson alternately cajoled, condoled, commanded, reprimanded, consulted and admonished her child. Happy she regarded with the tolerant eyes of the beginning mother-in-law. He wasn't good enough for Susanna, he wasn't rich enough, nor social enough nor handsome enough. But he loved her; and she loved him. And he was a nice boy; "bound to make his way," she caroled to her friends over the humming wires; and moreover he was, by his position of about-to-be-bridegroom, providing Mrs. Hudson's only child with the largest ray of limelight she would have for some time to come. Bridegrooms are always in the way before a wedding but somehow they are indispensable.

The apartment at the Luxor was being furnished. The southern honeymoon must be very brief as

Happy could not long be spared from his new duties. Even now he was available only at intervals when packing cases came or when Susanna rushed to the telephone to squeal . . . "Darling, a most priceless present . . . from old Mrs. Mathews. Dozens of crystal plates with gold monograms . . ."

"*Gold!*"

"Yes, isn't it terrible? Just as useful as chiffon ice picks and we can't exchange 'em. But we'll eat off 'em in lonely grandeur . . . they can send us up two rye sandwiches from the restaurant, and maybe a pickle. Won't that be swell?"

There were to be six bridesmaids. Three of them had been Linda's and Susanna's classmates. It was fun seeing them again and hearing them scold Linda—and Susanna, too—for desertion; fun listening to the campus news and gossip. But Linda felt curiously out of it all, a hundred miles, and a hundred years, away from the life which, during its course, was a complete small world in itself.

The other girls were old friends of Susanna's. All six of them were pretty, and Susanna had planned their frocks with very special care. Starting with two in palest green, the green shaded into two in springtime yellow and the yellow into two in cream. The hats were velvet toques in the contrasting shades, the little slippers strapped with black, the little jackets lace, all the colors in the softest pastel hues imaginable, and the great ribbon-fluttering sprays of flowers would repeat the tones in the green of ferns and leaves, in the yellow and cream of budding roses.

But Linda was to wear a shade brighter than shell pink and softer than flame, pale and clear and entirely lovely, and to carry masses of stock.

Susanna herself had rebelled against dead white and her bridal gown was fashioned of an ivory shading into palest pink. "I won't," said Susanna, "look like an oyster! Father's pearls would only enhance the resemblance." And tucked into the heart of Happy's white flowers would be a spray of pink orchids and a cluster of forget-me-nots. "No one will see them," she said, "and they'll make me feel a lot less like an attractive corpse. Do you think I want people to say 'Doesn't she look natural?'"

Fittings, teas, a shower. And Happy's bachelor dinner at his own hotel. And Susanna's hen dinner and theater party. "You only get married once," she told Linda when Linda worried about her, "that is, I only get married once. I know it's old-fashioned, but once suits me!"

New York, Linda observed, had still an aura of Christmas. The shops were gay with trees and holly, the weather perfect, crisp and cold, with a sprinkling of snow, like icing on a cake. The great tree still emblazoned the nights at Madison Square and the tree at the Arch still wore its blossoms of colored glass and light.

Linda had her "wedding present," a carved jade bracelet, and for Christmas the matching earrings. "Susanna, you shouldn't!" she said, for besides her frock, there was the fan of ruffled chiffon which would be carried when the flowers were discarded.

"If it hadn't been for you—" said Susanna, misty-eyed.

Linda's gift to Susanna had been typically Linda. A bond, all Susanna's own. "You'll spend the checks," she warned the bride. "This isn't much. It's the babiest bond on record, but you won't spend it."

Bonds and checks, her flat silver from her mother, her pearls from her father. Susanna commented: "Marrying's a good racket, isn't it?" Happy had given her the slim platinum band and pearls for her ears. "Later," said Susanna, "we'll have an engagement ring. Look what he's spending now . . . flowers and ushers and dinners and honeymoon and all. Isn't it grand he's a hotel man and gets cut rates?"

But Happy's salary was a good one; and Mr. Hudson had deposited "something" to his account, before the wedding. He said, when Happy expostulated: "Well, you and Susanna are all I've got. And I know you'll take care of her. Money—you get a lot more fun out of money when you're young. What's the use of waiting until it's a legacy instead of a gift? Susanna's mother and I come of long-lived families!"

Linda did not see Dick until the afternoon before the wedding. Then she saw him at rehearsal and everything was pretty much of a blur. But as they were turning in their march from imagined altar he asked her: "Linda, I haven't thanked you for your Christmas gift, have I?"

"Mine?" she asked, in astonishment.

"Didn't you drop it at my feet?" He had it in his pocket now, all the berries gone, the strange shining leaves a little wilted. A sprig of mistletoe.

Then someone claimed their attention and she was relieved of the necessity of an answer.

Susanna's wedding at noon on New Year's Eve was very lovely. The church was crowded. Happy's mother, and as many of the connection as possible, wept, to music, in their pews. Mrs. Hudson in brown chiffon with great cuffs of sable, wept in her own pew, surrounded by Susanna's aunts and cousins. Mr. Hudson, unusually nervous, and with his attention concentrated upon his spats, took Susanna up the long aisle. She looked as lovely as she had ever looked in her life; lovelier. The audience murmured, there was a sound like the gentle breaking of waves on a beach. . . .

Sometimes very pretty girls are not pretty brides. Trains and veils and orange blossoms, fatigue and excitement and setting eclipse them. But not Susanna, who lived up to her reputation of getting the most out of every situation.

Pale flame, the green of early spring, the yellow of daffodils, the cream of roses . . . "Prettiest wedding I ever saw," said Mrs. Mathews, very loudly, for she was very deaf. "Who's the stunning girl—maid of honor, ain't she?"

Mrs. Mathews could say "ain't" and get away with it. She was seventy-five and she had a million for every year of her life. She had had three husbands and had gotten away with that, too. She was an ample lady, massively upholstered in purple velvet, rose-cut diamonds and mink. She wore an ear trumpet.

At the altar Linda stepped forward to pull Susanna's train softly into place and received a dazzling and unofficial smile which filled her eyes with unexpected tears. Dick, paler than she had ever seen him, seemed preoccupied with the old problem of the ring. Did he have it? Of course, he had it. No, by Jove, he'd left it on the dresser of the hotel room! No, thank heaven, here it was!

Happy was not quite at ease. But Susanna's hand crept into his as they knelt and Susanna's small voice murmured in his ear, "Happy, I'm enjoying this—awfully."

It wasn't a usual comment but it was entirely sincere. He tightened his grasp on the confiding fingers and grinned at her, forgetting his discomfort, his goldfish-in-a-bowl sensation. He was looking very well. The hotel business had already accustomed him to striped trousers, morning coat, and, even, top hat. He rather fancied himself in a top hat.

Months of anticipation, weeks of planning, minutes of ceremony. It was over.

Susanna's behavior coming down the aisle was entirely her own. She waved at people. She conversed with her husband in an animated fashion. "Angel, there's Mrs. Mathews! You know, the crystal plate one. There, with the ear trumpet. You're to be very nice to her at the reception. Kiss her, yell sweet nothings into the gold-plated saxophone."

WHITE COLLAR GIRL

"Kiss her! She has whiskers!" objected the bridegroom.

"What's a whisker or two? Do you mean to say you'd deny me the first request of our married life? Tickets for one, to Reno! But Mat is a sort of godmother. She's a nice old thing, if pretty outspoken. Don't let her Victorian manners shock you, darling."

Crowds, strangers, gaping, impelled perhaps by a sort of mob sentiment, waiting patiently in the clear cold sunlight to see her—"There she comes . . . there comes the bride!" Cars. Ushers darting about frantically, top hats cocked to a crazy angle, policemen . . . guests pouring out into the open air, talking, laughing . . . "Going on to the reception, Grace?" "There—over there, there's my car . . ."

Fred Jarvis and his wife were talking to Mrs. Anderson, on the steps of the church; Mrs. Jarvis was saying: "Susanna made a beautiful bride," and her husband responded: "She did. But Linda, Linda took my breath away . . ."

The reception. People and warmth, food and drink, flowers and fans, an endless procession passing, and Susanna whispering to Happy: "Do you think it would be correct to send someone upstairs for my bedroom slippers? My feet are killing me! Next time I'll be married, and receive, in a sedan chair."

"There ain't going to be no next time!" said Happy.

Old women, young women, old men, young men. Among the young men several of Susanna's "discards," claiming their privilege of kissing the bride.

Happy glowered: "I don't like it," he told Susanna. "Why not?" she wanted to know, "it's an old Peruvian custom." "Well, for one thing, it isn't fair. If we'd been married up home now, I'd have produced a battery of old flames to offset your regiment," he told her.

"Well, Linda's here!"

"Oh, Linda!" He dismissed Linda with a smile. "Linda's all right," he said loyally and Susanna squeezed his arm. "All right? She's perfect!" she told him with indignation, "but just the same I'd rather say it for you."

"You're not alone in your opinion. Look at Dick!"

Susanna, between offering her slim hand to be shaken and murmuring thanks for felicitations and forgetting people's names, looked. She murmured:

"Just the same, he's a dumb bunny!"

Music. Dancing. The older guests drifting away; the younger ones remaining; the departure of the bride to dress, Linda and the bridesmaids following. But when they had reached the penthouse Susanna shooed them all away affectionately. "Just Linda, please, there's a good gang!"

Just Linda; and Susanna's mother. They took off the veil and the train and the gown, the sheer, sheer stockings, the little slippers. "Don't cry," said Susanna to her mother, "I'll be running home every six minutes with complaints."

Furred traveling suit, pumps, tiny French hat— "Where's my handbag, oh, for heaven's sake is that displayed with the presents? Linda, run and get it, the detectives won't eat you!"

Linda left her alone with Mrs. Hudson there, at the last, and fled down the stairs to the elevator. The penthouse living rooms had not been large enough for this occasion. Susanna mourned: "Why don't we live in a house? . . . I wanted to come downstairs!" she complained.

Back to the doors of the less crowded rooms where the guests still chatted, milled and laughed, came Susanna. Tiptoed, straining to her full height, which was very inconsiderable, she grumbled: "I told you a bride needs stairs." But Happy, equal to the occasion, lifted her in his big arms and held her there poised. She flung the flowers, looking down at the lifted laughing faces, the outstretched arms . . .

Dick caught them, mechanically. A chorus of protest arose. "That isn't fair," said the bridesmaids.

Mrs. Mathews glared at him. If he hadn't been so tall! He turned and presented them to her, smiling. She patted his face with her fat old hand. "You're a nice child," she told him, and to the amazement of the company, departed in triumph with her, it would seem, superfluous trophy of prophecy.

The bride had gone. But people still lingered and danced, still laughed and ate. Dick came close to Linda and stood beside her looking down at the close curve of her little hat, the lobe of her small ear, the curling tendrils of her dark bronze hair . . .

"What next?"

She answered uncertainly:

"Some of the wedding party are going to dance and supper; they just arranged it, didn't you know? I don't think I shall. It's very informal, they won't mind if I drop out."

"Tired?"

"Terribly," she admitted.

"Wouldn't it rest you to come out—with me," he asked, "and have dinner somewhere, very quietly? You're staying on here, aren't you? I promise to deliver you back in good season."

"I don't know," she began doubtfully, "Mrs. Hudson might——"

"We'll see." He hailed the lady, passing him, talking to one of the guests. "Mind if I carry Linda off to dinner somewhere?" he inquired.

"Of course not," Linda's hostess told him. She said, in astonishment, able to see clearly now that Susanna was no longer there. "You do look sweet, Linda!" and went on, toward the other room.

"You couldn't get away with it," Dick said to Linda.

"What time is it?"

He told her.

She said: "If I slip away now, and rest a little, and change . . . you . . . you could call for me, a little before seven?"

She gave him a bright smile, and vanished. He stood staring after her. His father came up and touched his arm. "People are beginning to go. What's the rest of your program?" he inquired.

Dick told him.

"I see. If your mother isn't too tired and we can get tickets, we'll go to the theater, I think. See you later, at the hotel," Mr. Jarvis said, perfectly concealing his satisfaction.

But before seven came Linda, dressed, regarded herself in the mirror; then she laid down the ribbon tied cotton which she had dipped into a powder bowl for a finishing touch.

She wouldn't go. She couldn't. She'd tell Mr. Jarvis that . . . all bets were off. It wasn't fair. It wasn't fair to her, nor to Dick. If he wanted her, he would have to find means of telling her so. She couldn't speak to him on the most casual topic, couldn't smile at him, in the most casual way, without wondering what her own motives were, whether it was part of the game she was playing. It wasn't, of course, a game, yet the conditions made it so. She found Mrs. Hudson's personal maid, gave her a message, and returned to her own room, to undress again and to lie down. Her head was beginning to ache . . . after all, her excuse hadn't been a lie.

Dick came; and Dick departed. He returned to the Luxor and exhibited to his father a face like a handsome thunderhead.

"She turned me down."

"What?" cried Mr. Jarvis.

Dick explained.

"The maid said, Miss Anthony was terribly sorry but she had such a wretched headache that she was going to dine quietly in her room and then go to bed."

"Oh, I see."

Jarvis ran his fingers over his smooth-shaven chin. Was Linda clever, or was she too clever?

"I'm pulling out," said Dick, "on the nine o'clock tonight."

His father regarded him in amazement.

"Stick around with us, for a little while," he suggested, "there's no great hurry. And after all, this is New Year's Eve."

"Thanks, no. I've had enough excitement," said Dick. "I'll get along back home, if you don't mind."

His father did mind; but held his peace. His mother minded and didn't hold hers. "Leave him alone," growled Jarvis, "he's a bear for work."

That was shortly after seven. Dick made his reservations by phone and ate a hurried dinner. He'd go back. He didn't care whether he ever saw her again or not. Every time he did see her he made a fool of himself. Asking her to dinner, begging her for a moment of her time. She didn't care whether she ever saw him again, that was pretty patent. Headache! She hadn't had a sign of it at five o'clock; she'd never looked better in her life—lovelier—more desirable. . . .

She'd forgotten what had happened—up at the cabin. What he'd said to her, kneeling there by her chair. As it happened, he'd never known what she'd thought about that, anyway. He'd told her he loved her and then, abruptly, they had been quarreling and—and that was all there was to it.

He thought: Perhaps I'll go back to the Lodge, for a few days, get out of town, get away from everybody . . . I've got to reconcile myself to meeting her as long as I live in Lawrenceton. That's about the size of it. But——

It wouldn't be easy.

He thought of the wedding. "Wasn't Susanna a dream?" his mother had asked him. He supposed so, a dream of Happy's, a dream come true. But he hadn't seen her. She'd been a blur, in white. He'd eyes only for one girl, a girl in palest flame color, with her arms full of scented stock, and her gray eyes shining and serious and her mouth tenderly shaped and gentle. . . .

At seven o'clock the maid knocked at Linda's door to ask her what she wanted for dinner. "Tea and toast," answered Linda, finding herself totally without appetite. She added, casually, and much against her will: "Did Mr. Jarvis leave any message?"

The maid replied instantly: "I'm so sorry, Miss Anthony. He said he would telephone you in the morning . . ."

"Thank you, Margaret."

At seven-fifteen the telephone in her room rang, it had been switched on from the hall, and was therefore a call for her. Dick. She stretched out her hand, and drew it back again. She picked up the receiver. Her mother's voice came to her, very clear and sweet. "Linda?"

She felt her heart stop; then race on again. "Mother? Is anything wrong?" she asked.

"No, dear, of course not. I couldn't wait to hear. How was everything? Was Susanna a pretty bride? Did you tell her how sorry I was I couldn't come?"

"Of course." They talked for a minute or two.

Linda hung up the instrument. She sat there a minute, thinking of her mother, smiling. Her smile faded. Tomorrow was another day. Dick would telephone.

Ten minutes later, Mrs. Hudson arriving in advance of the tea and toast to offer her sympathy and any help within her power, found Linda out of bed, and, her cheeks scarlet, packing.

"Why, Linda!"

"Mother phoned me, just now . . ."

"I hope she's not ill," Mrs. Hudson began, alarmed.

"No. But she hasn't been well for a time . . . you know, she sprained her ankle and it was so slow in mending," Linda went on, that much at least was true. "I—would you think me terribly rude if I went home, tonight? I have an idea she is lonely, without me. Myra couldn't arrange to sleep in."

"I understand perfectly. I'll have someone telephone for your reservation and order a car. I'm sorry you feel you must go, dear."

"It's been wonderful. The loveliest wedding. Susanna . . ." She stopped. She rose and kissed Susanna's mother, a little woman whose smart and restless sophistication seemed to have dropped from her like a cloak. "Don't cry, there's a dear. She'll be home soon. Happy's a lamb. You're going to love him—a lot."

"Susanna does," Mrs. Hudson admitted.

"I know, but no more than he loves her," Linda reminded her.

"Anyone would love Susanna!"

CHAPTER TWENTY-ONE

LINDA was running away. She was running away from Dick and the telephone call of tomorrow. Once at home she would reorder her life. She'd work, work hard. She'd have, eventually, her own office. She'd so fill up her days with work that there'd be no room left for remembering. She'd get accustomed to seeing him, suddenly, after a time. She'd school her heart to a normal tempo, she'd discipline her dreams. She'd take her mother away, vacations. Some day Dick would fall in love and marry and . . . there'd be an end to that.

But weddings are insidious things; and New York was, no matter what people said about it, a romantic place . . . Too romantic. If she stayed and saw Dick, if she went lunching and dining and bus riding and sightseeing . . . she'd . . . oh, she knew what she'd do. She'd win her bet, by all the wiles at her command. And she knew she had enough and to spare. Every woman in love and some not in love know that.

Man, say the philosophers moodily, prefers to think of himself as the pursuer; and is, in reality, the pursued.

Perhaps, thought Linda. She cast her mind back,

briefly, to Susanna and Happy. Perhaps, she thought again, smiling dimly. But Susanna had made no wagers with anyone, save perhaps, herself. . . .

She finished the tea and toast and set herself to packing again. She laid the maid of honor gown in its especial bag, and put it in her trunk-suitcase. She'd wear the bracelet Susanna had given her, carry the earrings. . . .

Mrs. Hudson's maid knocked and came in to take away the tray. "May I help, Miss Anthony?" she said, an attractive girl, demure, soft-spoken.

"Thank you, Margaret, I've almost finished. If you'd look around and see if I've left anything, please——"

Linda dressed for, she reflected wearily, the fourth time that day. She regarded herself in the mirror once more, as she had when, dressed for dinner with Dick, she picked up the fluff of powdered cotton.

Mrs. Hudson came in to say the reservations were secured. The drawing room, she said . . .

"But I don't need . . . I mean, a lower or, at most, a section," Linda began.

"No. You're tired out, you'll be traveling all night, and if you're anything like me, you won't sleep well anyway," her hostess told her. "When you're ready come down and talk to us, for a little while, before you go."

She had a few minutes with them both, looking strangely forlorn and deserted in the big drawing room. Mr. Hudson said gloomily: "Didn't think

you'd desert us, Linda. It's New Year's Eve, too
... Thought perhaps I'd persuade you two girls to
go out and make a little whoopee with me.''

He went with her to the station, kissing her cheek
as he delivered her into the hands of a porter. She
said: ''You've been awfully good to me . . .''

''You've been awfully good to our crazy girl.
Even if I do blame you for——''

''You don't really blame me, do you?'' she asked.
''And you like Happy. I know you do.''

''He's all right,'' Happy's father-in-law agreed,
''and once I get used to the notion perhaps I'll rejoice that that little gadget of mine is in good hands.''

On her way to the train, after picking up her reservations and with not very many moments to spare, Linda halted the porter and made her way to a telegraph desk. There she picked up a blank and wrote a wire. ''Leaving for home all bets off sorry love Linda,'' it read.

Then, with her porter beckoning frantically, she ran to the gates and down the steps and got herself on board by a very narrow margin.

The berths were made up. She went directly to her drawing room and proceeded to go to bed. A very noisy New Year's Eve party was seeing another party off. There was laughter on the platform, advice, wisecracks. Business men, she concluded.

Ready for bed, she put her shoes outside of the door to attract the porter's roving attention. They needed a polish badly.

After a long time she slept, but there seemed to be hours of just lying in the darkness of the little room, feeling the cool air through the ventilator, hearing the rattle of cinders on the roof, the creaking of the car, the sounds of steps; seeing flashes of light pass the drawn curtain, hearing the noises of pulling into a station, of pulling out again. The car swayed—the little hammock by her hand swung against the wall. There was something mysterious and lonely about traveling at night, boxed up with all these unseen, unknown strangers. Something frightening in the sound of the whistles, of bells ringing. . . .

Dick had arrived early, in more than good time and had made his way to the smoking compartment. A Wilson man whom he knew slightly was there, with two friends. They'd been doing the town, they told him, some of the gang had seen them off at the station. They urged him to a rubber or two of bridge.

Quite late he went through the train looking for the porter. He had decided against being called at six or so, at the way-station where a stop was made for breakfast. Everyone was asleep. The green curtains swayed. He passed the drawing-room door. A little light shone there and he stumbled, with an inaudible remark, over a pair of shoes. Looking down at them, he frowned. They were small shoes, they had a curiously familiar look. No, but that was absurd. They stood there, trim and polished, brown oxfords. He picked one up, looking about him guiltily. If anyone saw him they'd take him for a strange sort of thief. He looked inside the shoe.

"The Booterie——"

Well, there was a Booterie in Lawrenceton.

Yes, it was absurd. Still . . .

Smiling, he put his hand in his pocket, dropped something inside the little shoe, set it down gently and, forgetting his errand, made his way back to his section.

Linda had left a breakfast call. How she'd hate to get up, but, she reflected sensibly, tea and toast wouldn't stay by her very long and she would recover her healthy appetite by morning. She felt she hadn't slept at all when the porter knocked. "Time to get up, miss," he told her.

A new porter, she'd never laid eyes on him before. Presently she reached out a hand, opened the door, and retrieved her shoes. Putting them on, she walked to the washstand and mirror. She felt discomfort. She said, "Drat it, a cinder!" and sat down on her berth and removed her shoe. She sat there staring at what she had shaken into the palm of her hand.

A sprig of mistletoe. No berries, but the shining leaves and thick stem betrayed it.

How on earth?

It couldn't have been there when she put the shoe on, last night. Dick—he'd put it back into his pocket. Even if he hadn't, it wouldn't have made its way from the reception to a traveling costume accessory.

She was bewitched.

Someone passing through the car had dropped it. It wasn't her sprig of mistletoe. It was someone else's. A silly coincidence.

She put it in the buttonhole at her coat lapel. Ridiculous. And yet——?

The train had stopped. Washed, dressed, and in not very much of her right mind, she made her way to the platform and walked the considerable distance to the frame hotel. It was not very light, at six in the morning on January first, in the North Country. January first. People were saying, as they passed each other, "Happy New Year . . ."

Her eyes filled with tears.

She went into the little hotel, passed the cigar counter in the lobby and sat down at a small table. And a moment later, as the lanky waitress waited for her order, a tall young man walked briskly in and sat himself down beside her.

"Happy New Year, Linda, make it two," he said.

"Dick!"

The waitress lived up to her name. She waited. But trains were trains. She went muttering away, and made it two. But when she served them, they had no eyes for her, nor for the brownish oranges, the flattish cereal, the round yellow eyes of fried eggs, the coffee in the thick cups.

"Linda, were you running away?"

She asked, after a moment: "Were you?"

"I suppose so. When you turned me down last night, Linda . . ."

The room was full of people, talking, eating,

everyone in a hurry, mindful of the great animal of steel and wood and iron waiting for them, outside.

"Did you find the mistletoe? I took a long chance. But I told myself . . . there isn't another pair of feet in the world like hers——"

"Size three A—there are lots of them!"

She was trying to laugh. She wasn't succeeding. His hand brushed aside cups, plates, breakfasts—and covered her own.

"Linda? I'm not going to start all over again by asking you to forgive me. I was a fool—up there at Halfway Cabin. I—I thought your victory counted more with you than anything, that you didn't care what I thought—or felt—as long as you had the last word. I should have taken you in my arms and made you listen to me. I don't want your forgiveness, Linda, I want your love. For always. I want you. For always . . ."

She said, and her lips shook:

"You have it. For always. You haven't been more of a fool than I have, Dick."

"Linda—Linda——"

People were leaving. He looked around savagely. "I wish they'd all clear out!" he said, with violence.

A trainman was calling. "You'd better hurry," suggested the waitress, with complete indifference, regarding the untouched plates.

But they were looking at each other. Her hand lay under his own, her gray eyes were caught in the dark ardor of his deep, compelling gaze. She said, "We've been—so silly——"

"For heaven's sake," said Dick, a moment or so later, and flung money with mad liberality on the table. He rose, caught her hand in his, "Hurry, honey, we've got to run for it!"

But the train was pulling out.

Standing there, in the pale sunlight of New Year's morning, looking after the huge beast vanishing up the shining twin tracks, they began to laugh. He said:

"This is one way to start a New Year right. Miss your train. I know a better.

This was a deserted place. Flat scenery, the backs of barns, the frame hotel, the tracks running into the distance. He caught her in his arms and kissed her mouth. "Like this," he said, after a very long moment.

Her little hat at an angle, her eyes brilliant, her small face flushed, she cried, "Dick, our luggage!"

"They'll take it off at Lawrenceton. It's the last stop. I'll wire ahead. Speaking of wires. Wait, let's not speak of them now. Come on, we're going to go back and eat breakfast and then find a garage and hire a car to drive us home."

She followed him, docilely, to the hotel. The waitress, when they reappeared, gaped stolidly. "Did you miss your train?" she wanted to know.

"No," said Dick gravely, "we just didn't like it. Have you a garage, with cars in it? If so, may I use your phone? How about some hot coffee, freshly made, and some eggs, fried in butter, and a lot of orange juice? Can you give us your full attention now?" he suggested.

Something passed between him and the lanky lady. Something material and green. She smiled, exhibiting miraculous dental equipment. "Right away," she promised, and disappeared.

Dick telephoned the garage. Linda standing beside him. Turning, he reported:

"Car and driver will be with us in half an hour. Let's see, it takes the train three hours—wonder what kind of a car it is. I don't think we can beat the train though," he said regretfully.

"What's our hurry?"

"We have a date at City Hall. With the Mayor. The Mayor will have the honor of marrying us," said Dick, "this morning."

"Dick, are you crazy?"

"No, darling. Yes, about you. I'm taking no chances. I've just been through one wedding. I couldn't bear another. We'll have time to explain to your mother and bring her along as a witness. Bess can serve as the second."

He seized her, dragged her into the gloomy hotel parlor, kissed her some more, a great deal more. "Woman, you've had your way long enough. We'll be married today. That goes. And then we'll make for the Lodge. I'll wire your mother and Bert and my people from here. We'll break it gently—but firmly."

"But, Dick——"

"Do you love me, Linda?"

"I'm afraid—desperately."

"That's settled then. Now, explain this, if you can?"

He pulled a telegraph blank from his pocket. The wire had reached him when the train had stopped at the way-station, and it read: "Search fellow passengers for eloping lady stop make it elopement for two and don't stop your mother and I planning middle-aged honeymoon in New York stop suggest Canada for yours tell Linda bets are still on love to you both happy new year Dad."

"Bets?" asked Dick, endeavoring to torture his eyebrows into an alarming scowl.

"I can explain," Linda began.

But her heart failed her. After all there was only one way, and she thought, somewhat astray in her legal knowledge, a wife's testimony doesn't count——

"When?"

"After we're married."

The waitress stood at the door. Just like the movie fadeouts, she thought. Like her favorite Dorine Dunne and that handsome Jack Ormiston. She looked with grave appreciation. She said, Gee! under her breath, and then called:

"Breakfast's ready."